The Chosen One

"You were not ours," the letter read. "We loved you but you were not ours."

Reeling under the blow, lovely Marjorie Wetherill traveled from the warm, safe mansion in Chicago, from the brilliant life of private schools and debutante parties to a dark sordid street where she found her past—her real family broken by poverty and despair.

With a strange joy she accepted this new life— the unfamiliar hard work and the new duties— while in Chicago a young man waited with orchids and diamonds.

But Marjorie's heart now glowed with an irresistible passion for Gideon Reaver, a darkly handsome minister.

She would vow anything, do anything, if only she could some day be his!

Bantam Books by Grace Livingston Hill
Ask your bookseller for the books you have missed

Grace
Livingston
Hill

Brentwood

BANTAM BOOKS
TORONTO · NEW YORK · LONDON · SYDNEY

BRENTWOOD

*A Bantam Book / published by arrangement with
Harper & Row, Publishers Inc.*

PRINTING HISTORY

Lippincott edition published 1937

Bantam edition / January 1970

2nd printing .... March 1970	*6th printing .... June 1973*
3rd printing .... August 1970	*7th printing .... May 1974*
4th printing .... April 1971	*8th printing ...... January 1975*
5th printing .. September 1972	*9th printing ..... January 1975*
	10th printing .... August 1981

ISBN 0-553-14798-6

Published simultaneously in the United States and Canada

I

MARJORIE WETHERILL had always known she was an adopted child. She had been told when she was so young that it meant nothing at all to her. And as the years went by and she was surrounded by love and luxury, she thought little of it. Once when she was in high school she had asked about her own people casually, more out of curiosity than because of any felt need for them, and she had been told that they were respectable people who had been unfortunate and couldn't afford to bring her up as they would like to have her brought up. It had all been very vague. But Marjorie was happy, and her foster mother greatly stressed the fact that while Marjorie had not been born her own, she had been *chosen* because they loved her at first sight, and that meant more even than if she had been born theirs.

As Marjorie grew older however, she wondered now and then how a mother, if she had a true mother heart, could bear to give up her child. It seemed an unnatural thing, to surrender her permanently that way, and promise never to see her again. But there was even uncertainty as to whether her mother was still living. And so the thought passed by, and the happy days of her girlhood went on.

Mrs. Wetherill was a devoted parent, and she and Marjorie were dear companions. It scarcely seemed real to Marjorie that there had ever been any other mother, and as for another father, he wasn't even sketchily in the background.

When Mr. Wetherill died Marjorie was still in her school life, and she and the mother were brought even closer together, so that when Mrs. Wetherill was suddenly stricken with an illness that they both knew would be swift and fatal, the girl spent the last months of her foster mother's life in utmost devotion to her. When it was over and she was alone, she felt utterly desolate and life seemed barren indeed.

There were many friends of course, for the Wetherills had a large pleasant social circle, and there were instant invitations for prolonged visits here and there, but Marjorie had no heart to go. She longed for someone of her own. The world seemed empty and uninteresting.

People told her that feeling would pass and she tried to believe them, but she fell to wondering more and more about her own people and wished she knew whether any of them were living, and where. She wished she had asked more about them.

Then one morning about ten days before Christmas, because she could not settle to anything else, and because she had been almost dreading to go over her beloved foster mother's intimate papers she went bravely to Mrs. Wetherill's desk in the living room. unlocked it, and began to look over the papers in the pigeon holes.

The old lawyer had gone over all the papers of the estate with her, those that were kept at the bank, and there was nothing to worry about as far as money was concerned. The entire Wetherill estate was left to her without a question and it was a comfortable fortune. The income was ample for any possible needs.

But this desk was where Mrs. Wetherill used to write her social and friendly letters and seemed a very intimate part of her. Marjorie had known that sooner or later she must go over everything. and put away or destroy the things their owner would have wished disposed of. In fact Mrs. Wetherill had given her careful instructions about it.

But as she went from drawer to drawer, emptying every pigeon hole, and burning in the fireplace such things as had to be destroyed, she came finally to the little secret drawer, and there she found among several other important papers, a thick letter for herself.

In great surprise, for she had not known of any such

letter, she began to read it, the quick tears springing to her eyes as the precious handwriting seemed to bring back the dear one who had left her.

"Dearest Marjorie:" it read,

"There is something that perhaps I should have spoken of long ago, but did not, and I feel as if I must leave some word about it behind for you when I go. I cannot bring myself to *talk* about it to you and spoil our last brief days together, but I feel that it is something you should know.

I have never told you much about your own people. I did not really know much myself to tell, until about two years ago. My husband arranged everything about the adoption. He wanted me not to be troubled with details. He wanted me to feel that you were my own dear child, not adopted. So I never asked much about the facts.

I saw you first in the hospital. We were going through looking for a baby we could adopt, and when I saw you in the ward I fell in love with you, only to find you were not for adoption.

I never told you that you were one of twins. I did not want you to be drawn away from me by other ties. Perhaps I was selfish in that. I begin to feel now that I was. But anyhow it is past and cannot be undone. However, I feel that you should know. If you feel like blaming me I beg you to be pitiful, for I loved you.

You were a very beautiful baby, and so was your twin sister, yet she had a frailer look than you, and we found upon questioning that she had little chance to live unless she could have an operation and special treatment, which your parents were unable to give her.

But though neither of you were candidates for adoption, yet I had set my heart upon you. After seeing you, all the other babies looked common to me. So, my husband set about it to see what he could do. He discovered that your father was not strong and needed to get away to the country where he could have light work and be out of doors. My husband finally put it up to your mother while she was still in the hospital, that she should give her consent to our adopting you, Mr. Wetherill agreeing to finance the treatment of both your father and little sister, and to make it possible for your family to live on a nice little farm where they could be able to support themselves until better days came.

These details I did not know at the time. I only knew that to my great joy you were mine at last, adopted according to law, your parents signing over all rights and promising not to try to see you without our consent.

Once, when you were about three months old, your mother

wrote me, begging that she might come and see you, but I persuaded her that it would be better for us all if she did not, that it would be easier for her not to have seen you. Your father—Mr. Wetherill—went to see your own father and had some sort of an understanding with him, so that they did not come near us nor write any more. So the years went by and I was very happy with you. My dear, you know that you have always been to me all that a real child of my own could have been, and perhaps a little more, because I had picked you out from all the babies in the world to be mine.

It was not until after my husband died that I heard again of your people. It seems they had saved and saved, and gathered together enough to pay back all the money that Mr. Wetherill had given them when he adopted you, and they wrote begging Mr. Wetherill to accept it, and to allow them to come and see you at least occasionally.

I sent the money back of course, and wrote very firmly refusing their request, feeling that it would be most disastrous. I had no idea just what kind of people they were, and I felt it might hurt your life.

But then, about a year ago, just as you were graduating from Miss Evans' School, your mother came to see me.

I was surprised at what a lovely frail little woman she was. She was very plainly dressed, but she looked neat and pretty, and she had eyes like yours. It went to my heart. She said sometimes she could not sleep at night, thinking that she had given you up. She said it seemed at times as if she would go crazy thinking of things she might have done instead, to raise the money to save the lives of her husband and other child, and yet keep you.

I really felt very sorry for her. She looked so much like you that I began to feel like a criminal. She wanted to see you. But I would not let her. I felt it would be a catastrophe for you at your time of life. Your big photograph taken in your graduating dress was on the desk and I showed it to her, and finally gave it to her. You wondered what had become of it and I had to make up a story about something being the matter with the frame, till I could get another.

She went away sobbing and I have never forgotten it. When I have looked at you, and thought of her, I have felt like a criminal. I ought to have let her see you. I had no right to come between a mother and her child, no matter what she may have been, although she seemed quite lovely and respectable.

And now that I am about to die I feel that I should leave behind me this information so that you may do what you wish in the matter. Perhaps you will want to do something for your own mother. You will have quite a fortune, my dear, and you are free to do what you wish with it, of course.

After your mother had gone away I sent her quite a generous

check, but she returned it by the next mail, and sent with it also the amount of money which your father—which my husband—had given your own father. I felt quite badly about that. It seemed to put me very much in the debt of your parents.

But now I am leaving the matter in your hands, my dear, and if you feel there is anything you would like to do, or if you want to grant your mother's wish to see you, I want you to know that I am willing. I think perhaps I have sinned in this matter, and I want to make it right if I can. So I am giving you your mother's name and address. Do whatever your heart dictates.

You already know how much I have loved you, how I love you as my own, and so I need not say it again. If you feel, dear child, that I have done wrong, I beg you to forgive me, for I have loved you greatly, and I have tried to do my best for you in every other way,

Your loving Mother,
May D. Wetherill."

Below was an address in an eastern city:

Mrs. John Gay, 1465 Aster Street.

And below that, in pencil, had been written uncertainly as if with an idea of erasing it:

"The name by which they called you was Dorothy."

So then she was no longer Marjorie Wetherill but Dorothy Gay. How strange and fantastic life was turning out to be!

She bowed her head on the letter and wept. First for the only mother she had known, and then for the mother she had not known. How pitiful it all seemed! So many little babies in the world without homes, and yet she should have been loved so intensely by two mothers!

Her heart burned for the mother she had always known, whose conscience had troubled her, and then ached for the other mother who wanted her and might not have her! What a strange world, and a strange happening, that this should come to her! That suddenly her safe secure world should crumble all about her, death and change and perplexity staring her in the face.

And yet, she didn't have to pay any attention to this letter. Nobody but herself knew of it. She could go right on living her life apart from them, living in this lovely home that the Wetherills had left her, forgetting her own people, as she had always done. They had practically sold her out of their lives, hadn't they? They had no real claim upon her. And of course, they might be embarrassing! There was no telling what they were. She had nothing to give her a clue to what they were, except that her mother's eyes were like hers.

Then suddenly a thrill came to her heart. But they were her very own, whatever they were! How wonderful that would be! And her mother had *wanted* her, enough to come a long distance to see her!

All the rest of the day the thought of her real mother hovered in her mind, and grew into a great longing to go to her; yet somehow it seemed disloyalty to the mother and father who had brought her up and had chosen to keep her in ignorance of her own people.

It was not until she had read Mrs. Wetherill's letter over carefully several times that she began to see that the letter really was a permission, if not even a plea, for her to do something about her own people. As she began to read more and more between the lines of the letter, she felt that there was something demanded of her as a daughter that she should have done long ago.

That night she could not sleep and lay staring about in the darkness of her room—the room that Mrs. Wetherill had made so beautiful for her—realizing how safe and sweet and quiet it all was here, and how many complications there might be if she broke the long silence between herself and her own family. Yet the longing in her heart increased, to see them, even to find out the worst possible about them, just to have them for her own. Not to be alone in the great world.

There was a sister, too, and how wonderful it would be to have a sister! She had always wished for a sister. Or—perhaps the sister had not lived after all! The letter said she was delicate. Perhaps she had died. Perhaps that was the reason why her mother wanted her. Perhaps she had no others to love her and comfort her. Perhaps the father might be dead too!

Suddenly Marjorie buried her face in her pillow and wept.

The morning mail brought two invitations to spend Christmas week with friends.

Christmas was only ten days off and it loomed large and

gloomy. The thought of Christmas without the only mother she had ever known seemed intolerable.

One of the invitations was from a distant cousin of Mrs. Wetherill's, a kindly person with a large house, given to entertaining. The other was from an old schoolmate living in Boston. Both invitations spelled gaiety and good cheer, but they somehow did not appeal to her now. Her grief was too recent, and her feeling of loneliness too poignant to be allayed by mingling with a giddy throng of pleasure-seekers. In fact that kind of Christmas never did appeal to her at any time. She liked simpler pleasures. Besides, her heart was too restless just now to plunge into worldliness and try to forget her loss.

All day she went about trying to make a decision, now almost decided to accept one of the invitations and end her uncertainty, now playing with the idea of going to search out her people and learn once for all what they were like.

But when she reasoned that perhaps forgetting was best for the present, and tried to decide which invitation she should accept, she realized that she didn't feel like going to either place.

Oh, of course they would all be very kind, and put themselves out to make her have a good time, but Christmas couldn't be Christmas this year, no matter how it was planned.

She was still in her unsettled state of mind when evening came, and Evan Brower arrived to call upon her.

The Browers were one of the best old families, and among the closest friends of the Wetherills. Evan Brower was three or four years older than Marjorie, and though she had known him practically all her life, it had not been until the last year that he had paid her much attention. Mrs. Wetherill had been very fond of him, and of late he had been often at the house, one of the closest friends Marjorie had Yet the two were still on the basis of friendship, nothing closer.

Marjorie was glad of his coming as a relief from the perplexities that had been with her all day, and smiled a real welcome as he took her hand in greeting.

"You are looking tired and white!" he said scrutinizing her face sharply. "You need a change, and I've come to offer one. Mother wants you to come over and stay a couple of weeks with her. She thought you might like to help her get ready for the family gathering at Christmas time. It will take your mind off your loneliness. You know your mother would never want you to mope. Mother thought maybe you would come over tomorrow and just consider you are on a visit."

Marjorie's heart sank. Here was the question again! And a family gathering! The hardest kind of a thing to go through, with this thought of her own unknown family in the back of her mind. Suddenly she knew she could not go anywhere till that matter was settled! She had got to know just where she stood before ever she went among people again. She lifted her eyes to Evan's kindly pleasant face and tried to decline his offer in a gracious way.

"Oh, that is dear of your mother, Evan!" she said. "I do appreciate it a lot, and some other time I'd love to come, but just now I don't feel I could."

He settled down comfortably to combat her, just as if he had expected to have to do so.

"Now, you know that isn't a bit sensible, Marjorie. There's no point in stretching out your grief. You've got to go on living, and you know perfectly well your mother would want you to be happy."

"Yes," said Marjorie sweetly. "I know, and I'm not stretching out my grief. Mother and I talked it over together, and she told me all that. I understand, and I don't intend to mope. But somehow I don't feel I can stand gaiety just yet. I've had two other invitations but I'm declining them both—"

Marjorie hadn't been quite sure till this minute what she was going to do, but now it was all very clear in her mind.

"But, Marge, it's only our house. It's almost like home, you know. It isn't as if we were going to have a lot of strangers either. There will be just the cousins and aunts and uncles. You've always known them, and Mother intends to plan it all very quietly. I'm sure there won't be anything to upset you. If you find it's too much I'll take you off in the car to some quiet place for a few hours and rest you up, and you really must see it will be better for you than moping here in this lonely house."

"You're very kind!" said Marjorie with troubled gaze, but more and more certain that she wasn't going to accept. Then suddenly she lifted frank eyes to his:

"You see, Evan, there's something I have to do first before I can go anywhere and begin life again."

"Something you have to do? What do you mean?" He turned puzzled, dominating eyes upon her.

Marjorie hesitated, then spoke decisively. After all, he was her good friend, why not confide in him? Perhaps he could advise her.

"You know I'm an adopted child, don't you? You've always known that, haven't you, Evan?"

A startled, almost cautious look came into his eyes.

"Why—yes, of course, but what has that got to do with it? You don't mean, Marjorie, that after all these years your mother has cut you out of the property she promised you? I heard her say myself that she was leaving you everything. You don't mean that she tied it up or anything?"

Marjorie laughed, and drew a deep breath.

"Oh, no, nothing like that, Evan. I'm very comfortably fixed, of course."

A relieved look came into the young man's handsome eyes.

"Well, then, why worry?" he said playfully, and his hand stole across and dropped familiarly, warmly, down upon hers.

They were sitting on the deep couch, Marjorie at one end, Evan near the other, but now he leaned across with a comforting manner and looked into her eyes.

She was quite serious as she answered:

"It's no money worries," she said. "It's something entirely different. It's my family. My *own* family, I mean."

"Your own family?" he looked at her startled. "Have they dared turn up and annoy you?"

"Oh, no!" she said quickly. "Of course not!"

"Why 'of course not'? They likely would if they knew you were alone and unprotected. A girl with a fortune is never quite safe alone. You ought not to stay a night alone here!"

"Why, I'm not alone!" smiled Marjorie. "The servants would protect me with their lives if there were need. I'm quite safe. But it's absurd, Evan, for you to talk that way about my own people! Don't, please! It hurts me!"

"*Hurts* you?" he said, looking at her incredulously. "Hurts you to hear that people you never saw in your life, and about whom you know nothing might possibly have some motives that were not of the best?"

"They are my own people, Evan!"

"Nonsense! Nothing of the kind!" said Evan lifting his

well-modeled chin haughtily. "You are no more connected with them than I am. They gave you up! I should think you would never want to see or hear of them! I should say you are fortunate that they are not troubling you. Let sleeping dogs lie! You have no obligation whatever toward them!"

Something in the harshness of his tone made Marjorie give a little shiver and draw her hand quietly away from under his.

"I don't feel that way, Evan!" she said gently, marveling that after her hours of doubt she suddenly felt clear in her mind about the matter. "You don't know all about it, or you wouldn't say that either, I'm quite sure. Mother left a letter telling me about my people and suggesting that I might want to hunt them up and see if there was anything I could do for them."

"And I still say, 'Let sleeping dogs lie,'" said Evan coldly. And then he laid his hand once more on hers in a possessive way as if he owned her.

"Of course, if you were very anxious to do a little something in a quiet way for them, it could be arranged anonymously," he added. "I would be glad to see to that for you, and it might ease your conscience, since you seem to be exercised in the matter. But on no account let them know that you have done anything for them. They will just be after you all the time, begging and whining, and making your life a misery. They are all suckers, those people! They never cared anything for you or they wouldn't have sold you in the first place. And now you are a being of another world than theirs and they have no right to intrude into your life and try to get your property away from you! I insist—!"

Marjorie drew her hand decidedly away from under his again and stood up, her own chin lifted defiantly, her eyes bright and indignant.

"Evan! You must not talk that way! You simply don't understand at all. I thought you were my friend and I could talk it over with you, but you don't seem willing to listen. I'm sorry I mentioned it, but since I have started I must finish. I tell you Mother left me a letter in which she tells me more about my people than I ever knew, and than she ever knew until a few months before Father died. I think she meant to *tell* me, but found it hard to talk about, and so left this letter. She gives me all the circumstances of my adoption, and how my own mother afterwards was grieved that she had given me up and begged to see me, and—"

"Yes! *Exactly!* Didn't I tell you? People like that can never honorably abide by a bargain—"

"Please don't interrupt me, Evan. You must hear me to the end. Mother felt I ought to know about everything, and that I was free to do what I liked about hunting up my people and doing everything I liked for them. She says in the letter that they positively refused money. Sent back a check that she sent them!"

"Oh, probably only a fine gesture!" sneered Evan. "My dear, trust me! I know that class of people—"

"Be careful, Evan," said Marjorie drawing herself up. "Please don't say any more! It is my own mother and father you are talking about! This is something I have to work out myself. I'm sorry I said anything about it until I had made my decision."

"But, darling, be reasonable!" said Evan softening his voice. Marjorie didn't even notice he had called her darling. It was such a common phrase of the day, and Evar was a very close friend. But his voice was less aggressive now, more gentle. He got up and stood beside her, taking her hands in his and drawing her nearer to him. "Listen, little girl! If you are really serious about this thing, of course it will have to be investigated. I still think it would be better not, but if you have set your conscience to it, I beg you will let *me* do the investigating for you. I am a lawyer. I know how to protect your interests, and I will do whatever you want done conscientiously. I am sure you can trust me, Marjorie. I love you, don't you know it, little girl?"

She looked up at him startled. It was the first time he had ever spoken of love. He had just been a good friend, somewhat as she supposed a brother might be, only more polite than some brothers. One who would protect and advise and care for her when she needed it. And even now she was not sure but it was just in this way that he meant that he loved her, as a man might love a dear sister whom he wanted to guide and protect. But somehow he had created a doubt in her mind as to his full willingness to understand and do all that she needed now. She could not get away from the harshness in his voice when he had said "Let sleeping dogs lie!" The very words by which he had hoped to turn her away from her purpose had served to clarify her decision, and give her a certain loyalty to these unknown ones of her family.

Her eyes searched his for an instant, keenly, doubtfully. There was a light in his own as he looked possessively down at her now, that seemed to be different from any look she had ever noticed there before, but it did not stir her deeply. She tried to think that perhaps this was the rest she sought, Evan's love and care, but the thought failed to bring any joy or rest. If this was love she wasn't ready for it yet, not until she had found out the whole truth about her people.

She drew back and tried gently to take her hands away from his clasp, but he held them firmly and drew her closer.

"Dear little girl!" he said suddenly, putting his face down and laying his cheek against hers, seeking her lips with his own and pressing a kiss upon them.

For an instant she yielded herself to that embrace, her lips to that kiss; but only an instant so brief it might scarcely have been recognized by the man as yielding. For suddenly she sprang away, and put out her hands in protest.

"No, please, not now! I can't think of such things now!"

He snatched at her hands again, trying to draw her back quietly to his embrace.

"Poor child!" he said stooping and kissing her fingers gently. "Don't you realize that this is where you belong, in my arms? Don't you love me?"

"I don't know!" said Marjorie turning unhappy eyes away from him. "I haven't ever thought of you in this way. And my heart is full of so many other things now."

"I know, poor child!" he continued. "But you do love me. I'm sure you do. I've seen it in your eyes a thousand times when you have looked at me. You love me only you haven't recognized it as love yet! But I will teach you what love means!"

And he suddenly drew her close again and pressed hot kisses on her lips.

But now she sprang away again, covering her face with her hands.

"No! No!" she cried out. "I will not let you kiss me until I am sure, and I am not now! Please, won't you go away and let me think? My mind is so tired and all mixed up!"

"Poor child!" he said gently. "I am sorry if I have seemed to hurry you. I only wanted to show you that I am your natural protector. But I am willing to wait, to go slow, till your sorrow is not so sharp. I only ask one thing of you and that is that you will not make any move in this matter of your family till you have talked with me again. That you will think it over, and if anything has to be done you will let me handle it for you. Will you promise?"

Marjorie was still for several seconds, looking down at her hands clasped tightly before her, then she said slowly, seriously:

"I will promise to think over what you said. *Every*thing that you have said."

She looked up at him quietly, and smiled a cold little wistful smile. Then she added:

"I'm sorry to seem so—uncertain—and so—unappreciative—of your—love. But I just can't seem to think tonight!"

"Well, that's all right, little girl!" he said and his voice was very gentle again, as if he were talking to a child who didn't quite understand. "I know you've been terribly upset, and I don't want to rush you. But I do want you to understand that you can come to me for everything!"

"Thank you!" she said simply, but her face looked white and tired.

He was a wise young man and he saw that he couldn't get any further tonight.

"Well, then, we'll say good night. Are you going to let me kiss you again?"

"Please, no," she said with a troubled protest in her eyes.

"All right," said the young man gravely. "It shall be as you wish, but I wish you would consider that we are engaged. I'd like to put a ring on your finger tomorrow and feel that you are my promised wife."

Marjorie turned her head away and looked troubled again.

"I can't think of these things now!" she said. "Please let us be just friends, as we have always been!"

He studied her for a moment and then his lips set in a firm line of determination.

"Very well," he said quite cheerfully. "I am just your friend for now, but a very special friend, you know. One whom you can call upon for anything. Will you feel that?"

She smiled with relief.

"Yes," she said. "Thank you! Good night!" and she put out her hand and gave his a brief impersonal clasp.

Then he was gone, and she stood alone, looking down at the gardenias he had brought, and wondering why she had not thrilled to his touch. Why, somehow, her feeling of his friendliness had been lost in a new something that she did not understand nor want. Not now, anyway.

II

MARJORIE found she was too excited to sleep when she laid her head on her pillow. But strangely enough it was not on the eager protests of love that her mind dwelt most during that night's vigil, but more on his insistence that she should not search out her people. And the more she thought of it, the less she thought of Evan.

Still, she knew that was not fair either. If Evan really loved her as he said he did, it might be natural, if not noble, at least for her sake, to wish to protect her against anything that might annoy or embarrass her. And yet the more she faced the possibility that her family might be embarrassing, the more she felt it her duty to search them out and know the truth.

After all, even if she wanted to accept the love that had been offered her—and she wasn't at all sure that she did —it was all so new and unexpected, and her reaction to it was tempered by his utter distaste for having her people in her background. Could she honestly marry any man without knowing the truth about her family?

And of course she could not get away from the fact that they *were* her parents, and had a right to a place in her life, whether she or her friends or anybody else wanted them there or not. What that place was to be must be decided before she went on another step in life. No other questions of life or love or future happiness could be settled until she dealt with that. And she would have to deal with it alone. No one else could settle it for her.

She awoke in the morning with the definite purpose in her heart to get the matter over with at once. She would start right away before anything else could possibly delay her. If any more people came in and tried to turn her from her purpose she would become bewildered again.

She dressed hastily and sat down at her desk at once, determined to burn all bridges behind her. She wrote charming little notes declining all her invitations, and then wrote to Evan Brower:

"Dear Evan:

I have kept my promise and thought over carefully the matter of which we were speaking last evening, and have decided that I must visit my family at once. When I come back I hope to be able to talk about the question more intelligently.

Please don't think I do not appreciate your kind thought for me, but I feel that this is a question I must investigate and decide for myself, and I must settle it before I do anything else.

I have written your mother, thanking her for her kind invitation, and telling her how sorry I am that it doesn't seem possible for me to visit her just now.

I shall probably return sometime after New Year's Day, or perhaps sooner if I get homesick. But I will let you know when I get back.

Thanking you for all your kindness, and trusting that you will try to understand,

Most gratefully,
Marjorie."

She felt better when the notes were written. It seemed as if she were already started on her journey. But she decided not to mail them until just as she was leaving. She did not want anybody coming in to try and hinder her. Evan would not be able to get away from his office before evening, and if anyone else came she would merely say she was about to visit relatives for the holidays.

She called up the station and made her reservations on a train that left the city a little after six that night. Then she went down to the kitchen and gave the house servants a vacation for the holidays, all except the chauffeur and his wife who lived over the garage and would care for the house.

After all it was very simple. The servants were delighted, and did not ask her plans. She told them she would be visiting relatives. The house became a hive of industry for the next few hours. Though there wasn't much to be done toward closing up as the chauffeur's wife would look after all that. Marjorie went at her packing. It didn't take long. She took some of her prettiest sport dresses—the Wetherills had never approved of wearing mourning—and two or three plain little house dresses in case she found her relatives in poor circumstances. She must remember not to remind them that she had been brought up to plenty.

She took her check book and plenty of money, carefully stowed as she had been taught to do when traveling. She left no address with anybody. She did not want anyone coming after her to try and hinder her in whatever she should decide to do.

At the last she almost turned back, her heart failing her at what might be before her, for she was gifted with a strong imagination, and had in the night visioned a number of situations that might arise which would make her greatly regret this step she was taking. But the servants were gone now, and it was too late to turn back. The taxi was at the door to take her to the station.

She waited long enough to telephone her lawyer that she would be out of the city for a few days, perhaps till after Christmas, and would let him know her address later. Then she locked the door and went down the walk to the taxi, winking back the tears, feeling as if she were bidding good-bye to her former lovely life and stepping off into the great unknown. What a fool she was, she told herself, she didn't have to stay if she didn't want to. She could come right back the day she got there if she chose.

And so at last she was on her way, quite worn out with the tumult of her decision and her preparations.

The next morning she arrived in the strange city and went to a hotel. After attempting a sketchy breakfast she took a taxi and drove to the address that had been given in the letter.

She had meant to do a great deal of thinking before she went to sleep in her berth, but the day of excitement had wearied her more than she knew and she had dropped to sleep at once and had not wakened until the porter called

her in the morning. So now, as she rode along in her taxi
she suddenly felt unprepared for the ordeal that was before her. She had intended to plan just how she would
open the interview, always supposing she found anybody
to have an interview with, but now it seemed too absurd
to plan anything for so vague a scene as she was about to
stage. She found herself shrinking inexpressibly from the
whole thing. If she had it to decide all over again this
morning she would certainly have turned it down as an utterly preposterous proposition. Certain words and phrases
of Evan Brower's came to her mind, a tiny reflection of
his sneer when he had told her it might be embarrassing
for her to hunt up her relatives.

Then her own honest loyal nature came to the front and
declared to her that whoever or whatever they were they
were hers, something God had put her into the world with
as her own, and nobody, not even themselves, had a right
to put them asunder. They were her birthright, and something she must not disown.

Now and then it came to her that her foster mother
should have faced this problem with her long ago, when it
wouldn't have hurt her so much, but instantly her love defended the only mother she had ever known, and her heart
owned that it would have been very hard for Mrs. Wetherill. On the whole it was just as well that she should decide
this thing for herself and act as she chose. And it was generous of course of Mrs. Wetherill to give her a free hand
to do what she chose for her people.

So her thoughts battled back and forth as she rode
along through the strange city, looking out but not seeing
the new sights, not taking in a thing but the breathless fact
that she was on her way unannounced, to meet the people
to whom she had been born, and she was frightened.

It seemed a very long drive, out through a scrubby part
of the city, and then into a sordid street of little cheap
houses all alike, brick houses with wooden porches in an
endless row, block after block, with untidy vacant lots
across the street, ending in unpleasant ash heaps. It was
before the last house in the row that the taxi stopped, on
the far outskirts of the city, with a desolate stretch of city
dump beyond. Marjorie's heart almost stopped beating,
and she nearly told the driver to turn about and take her
back to the hotel. Could it be that her people lived in a

house like this? A little two-story, seven-by-nine affair, with not even a pavement in front, just a hard clay path worn by the feet of many children playing?

The driver handed her her check, opened the door, and she got out her purse.

"I think perhaps you had better wait for me a minute or two until I make sure this is the right place," she said hesitantly, as she eyed the house with displeasure.

"Yes ma'am, this is the number you give me," said the man, "1465 Aster Street."

"Yes, but they might have moved, you know," said Marjorie hopefully.

So, on feet that were strangely unsteady, she got out and went slowly up the two wooden steps to the door that sadly needed paint. There was no bell so she knocked timidly, and then again louder as she heard no sound of life within. She was just about to turn away, almost hoping they were gone, and she would have no clue to search further, when she heard hurried steps on a bare floor, and the door was opened sharply, almost impatiently. Then she found herself face to face with a replica of herself!

"Does Mrs. George Gay live here?"

She said the words because she had prepared them on her lips to say, but she was so startled at the apparition of herself in the flesh standing before her that she did not realize she had asked the question. She just stood there and stared and stared at this other girl who was so like and yet so unlike herself.

The other girl had the same cloud of golden hair, only it was flying in every direction, not smoothly waved in the way it ought to lie; the same brown eyes, only they were full of bitterness, and trouble, and a kind of fright in the depths of them; the same delicate lips, only they were set in hard lines as if the grim realities of life had been too close to her. She was wearing a soiled and torn flimsy dress of flowered material that was most unbecoming, and a cheap old coat with all the buttons off or hanging by threads. Her hands were small but they were swollen and red with the cold and she shivered as she stood grimly there staring at her most unwelcome guest.

"Well," she said with a final little shiver, opening the door a trifle wider, "I suppose you must be my twin sister! Will you come in?" Her voice was most ungracious, but she stood aside in the tiny hall to let the other girl pass in.

"Oh! Are you—? That is— I didn't know—!" said Marjorie in confusion. Then she turned suddenly to the taxi and nodded brightly.

"It's all right," she said. "They still live here!"

"But they probably won't for long," added the other girl grimly.

"Oh, are you going to move? Then I'm glad I came before you did, for I might have had trouble finding you."

"Yes," said the other girl unsmiling, "you probably would." Then she motioned toward a single wooden chair in the middle of the room. "Won't you sit down? We still have one chair left. though I believe Ted is going to take it to the pawnshop this afternoon. There isn't any heat here. Will you take cold?" There was something contemptuous in the tone of this hostile sister. Marjorie gave her a quick troubled glance.

"Are you really my sister?"

"I suppose I must be," said the other girl listlessly as if it didn't in the least matter, "there's your picture up there on the mantel. Maybe you'll recognize that. If you had waited till afternoon that would probably have been gone too."

Marjorie turned startled eyes toward the stark little high wooden shelf that ran across the narrow chimney over a wall-register, and saw her own photographed face in its silver frame smiling at her and looking utterly out of place in that bleak little room. She turned back to look at the other girl wistfully.

"You know, I didn't even know I had a sister until day before yesterday!"

The other looked at her with hard unbelieving eyes.

"That's odd, isn't it? How did that come about?"

"No one told me," she answered sadly.

"Oh, yes? Then how did you find out?"

"I found a letter—from Moth—that is from my adopted mother after she died. She left a letter to tell me about my people."

"You mean Mr. and Mrs. Wetherill are both dead?" The tone was incredulous.

"Yes. I am alone in the world now, except for you—my own family."

The other girl's face grew very hard and bitter now.

"Oh!" she said shortly. "I wondered why you came after all these years when you haven't paid the slightest attention to us. Not even a Christmas card now and then! You with your grand home and your aristocratic parents, and your fine education! What could you possibly want with us? But I see it now. They have died and left you penniless, I suppose, after all their grand pretensions, and you have come back on us to live. Well, we'll take you in of course. Mother wouldn't have it otherwise, but I'll say it's something like the end of a perfect day to have you turn up just now."

"Oh, I'm sorry," said Marjorie distressed at once. "I ought to have telephoned to see if it was convenient, but I was so eager to find you. And you don't at all realize anything about it. I've not come to be a burden on you. I thought maybe I could spend Christmas with you. I know how you must feel. You are moving, and frightfully busy, but you'll let me help, won't you?"

"Moving!" sneered her sister. "Yes, we'd be moving right away today if we had any place to move to! And any money to move with! And anything to move! *Christmas!* I didn't know there was such a thing any more!" And suddenly she dropped down in the vacant chair, jerking her hands out from the ragged pockets of her old coat, put them up to her face and burst into tears, sobbing until her slender body shook with the force of the sobs. Yet it was all done very quietly as if there was some reason why she must not make a noise.

Marjorie went close and put her arms about her, her face down against the other's wet cheek.

"Oh, my dear!" she said brokenly. *"My dear!"* And then her own tears were falling. and she held the weeping girl close. "But you are *cold!* So cold you are trembling! Can't we go into another room where it is warm and let me tell you how you have misunderstood me? I won't stay if you don't want me, but I can't bear to have you misunderstand me. Come!"

Then the girl lifted her face and spoke fiercely again.

"Come?" she said. "Where shall we come? Don't you know there hasn't been a teaspoonful of coal in this house for two days, and that we've burned up all the chairs that aren't sold to try and keep from freezing—except this one that has to be sold to get some medicine for Mother?

Don't you know Father hasn't had any work for nine
months, and Mother is sick upstairs in bed with all the
blankets we own piled around her and a hot-water bag at
her feet? I borrowed the hot water from a house in the
next block, and it won't stay hot long, I had to bring it so
far. She's getting pneumonia, I'm afraid, and I had to lose
my job to stay home and take care of her. Don't you
know that Dad is sick himself, but he had to go out and
beg the landlord to let us stay a few days more till Mother
is better—? And I guess Ted has lost his newspaper route,
and I've had to take the children to the neighborhood nursery, to keep them warm and fed! If you stay here with us
you'll have to pawn that fur coat to get enough to eat!
You'd better go back to your fine friends and get a job or
something. We haven't anything in the house to eat but
two slices of stale bread I saved to make toast for Mother.
She'd likely give them to you if she knew, for she's cried
over you night after night lately. Dad has been eating at
the mission for two weeks to save what we had for the rest
of us. We pawned everything we had for a pittance to live
on. We just finished Mother's silver wedding spoons, and
there isn't anything left but your picture frame and
Mother's wedding ring, and I can't bear to go and take
that off of her. It would break her heart!"

Suddenly the sister's head went down again and more
silent sobs shook her. It was terrible to look upon. Marjorie felt it was the most awful sight she had ever seen.
She stood there appalled as the bald truths were thrown at
her like missiles. And that was *her sister* sitting there shaking with cold and misery! And she was standing here done
up in costly furs, never having known what it was to be
cold or hungry or frightened like that! How she despised
herself!

Suddenly she stood back and unbuttoned her coat, slid
out of it and wrapped it warmly around her sister.

"There! There! You precious sister!" she said softly, laying her lips on the other girl's.

But her sister struggled up fiercely, her pride blazing in
her eyes, her arms flinging off the coat. "No!" she said,
"no, I won't wear your coat even for a minute."

But Marjorie caught it together about her again and
held it there.

"Look here!" she said with authority. "Stop acting this way! I'm your sister and I've come to help you! You can't fling me off this way! And we haven't time to fight! We've got to get busy. What's the first thing to do? Make a fire! Where can I find a man to send for coal? Where is your telephone?"

"Telephone!" laughed the sister hysterically. "We haven't had a telephone in years!"

Marjorie gave her a startled look. "Well," she said suddenly, "we must get a fire going before that hot-water bag gets cold. Mother has got to be thought of first. Where can I find a man to make a fire?"

"A *man!*" said the other girl. "A *man* to make a fire!" and she suddenly gave that wild hysterical laugh again. "*I* could make a fire if I had anything to make it with. I tell you there isn't even a newspaper left."

"Well, where do we get coal? I'll go out and get some," said Marjorie meekly.

"You can't," said her sister sullenly, "they won't trust us till the bill is paid, and we've nothing to pay it with." Her eyes were smoldering like slow fires, and her face was filled with shame as she confessed this, but Marjorie's eyes lit with joy.

"Oh, but *I* have!" she cried eagerly, and put her hand into her purse pulling out a nice fat roll of bills and slipping them into her sister's hand.

"There," she said, "go quick and pay the bill and get the coal!"

The other girl looked down at her hand, saw the large denomination of the bills she was holding, and looked up in wonder. Then her face changed and an alert look came, pride stole slowly up, and the faint color that had come into her cheeks faded, leaving her ghastly white again.

"We couldn't take it!" she said fiercely. "We couldn't ever pay it back. There is no use!" and she held it out to Marjorie.

"Nonsense!" said Marjorie. "You are *my family*, aren't you? It's *my mother* who is cold, isn't it?"

"After all these years? You staying away and never sending us any word? No! You're adopted and belong to that other woman, and it's her money, not ours. We can't take it!"

"Look here!" said Marjorie, her own eyes flashing now till they resembled her sister's even more strongly than at first, "I didn't *ask* to be adopted, did I? I didn't have any choice in the matter, did I? I was adopted before I knew what was going on, and I didn't know anything about you. You have no right to blame me that way! I couldn't *help* what was done to me when I was a baby! If she had happened to adopt you, you probably would have been just what I've been. But I came to you just as soon as I found out, didn't I? And I want you to know that I'm *here*, and I'm going to *stay*, and I'm going to help just as much as if I'd been here all the time. And as for the money, it's mine, not hers. She left it to me, and she said in the letter I was to use it in any way I pleased. She even seemed to feel that she would like me to come and find you. But anyway I'm here, and I'm going to stay, and please don't let's waste any more time. It *is awfully* cold here!"

Then suddenly the other girl jumped up and flung Marjorie's coat back to her.

"All right!" she said. "Put on your own coat. Maybe it's all true. I don't know. I've hated you and the Wetherills so long that I don't know whether I can ever get over it or not, but I've got to try and save my mother's life, even if it is with that other woman's money!"

"But it isn't her money now! It is mine! And I am going to look after my family. We are going to do it together! Quick! Tell me where to begin. Do I get to see my mother first or had we better have a fire? I guess the fire comes first, doesn't it? Or you will be sick too. Tell me where to go, and I'll have the fixings here in short order."

"It's two blocks down, and a block to the right. Brown's Coal Yard. But there's a bill for twenty-three dollars. They won't send any coal till it's paid. Here! Take back the money!"

She held out the roll of bills half reluctantly, looking at it with a sort of fierce wistfulness.

"No," said Marjorie. "You keep that. I've more in my purse. You might have some need for it while I'm gone. But can't you put something more around you? Your lips are blue with cold!"

"I'll be all right! I'm used to it. I really ought to go myself, I suppose. Maybe you won't be able to find your way. But I hate to leave Mother, if anything should happen."

"Of course!" said Marjorie. "And it might startle her too much if I went to her before she knew I had come. Don't you worry, I'll find my way. But say, what shall I call you? I can't exactly go around calling my own sister 'Miss Gay,' can I? And you know I never knew your name."

The other girl stared.

"You don't mean they never told you your own sister's name? Well, that certainly is funny! I'm Elizabeth. They call me Betty."

Her voice was a trifle warmer.

"That's a pretty name Betty Gay! I like it. And——I'm Dorothy——isn't that it? The letter told me that."

"Yes, but *they* called you Marjorie!" Betty's voice was suddenly hard again.

"Well, I couldn't help that either," grinned Marjorie. "Say, suppose you stop having grudges awhile and tell me if there is anything else I need to get before I come back. When we get the house warm and everything going all right we'll get out the grudges and settle them up, but we haven't time for them now, have we?"

Betty suddenly softened again and almost smiled, and Marjorie saw that her eyes were really lovely when she smiled.

"I'm sorry!" said Betty. "I guess I've been pretty poisonous to you. But maybe if you'd been here and seen your people you loved suffer, you'd be poisonous too."

"I'm sure I should!" said Marjorie with a sudden quick setting of her lips "I'm quite sure I would feel just as you feel. And now let's forget it till we get this place comfortable for you all. What else shall I get besides coal? You said there wasn't much in the house to eat, didn't you? Are there other stores down there by the coal yard?"

"Yes, there's a couple of grocery stores, and a drugstore," said the girl reluctantly, "but don't you worry. I'll get things You've given me all this money."

"You'll have plenty of use for the money, I imagine. I'll just get whatever I see that I think would be nice and you can get later what I've forgotten. Now, go up to Mother and see that she's all right, and I'll get back as soon as possible."

Marjorie turned and put her hand out to open the door,

but before she quite touched it someone fumbled at the knob from the outside, the door was suddenly flung open with a bang letting in a rush of cold air, and someone stumbled into the hall bearing a heavy burden.

III

MARJORIE stepped back startled, staring at the tall man carrying a heavy sack of coal upon his back and another of small pieces of wood in his arms.

But Betty rushed forward and put up her arms to take one bag from him.

"Oh, Father!" she cried, "where have you been? How did you get it?" And then, giving him a quick searching look, "Where is your overcoat, Father? Oh, you didn't sell your overcoat, did you? Your nice overcoat? Oh, Father, and you *are sick!*"

"It couldn't be helped, Betty," said the man in a hoarse voice. "I had to get this house warm somehow for your mother. I couldn't let her freeze to death!" There was something warm and tender in his voice that brought the tears to Marjorie's eyes and a great rush of love for her unknown father to her heart.

Then the man suddenly dropped the bag from his back to the floor, put his hands up to his head with a bewildered look, and staggered over to the stairs, dropping down upon the second step, his face in his hands, and Marjorie saw that his bare hands were red and rough with cold, and that he seemed to be shivering.

"Father! Oh, Father! What is it?" cried Betty rushing over to him.

"Oh, it's nothing!" murmured the man with an effort. "Just a little dizzy, that's all. I'll be all right in a minute!"

27

"You had no breakfast! That's what makes it!" cried the girl in deep distress. She did not look toward her new-found sister. She seemed to have forgotten her presence. And the man on the stairs had not even seen her. She was getting an inside glimpse of her family off their guard, and a sharp new thrilling pain went through her heart. This was what they had been enduring part of the time while she rode on the top wave of luxury. Hungry! And she had often had to be coaxed to eat!

That picture of her father sitting on the stairs, his head bowed in his hands would stay with her always, she knew. Tall and well-built, but stooped Shapely hands, thin and blue-veined, the hands of a scholar or a gentleman. Shabby in his summer-weight business suit, yet with an air of having known better days All this she saw in a flash. And Evan Brower had dared to suggest her family might be an embarrassment! Her heart suddenly arose in defense.

"I'll get you a drink of water!" Betty was saying. "Thank fortune, they haven't turned off the water yet!" and she vanished through the door into the kitchen.

Marjorie saw there was a door from the little parlor where she stood and opening it she followed and found her sister as she brought back the water.

"I'll get him something to eat right away," she whispered. "Is there a restaurant or any place near by where they have food?"

"Only the drugstore. You can get a bottle of milk. Yes, bring it back quick. He didn't go out to the mission last night, he felt too miserable to go in the cold. And I suspect he hasn't been going there very often. It hurts his pride terribly. Yes, bring some milk quick. He's probably brought enough fuel to start the fire, and I can get it going while you're gone."

Marjorie ran down the uneven little sidewalk, breathless with the thought of her father sitting there in the bare ugly house, cold and hungry, dizzy with faintness, and her mother, no telling how sick upstairs! It was too dreadful! Why hadn't she come sooner? Why hadn't she taken the first train after she found the letter? Why had she dared hesitate? Why didn't her heart tell her how much her own were in need?

Then her quick mind began planning what to do. Her father should have something hot, like soup or coffee.

Probably both. In all probability her sister hadn't had much to eat either. And likely the mother had had very little, although they seemed to have saved everything for her. She must somehow manage to get some strengthening food to them at once. But how, and what? How far would it be to a good restaurant? Well, the drugstore would have hot-water bags. She could perhaps get them to fill one or two. And thermos bottles. Would there be any way to get a can of soup heated and fill a thermos bottle?

Arrived breathless at the diminutive drugstore she found to her joy that they had a soda fountain and served soup or coffee with sandwiches. The service wasn't very efficient and there was very little choice. But there was hot coffee and there was hot tomato soup, that is, it wasn't hot yet but the man said he could heat them both in a jiffy. And he had just two thermos bottles left. He agreed to rinse them out and fill one with coffee and the other with soup, and also to fill two hot-water bags with hot water and wrap them in newspapers. He hadn't had such a large order in weeks.

While he was getting them ready Marjorie hurried across the street to the grocery and bought two baskets big enough to carry her purchases, and also a dozen oranges, a loaf of bread, a pound of butter and a pound of sliced ham.

Back at the drugstore she added a quart bottle of milk to her other purchases and started back to the house. But she found she could not make very good time, a great basket in either hand. It was the heaviest load that she had ever carried in her life. She fairly staggered under it, but she would not waste time resting.

Arrived at the house she found the front door unlatched, but her father was no longer sitting on the stairs, and she heard sounds from the cellar.

Betty came hurrying up the cellar stairs as she came out to the kitchen, a long streak of soot on one white cheek and her eyes wide and worried.

"He would go down and start the fire," she said in a distressed voice. "I couldn't do anything with him." Her voice was almost like a sob. "He always thinks a woman has to be waited on, but he's had another dizzy spell and he's sitting on the cellar stairs now. Did you get anything?"

"Yes," said Marjorie eagerly, "I brought hot soup and

coffee, and here's some aromatic ammonia. Perhaps that will help too. And here, I have two hot-water bags nice and hot. Take one down and put it on his lap. Haven't you got a flannel or bit of old something to wrap it in? He ought to get warm right away."

"Oh, you're great!" said Betty and the tears were rolling down her cheeks, tears of relief.

She snatched a nicked cup from the shelf and poured out coffee and with a hot-water bag under her arm hurried down cellar again.

Marjorie hunted around and found plates and more cups and a knife, and cut some slices of bread, buttering them and putting ham between them. When Betty came back upstairs she had a plateful of nice sandwiches ready for her, and a cup of coffee.

"Take a swallow of this," said Marjorie holding out a cup of coffee, "and take this sandwich in your hand. You'll be sick next if you don't look out."

Betty looked hungrily at the food.

"But I must take something up to Mother, first," she said.

"No, drink this first, quick. It won't take you but a minute, and you can work better with something inside of you. Take this sandwich in your hand, and carry a cup of something up to Mother. Which should it be? Coffee first, or soup, or isn't she able for those? I've got oranges here. I can fix her a glass of orange juice in no time."

"Oh, wonderful!" said Betty gratefully, her eyes filling with relieved tears again. "I—don't know—what we would —have done if you—hadn't come!"

"There! Never mind that now. Just drink a little more and then go up to Mother. As soon as she knows about me I can help you care for her. I know how to take care of sick people. And now, shall I just slip out and have that coal sent up? You haven't got enough to last long in those bags and the house ought to get thoroughly warm and stay so. And while I'm out I'm going to order some groceries. Is that store I went to the best, or is there a better one somewhere else?"

"That's the best near here. They're all right. Ted will be home by and by perhaps and bring the things up for you."

"Don't worry about that. I'll find a way," said Marjorie brightly. "Did you tell Father I had come?"

"Not yet. He seemed so sick. And he was so determined to get that fire started. I'd better run down and see if he is all right now, and while you are gone I'll tell him."

Betty with her sandwich in her hand went down cellar, and hurried up again.

"He's eaten all the soup and is eating his sandwich now. I think he feels better. He said he would stay down for a few minutes to be sure the fire was started all right. He had one of those patent lighters, you know, and he wants to be sure the kindling catches. Now, I'm going up to Mother."

"Well, take this other hot-water bag," said Marjorie, "and I'll wait here at the foot of the stairs a minute to see if there is anything else you want me to get."

So Betty flew away up the stairs, and back again in a moment.

"She is still asleep," she whispered. "I laid my hand on her head and she didn't feel quite so hot as before. I think the hot-water bags helped. I slipped the other one in beside her back."

"Has she had a doctor?" asked Marjorie.

"No, she wouldn't let us. She said we hadn't the money to pay him. But Father is almost crazy about it. I think we ought to have him come just once, anyway, don't you?"

"I certainly do!" said Marjorie. "Where is he? I'll get him before I do anything else."

Betty gave the name and address.

"He's supposed to be a good doctor. I guess his prices are rather high," she said sorrowfully.

"What difference does that make?" said Marjorie. "We want the best there is. I'll send him as soon as I can, and you'd better make him prescribe for Father too. I'll tell him about it, and you make him. And, where do I talk to the gas people to get that gas turned on? We want to be able to cook some real dinner tonight!"

"Oh!" said Betty, quick tears stinging into her eyes. "You are going to be wonderful, aren't you!"

"No," said Marjorie smiling, "I'm just going to be one of the family, and try to make up for lost time. Does the water bill need looking after, too? We can't have that shut off. And what about electric light?"

"Oh!" cried Betty softly, sinking down on the lower step of the stairs, "you'll use all your money up!"

"Well," said Marjorie happily, "that's what money is for, isn't it? To be used up?"

"You're really real, aren't you?" said Betty, "I can scarcely believe it."

"What did you think I was, a spirit? Here, write those addresses quick. I want to get things started and get back to help."

She handed her sister a little note book and pencil from her handbag.

"We could get along without electric light if you get a couple of candles," Betty said with a troubled look.

"Why should we?" said Marjorie, and stooping kissed her sister's forehead lightly.

"You'll be sorry you ever came near us," said Betty sadly, "having to spend all this money and go on all these errands."

"I'm already glad I came," said Marjorie, "and if Mother and Father get well, and you don't get sick, I'd say I'm having the time of my life. It makes me greatly happy to be able to help and I only wish I'd known before that you had all this suffering. *And me with plenty!*"

Then although she was almost choking with tears, she gave a bright smile and hurried away on her errands.

She betook herself to the drugstore where there was a telephone booth and did the doctor, the coal, the gas, and electric light by telephone, and her crisp young voice, accustomed as it was to giving orders that were always promptly obeyed, brought courteous service at once, especially since full payment of the bill was promised when the agent would call. Then she went over to the little grocery and astonished the manager by selecting a large order from the best of his stock. She found also that there was a certain Joe, with a rusty little flivver, who would, for the consideration of a dime, deliver the order at once. And so, in an incredibly short space of time considering all she had accomplished, she arrived back at the house. She was in plenty of time to let in the gas man who had come posthaste because of her urgency, and her statement that there were two sick people in the house.

Then the groceries arrived and filled the shelves with stores.

In the midst of it Betty came down with round eyes of astonishment at the magic that had been wrought.

The chill was partly gone in the house by this time, and Marjorie took off her fur coat and her smart little felt hat, and hung them in the almost empty hall closet. She was rejoiced to feel a strong puff of hot air coming up the tiny register in the hall.

"Now!" she said, "I'm ready for work! Where do I put these things? Are there special places for them, or do I park them wherever I like?"

"Wherever you like!" said Betty throwing open the little pantry door and displaying a vista of empty shelves.

"And there comes the coal!" said Marjorie. "You'll have to tell him where to put that!"

Marjorie enjoyed putting away the things. She found the empty sugar jar and filled it. She put the vegetables and fruit in baskets. She found the old tin bread box and filled it with loaves. She had bought with a lavish hand, as far as the selection of the small store had afforded. Tin boxes of crackers and cookies and sand tarts, cheese and pickles and olives, coffee and tea and flour and meat. But there was no refrigerator and she decided it had probably been sold. Well, it was good it was cold weather. And they could remedy most of the discrepancies tomorrow.

Betty came up from the cellar and looked at her, watched her as she put things away.

"Well," she said in her sharp young voice that had a mingling of tears in its quality, "I suppose you must be pretty wonderful, and I'm crazy!"

"Nothing wonderful about it! I'm just an ordinary sister, Betty, that's mighty hungry to be taken in and made one of you!"

"Well, I should say you'd taken us in, if you asked me! I thought we'd reached the limit and tonight would see us all well on our way out of this life, but you've somehow brought us back again where we have to go on." Suddenly Betty dropped down on a box by the kitchen door and putting her head down in her hands burst into tears. Betty was worn out.

Marjorie was at her side at once, her arms about her, soothing her, putting the hair back from her tired forehead, putting a warm kiss on the back of her neck.

"Why, you're cold yet, you poor dear!" she said. "Come into the hall and sit over the register and get your feet warm."

"No! No, I'm all right," insisted Betty, raising her head and brushing away her tears. "I just can't understand it all, everything getting so different all of a sudden. Food in the house, and heat, and a chance to sit down."

"But, my dear, you've scarcely eaten a thing. Come, let me get you a nice little lunch. Have another sandwich! And here are eggs. I don't know how good a cook I am, for I haven't had much chance to practice, but I can scramble eggs beautifully, and the gas is on now."

Marjorie made Betty sit down and eat.

"Mother said the soup was the best thing she had tasted in weeks," she said as she ate hungrily.

"Have you—told her about me—yet?" asked Marjorie anxiously.

"No," said Betty. "I didn't have a chance yet. I didn't want to excite her while she was eating. And besides Father had come in and dropped down on the other edge of the bed. He went right off to sleep. And when Mother finished her soup she put her head back and said in a whisper, 'That was good! Now I'll go to sleep awhile and then I'll be all right.' And they never either of them asked where the things came from! Mother knew Ted had gone out to try and get a few subscriptions for a magazine. She likely thinks he has picked up a few pennies. But I thought it would be better for me to wait till they woke up to tell them about you."

"Of course!" said Marjorie. "Now, what should we do next? The doctor won't be here till two o'clock. He had gone to the hospital, but I got him on the wire and he promised to come here right from there. He had an emergency operation this morning. Is there anything to do to get ready for him?"

"There isn't anything we can do," said Betty. "I used the last clean sheet when I made up her bed fresh last night, and I haven't had any hot water to wash them with since."

"Well, if the sheets were clean last night they ought to be all right. Anyway I guess it's more important that they both should have a good sleep than that the bed should look stylish and uncrumpled. Let's bend our energies toward getting everything ready for a comfortable dinner. But first, tell me about us, just a word or two more. You spoke of Ted. Is he our brother?"

"Of course. Hadn't you heard of him, either? He's almost seventeen, and he's a dear. I don't know what we would have done while Father was sick, if it hadn't been for Ted. He worked early and late, just like a man. Like two men! He got a job in a grocery, and he got up before daylight and delivered papers, and then he worked from eight in the morning till sometimes nine at night. He's out now hunting for some kind of a job. And he hasn't had much to eat for a day and a half. He wouldn't take it away from us. He had a real desperate look on his face when he went away this morning. I wish he would come back and get something to eat. But he won't come until he finds something."

"Oh," said Marjorie, "couldn't I go out and find him? Or couldn't you, and let me stay here and look after things? It wouldn't do any good for me to go, of course, because I wouldn't know him. But I could look after Father and Mother if worst came to worst. I could perhaps get away with playing I'm you if I put on one of your dresses. I'm a pretty good nurse, you know."

Betty's eyes filled with tears, but she smiled through them, and shook her head.

"I wouldn't know where to find Ted. He goes all over the city when he gets desperate. He'll come pretty soon perhaps, because he said if he couldn't find something else this morning he'd come back and get that chair and take it to the pawnbroker. He felt we ought to have some coal as soon as possible, but he hated to give up the last chair."

"Oh, my dear!" said Marjorie, her eyes clouded with tears of sympathy. "Oh, if I had only known sooner!"

"Oh, don't you cry!" said Betty. "You've come, and I can't tell you how wonderful it is just to have it warm here again and have something to eat, and not be frightened about Mother and Father. That sounds awfully sordid, I know. But those things had to come first. And you don't realize how awful it's been. I'm sure I'll love you afterwards for yourself, but just now I can't help being thankful for the things you've done. Maybe I can make you understand sometime, when I'm not so tired. But you see I've hated you and blamed you for being better than we were so long! I see now it wasn't fair to you. You couldn't help what they did to you when you were a baby of course. Only I never dreamed they wouldn't tell you anything about us. Mother said Mrs. Wetherill had said they would tell you you were adopted, and I supposed of course you knew, and didn't care to have anything to do with us."

"I don't think Mrs. Wetherill knew much about you either," said Marjorie slowly, thoughtfully. "Not till Mother came to see her. And she never told me about that at all. She just left a letter. I think she couldn't get courage to talk with me about it when she knew she was going to leave me so soon. You see, when I was little, they just told me they had picked me out from all the babies in the world to be theirs, and I was more to them than if I had even been born to them. That satisfied me when I was small, but as I got larger and went to school and heard more about adoption I began to wonder why my parents had been willing to give me up. It seemed very heartless of them. But when I asked more questions about them I got very little satisfaction, just that somebody had been sick and they couldn't afford to keep me. So I confess I grew up feeling rather hard toward my own parents. Oh, I was having a good time of course, and not a hardship in the world, everything money could buy heaped upon me, but sometimes I got a little depressed or sentimental or something, and felt that I had been cheated by my own folks. You aren't the only one, Betty, that had hard feelings! I sometimes felt like a castaway. My own mother being willing to give me up when I was tiny and helpless. And of course I loved Mrs. Wetherill all the more fiercely in consequence, because she had come to my rescue. There! That's the way it looked to me! Now I guess we're somewhat even, and perhaps we can understand each other better. Anyhow it wasn't any of it our fault."

"I see," said Betty sadly. "I was all wrong of course. But I guess that was what made Mother suffer so, thinking she had let you go. She has cried and cried over that. Whenever she wasn't well she would cry all night. She said Mr. Wetherill came to her when she was weak and sick and didn't realize fully what she was doing. Father was threatened with tuberculosis. He had had lung fever and the doctor said he simply must get away from the office and out into the open for a few years, and Mr. Wetherill promised to put him on a farm and start him out, with the privilege of buying the farm if he wanted to. Besides he gave them quite a sum of money to have me treated. It seems I wasn't very strong and had to be under a specialist for a long time. They said I wouldn't live if I didn't have special treatment."

Betty's eyes grew stormy with bitterness.

"I used to wish sometimes they had let me die. I thought Mother didn't love me at all, she mourned for you so much."

"Oh, *my dear!*" said Marjorie coming close and putting her arms about her sister. "My dear! I think we are going to love each other a lot!"

It was very still in the dreary little kitchen for a minute while the two sisters held each other close. Then Betty lifted her head.

"I'm glad you've come, anyway!" she said. "You've been wonderful already. And I'm glad for Mother that she needn't fret for what she did any more. As soon as the doctor's been here I want to tell her. It will cure her just to know you are here, I know it will."

"Well, you'd better ask the doctor if it won't excite her too much. There! Isn't that the doorbell? Perhaps he's come! But it isn't quite two o'clock!"

Betty hurried to answer the bell, and Marjorie lingering in the kitchen saw through the crack of the door that it was the doctor. Betty took him upstairs at once, and Marjorie stood for a minute by the kitchen window looking out, staring at the minute frozen back yard and its dreary surroundings, wondering if her mother were very sick, wondering at herself that she cared so much already for a mother whom she had not yet seen. And this dear, fierce sister seemed already another self. And yet they had lived such different lives! Marjorie felt almost ashamed of her own sheltered existence. It seemed terrible to think of her leisurely, butterfly life, when everything Betty had had seemed to have been gotten by the hardest. Well, perhaps not all the time. She had spoken as if there were times when they had nice things. But the last few months must have been simply terrible! If she had only known sooner! If she might only have saved her mother and father in their distress. Oh, suppose it should be too late for either of them? She recalled the ghastly look of her father as he stumbled into the hall a little while ago with that great burden in his arms. How white and desperate he looked. How his voice shook as he said he must get it warm for the mother! Her heart thrilled at the desperate love in his voice. It was so grand to have them love one another that way! Even through trials and adversity!

Then she remembered the pantry which she had been putting to rights, setting the supplies up in an orderly manner on the shelves. She might as well get it done before her sister got back. It was better to be doing something than just standing there waiting to know what the doctor said.

She dampened a cloth she found, wiped off the shelves, and set about putting things away systematically. She stepped on a box to reach the top shelf, and there she discovered a handleless cracked cup with little tickets in it. Were they milk tickets or what? She wiped off the shelf, stepped down with the cup in her hand, and stood there examining the bits of paper. Each one had something written on it.

"Six plain sterling spoons," one said. "One brussels carpet," said another. "Three upholstered chairs."

Marjorie stared at them in dismay as she realized what these bits of paper must be. They were pawn tickets! She had never seen pawn tickets before. They represented the downfall of a home! A precious home where these her own flesh and blood had lived!

She went on with the tickets. "One child's crib-bed." "Six dining room chairs."

And now she noticed there was a date on each one and a price. Was that all they got for each of those articles? How pitifully little in exchange for surrendering their household necessities! "Two double blankets!" And they had been cold! Her mother was threatened with pneumonia—perhaps more than threatened! She went on with the tickets. "One wrist watch. Fifty cents."

She stood studying them, trying to make a rough estimate of the entire amount loaned for all those articles, when suddenly she heard the kitchen door open and a boy's voice said:

"What's the idea, Betts, of having the cellar window open? Did you think it was milder out than in?"

And then as the door shut to behind him:

"Gosh! You've got a fire! What did you do? Burn up our only chair? That's too bad. I found a place where they would pay sixty cents for it, since it's almost new!"

Marjorie turned startled, letting the pawn tickets fall

back into the cup, and facing him, not realizing that she still held the cup in her hands.

"Gee, but it feels good in here, anyway! But how did you manage a fire? There wasn't even a match! Did Dad —?" And then he turned and looked her straight in the face!

IV

SHE saw a tall boy, lean and wiry, with a shock of red hair and big gray eyes that had green lights in them. Under the mahogany brows and lashes they looked enormous; and they were weary, haunted eyes that seemed to have been perpetually puzzling out some anxious problem. There were shadows under them, too, and he looked too utterly worn for one of his age.

He stared at her first with a bewildered gaze like one who had come in out of the sun and could not rightly see in the dimmer light. He put up his hand and passed it over his eyes, and then his gaze grew puzzled, and then frightened, almost as if he were afraid his sight had played him a trick. Marjorie began to sense what he was feeling, and spoke quickly.

"You are Ted, aren't you?" She did not know how much her voice was like Betty's, only for that rich silken note that a luxurious surrounding had given her, and the boy was still more startled. He stiffened visibly, realizing that he was in the presence of a stranger.

The light of the pantry window was behind Marjorie's head which made the likeness to Betty still more illusive.

"Yes?" he said coldly, lifting his head a trifle, with a gesture that in a man would have been called haughty. He was alert, ready to resent the intrusion of a stranger into their private misery.

Then he saw the cup in her hand, and putting down the bucket of coal he had picked from the dump he stepped over and took the cup possessively.

"That wouldn't interest you," he said coldly, reprovingly.

"Ted!" said Marjorie impulsively, "I'm your sister! Don't speak to me that way!"

"My sister!" said Ted scornfully. "Well, I can't help it if you are, that doesn't give you a right to pry into our private affairs, does it?"

An angry flush had stolen over the boy's lean cheeks and his eyes were hard as steel.

"Oh, please don't!" said Marjorie covering her face with her hands, "I wasn't prying. I was trying to help!"

"Well, we don't need your help!" said the boy with young scorn in his eyes, "and it would be much better if you were to go back wherever you came from. This wasn't a very good time to select to visit us. We've got sickness in the house, and we've—been unfortunate—!"

"Oh, I know—!" moaned Marjorie, "but you see I didn't know anything about you till three or four days ago. I didn't even know I had a brother! But now I've come and I want to help."

"Well, I don't think there is anything you can do," he said icily. "We'll manage somehow by ourselves. You might leave your address and we can let you know when things are more prosperous, and then you could come and see Mother. Just at present it wouldn't be possible for us to have visitors."

"But you see, Ted, I'm not a visitor. I'm one of the family, and Betty and I are working together."

"Betty! Does my sister Betty know you are here? Where is she?"

"She's upstairs now with the doctor."

"The doctor! Is my mother worse?"

"I don't know. I haven't seen her yet, but as soon as I heard she was so sick I begged Betty to get the doctor. You know pneumonia is a very treacherous disease."

"Yes, and who did you think would pay the doctor?" asked Ted in that hard cold young voice so full of anxiety and belligerence.

"Oh, Ted! I'll pay it, of course!"

"Yes, and what do you think Mrs. Wetherill will say to that?"

"She won't say anything, Ted. She's dead!" There was a bit of a sob in Marjorie's voice in spite of her best efforts. She was tired, and this strange manly boy's repulsion hurt her terribly.

"Dead?" said Ted. "Well, that's just too bad for you, but I guess somehow we'll get along here without having outside help!"

"Oh, please, Ted, I'm not outside! I'm family!" she said, and now there were tears on her cheeks.

The boy looked at her speculatively and frowned.

"If you are family why didn't you ever turn up before when Mother was fretting for you?"

"Because I didn't know anything about her or any of you except that you had let me be adopted! I thought my mother didn't want me. I only found out three days ago who she was. Mrs. Wetherill left a letter for me in her desk. I found it after she died. It was there I discovered my mother's address. I didn't even know whether my father was living, and I didn't know there were the rest of you. But I came as quick as I could, and now I'm here I'm going to do my best to make you love me a little."

The hardness in the boy's face relaxed.

Then they heard the doctor coming downstairs, with Betty just behind him, and by common consent they froze into silence, Marjorie with a hand at her throat to still the wild throbbing of her pulses. Then they heard the doctor's voice:

"No, I don't expect her fever to go higher tonight. Oh, perhaps a little more. All she needs is rest and nourishment and good care. Be careful about the temperature of the room. Of course don't let her get chilled. That is the greatest danger. No, I don't think her lungs are involved yet. Good care and rest and the right food will work wonders. But I do think, as I said, that you should have a trained nurse for a week at least. If you want me to look one up for you I'll do it."

"Oh!" said Betty in a frightened voice, "I don't believe Mother would like that. I'm sure I can take care of her. I have before."

"Well, all right if you think so, but you look to me as if you needed a little nursing yourself."

"Oh, I'm all right!" said Betty summoning a cheerful voice. "I've just been worried about Mother."

"Well, don't worry any more. Just be cheerful. That's what your mother needs above all else, cheerful surroundings and no anxiety. Don't let her worry about a thing!"

"Doctor, my sister—has been away some time. She has just come back. Do you think it will hurt Mother to know she has come? She has been grieving to have her at home."

"What kind is she? Will she worry your mother, or will she be a help?"

"Oh, she'll be a help. She's rather wonderful!"

Ted stole a sudden shamed glance at Marjorie, with the flicker of a grin of apology in his young face.

"Well, then, tell her about it by all means. Joy never kills. Perhaps you'd better wait till she wakes up. Give her a sleeping tablet after her egg and milk and she'll settle down to sleep, I think. And don't you worry about your father. He's just worn out. Told me he had had reverses in business. A lot like that today. But he'll be all right after a few days' rest and feeding up. Give him plenty of fruit and vegetables. I suggested his getting away but he didn't seem to think it possible. However, if you just lift the worry from his heart he'll be all right, I think. No, I don't think there's any organic trouble with the heart, not yet. But you know hearts can't stand everything, especially when they are beginning to get older. Well, I'll step in again in the morning just to see if all is well, and don't hesitate to call me if you need me, or if there is any change. It's better to come unnecessarily than to wait too long, you know."

When the door closed behind the doctor Marjorie had a sudden feeling of letdown as if she wanted to sit down and cry with relief.

Betty's face was eager as she came out into the kitchen. She looked straight at Marjorie. Perhaps she didn't see Ted at first.

"He thinks maybe she won't have pneumonia after all," she said with relief. "And he says she must be fed every two hours. He wants her to have an egg and milk right away."

"I'll fix it," said Marjorie. "I know how to make won-

derful ones. Have we got an egg beater? A fork will do if
we haven't."

"Sure we've got an egg beater!" volunteered Ted.

Then Betty whirled upon her brother.

"Oh. Ted. you've got back. I've been so worried! You
went off without any breakfast, and you had no dinner last
night!"

"Aw, whaddaya think I am? A softie?" said Ted.

"I've been keeping the soup hot for him." said Marjorie.
"Here it is. Ted." She placed a bowl on the box and
brought the thermos bottle. "There's coffee too, and a
plate of sandwiches." She set the things before him.

"Gosh!" said Ted, dumbfounded. "Where did you get
all this layout?"

"You don't know what's happened since you left. Theo-
dore Gay! A miracle has come. that's what!" said Betty.
"We've got another sister, and she's just like Santa Claus.
She did it all!"

"Gosh!" said Ted, wrinkling his nice mahogany brows,
"but I don't think we ought to take it."

"Well," said Betty "I thought so too, but I found out it
was a choice between that. and dying, and she seemed determined to die with us if we did. so I let her have her way.
Sit down and eat that soup while it's hot. You'll be down
sick next if you don't, and we can fight it out later when
things get straightened out again. I'm so glad Mother and
Father aren't so sick as I thought that I'm willing to take
anything anybody hands me. But, Ted, you're mistaken
about that egg beater. It was in the kitchen table drawer
when you took it away to sell it. I missed it after you were
gone."

"Okay! I'll beat yer eggs with a fork!" said Ted, settling
down on another box and diving into the bowl of soup.
"Say, is this good! Or *is* it good!" he murmured, and then
ate away in silence.

"I'm going up to fix Father in the other room so he and
Mother won't disturb each other," said Betty. "I'll be back
for the egg and milk."

"No, I'll bring it up when it's ready," said Ted.

Marjorie got out the milk and eggs and fixed a tray.
Ted eyed her silently.

"How did you get a fire?" he growled out suddenly as
he took a big bite from the sandwich.

"Why—Father—" Marjorie brought out the name hesitantly, it was so new a name for a father she had never known—"Father came just as I was starting out to try and find the coal yard. He had two big bags in his arms, and he was dizzy. He had to sit down on the stairs."

Ted suddenly put down the cup of coffee he was drinking and half rose.

"Dad hasn't had a thing to eat!" he said horror stricken. "It was raining last night and he didn't go out to the mission to get his dinner! He said he wasn't hungry!"

Ted had forgotten the new sister. He was talking aloud, accusing himself for having eaten when his father was hungry.

"I'll take this right up to him! I ought to have thought."

"No," said Marjorie putting out a protesting hand, "he has had plenty now. I went right up to the drugstore and got soup and coffee. But while I was gone he had insisted on going down cellar and starting the fire. He had matches and a patent kindler. Betty took some coffee down to him and then made him go up and lie down afterward."

"That fire won't last long," said Ted wisely, "not on one bag of coal. I'd better go out and rustle some more. I've got one bucket full here, but it isn't very good, all partly burned. I mustn't let this house get cold again."

"Oh, there's plenty of coal in the cellar now," said Marjorie happily. "The man said the bin would hold two tons so I got that. He's just got done putting it in. That will last a good while, won't it?"

"Two tons!" the boy stood aghast. "How'll we ever pay for two tons? You didn't get that from our regular coal man? He said he wouldn't let us have any more till the bill was paid." He looked at her with accusing eyes, such young, frightened, stern eyes. She loved him for the way he was trying to be a man and take responsibility.

"But it's all paid for, brother dear!" said Marjorie with shining eyes. "Bill and coal and all. I told him I would pay cash if he would send it at once, and I certainly did!"

The boy looked at her astounded.

"Gosh!" he said, and then he turned and ran down the cellar stairs. She could hear his footsteps, going over to the coal bin, then back to the furnace a few paces, opening the furnace door, looking in, closing it again, and then more slowly coming up the stairs. She glimpsed him brushing his hand quickly across his eyes as he appeared in the kitchen, his young face filled with relief.

"Gosh, that's a break!" he said flinging himself down on the box again and reaching for what was left of his sandwich. "I never expected to see that much coal again, not in that cellar! I'll say you're some sister!"

Marjorie smiled, her heart warming.

"Will you have another sandwich?"

"No, I mustn't eat things up. I can get along on what I've had. It's more than I've had at once in six months. Save the rest for Mother and the others."

"But there is plenty," said Marjorie happily. "I got several loaves. And how about some scrambled eggs? I can make lovely scrambled eggs!"

"You couldn't, not here!" said Ted with finality. "The gas company turned off our gas. You can't scramble eggs in the furnace, can you?"

"Oh, but the gas company have been here and turned on the gas. See?" and she struck a match and lighted a burner. "There's no reason why you can't have scrambled eggs." Marjorie put on a bent little frying pan over the flame, flipped a bit of butter into it and broke three smooth brown eggs into it.

Ted watched her fascinated as she scrambled the eggs, finishing with a shake of pepper and salt.

"Say, you can cook, can't you? I thought you'd be too high-hat to cook."

"I can cook a little," said Marjorie, "not much. Probably Betty can do much better than I. I never had a chance to practice much."

"Well, neither had Betts. She's been in an office ever since she got out of school. Say! These eggs are great! Gosh, I haven't tasted anything so good in weeks. You're sure I ought to eat all of this? It seems enough for the whole family. Why, if we'd had this much yesterday we would have thought we were rich!"

Marjorie felt a sudden lump coming into her throat that betokened tears near at hand. She felt so glad to have got here in time before her family starved to death! How awful to think they had been in such straits while she feasted on the fat of the land!

He studied her for an instant and then he said gravely:

"But we can't live off of you! It's great of you to help us out a little till we get on our feet, but we can't keep on letting you feed us. Perhaps I can get a job soon and pay you back."

The brightness went out of Marjorie's face.

"Listen, Ted, if I had lived here, and you had plenty, wouldn't you have shared it with me?"

"Of course!" said Ted crossly, "but that's different! I'm a fella!"

"Well, that's all right, 'fella' dear, but it isn't different. I'm a part of this family, unless you throw me out, and what's mine is yours. And now, come, I'd like to say a word about what you did to me when you first came in. You took that cup of tickets away and told me they wouldn't interest me. But they do interest me. They interest me very much. They're pawn tickets, aren't they? Well, what are we going to do about them, Ted? Are those Mother's things that she's fond of? Oughtn't we to go and get them?"

"That would take a lot of money," said Ted hopelessly. "Yes, of course, they're her things, but we had to pawn them. She had to have food and heat and medicine."

"Of course," said Marjorie, just as if she was used to going out and pawning her furniture and clothes whenever she had to have something else, "but are they things she cares about? Or would she rather have new things?"

"They're her things. They're all the things she has. And she couldn't get new things even if she did want them. She can't get these either," he added dejectedly. "I tell you it costs a lot of money."

"Yes, but how much, Ted?" persisted Marjorie. "That is what I was trying to find out when I was looking over those tickets. I wasn't wanting to pry. I was trying to find out what to do."

"It isn't your responsibility," said Ted doggedly. "It's mine. I pawned them."

"Now look here, Ted, you just stop pushing me out of the family like that. I'm trying to make up a little for all the good I might have been to the family if I had been here. Don't you see I want to be in and be loved and be a part of things, even of your troubles? That's what it would have been if I had lived with you while I was growing up instead of with the Wetherills. And I'm certainly sharing in everything from now on. Now you reach up to that top shelf and take down the teacup and we'll add those tickets up and see what it comes to. Please!"

Half shamedly Ted did her bidding.

They got out the tickets and Marjorie added them all up, a pitifully small sum it seemed to the girl, to represent the household goods of a home, but to the boy it seemed a breath-taking fortune.

"Is that all!" said Marjorie when he handed her the sum. "Why, I can give you that right away. I was afraid maybe I'd have to go out and cash a check. But is this all? Aren't there some things somewhere else?"

"No," said Ted. "The rest we had to burn up to keep warm with, but they weren't much account. The old rickety kitchen table, and a few shaky chairs. Oh, yes, and Betty's bedstead and mine, they went first, but they weren't anything great. We just put the mattresses on the floor."

He grinned, and Marjorie stifled a gasp and grinned back. What a lot of things she was learning about the makeshifts of poverty.

"All right!" she said briskly, "then let's get those things back and make the house look natural before Mother gets up to see it. That will do a good deal toward making her cheerful, and there is no need for her to know how we did it either. Have these things been out of the house long?"

"Not so many of them. The spoons went first. Mother felt awfully down about those, and soon after that she was taken so sick she had to go to bed. She doesn't know about most of the rest. We kept her room like it was when she went to bed. I guess she thinks we've been living on the spoons all this time. She doesn't know how little they gave for them. She thought an awful lot of those spoons. They were her grandmother's."

"Oh!" said Marjorie pitifully. "Well, now, do you think you could get those back this afternoon? Or should I go for them?"

Ted flashed a quick negative.

"I'll get them," he said. "It's no work for you. I'll have to bring the big things one at a time. I'm not sure I can borrow the hand cart I had when I took them away either.

I took them at night, you know, so the neighbors wouldn't see. Probably I can get the cart after the store closes tonight, but it will take several nights to get them all."

"Oh, my dear! Don't try to bring them yourself. It won't cost but a few dollars to hire a truck and have them brought."

"A *few* dollars!" laughed Ted excitedly. "I can get Sam Sharpe to bring them all after five this evening for a dollar. He'd be glad to get it. He takes the truck to his Dad's garage for the night and has the privilege of using it for any little odd jobs he gets. But a dollar's a dollar, you know, and I've been too near to the edge of nothing to throw dollars away when I can do the thing myself."

"Oh, Ted!" said Marjorie pitifully. "But in this case I think a dollar is cheap, just to get the things here tonight and make things look like home again."

"Okay with me," said Ted, "but it won't likely look like your home at that. Mother's told us how it looks where you were brought up."

"Yes, it was a lovely home," said Marjorie with a sudden rush of feeling, "but we're going to make this as lovely as we can. Now, can you go right away and see if you can get the truck?"

"Sure thing!" said Ted. "But he can't bring them till after five. I might as well stick around here and see if there is anything else I can do till then. That will be after dark, too. The neighbors are so curious. Mother hates that! Having them all find out just what we've got and what we haven't. You know we used to have a nice home over in a suburb on the other side of the city. Nice big house, built of stone. Plenty of room. We each had a room to ourselves, and there was a garage and a big garden, and flowers and fruit trees. It was a swell place. And Dad had a position with a good salary. That was before the depression, you know. We had a car, too, and Dad used to drive in town every morning. It was swell living there. Dad had money in the bank. That was about the time Mother tried to get to see you. She did so want to have you visit us. She was all in when she came back with that picture of you and said they wouldn't let her see you. She'd counted on bringing you home. We'd all counted on it. And then all of a sudden the man where Dad worked

died, and his business went flooey, and Dad couldn't get
anything else right away except a little accountant job that
didn't pay much. He took it and kept on trying for something better, but things were going bad, and Mother had to
have an operation, and the kids were sick, and Dad had to
put a mortgage on the house, and the next thing that happened the Building Association that had the mortgage
went up, and they demanded the money right away, all of
it, and Dad hadn't been able to pay the interest for a couple of times, so they took away the house. Oh, it was a
mess, and then Dad got sick, and everything's been going
from bad to worse ever since."

"Oh, my dear!" said Marjorie quite honestly crying
now. "My dear! I'm so sorry you've been going through
all that!"

"Well, don't bawl!" said Ted crossly, brushing his hand
over his own eyes. "I can't stand bawling! I just told ya
because I thought you'd wantta know. We haven't always
been down and out this way. We had a swell home!"

"Well, now let's make this one as cheerful as we can before evening," said Marjorie taking a deep breath. "I'll get
the money!"

She went into the parlor to her handbag that she had
left on the bare little high mantel shelf and brought back a
roll of bills that made Ted's eyes open wide.

"I put in a little extra," said his sister smiling. "I
thought perhaps you'd think of something we need that
I've forgotten."

"Gosh!" said Ted gazing down at the roll of bills in his
hand. "Don't know's I can trust myself out alone. I might
get held up carrying all this wealth."

She smiled. It seemed a very small amount of money to
her.

"Get anything you want, you know. I'm not used to
providing for a family. I got everything I could think of at
the little store down here, but I suppose I've left out a lot
of things. Soap is one. Better get plenty. Betty says there
isn't any in the house. And potatoes. We could have
roasted potatoes for dinner tonight. I got a beefsteak!"

The boy grinned.

"I can see where you're going to spoil us for living
again when you're gone."

"Gone!" said Marjorie with dismay in her voice. "Do you want me to go?"

"No, not on yer life! But you're not going to stick around these diggings. Not with the home you've been used to! You'll be spreading your wings and flying away!" and he gave her a sudden quick look. "Say!" he added irrelevantly, "you look a lot like Betts, and yet you don't. I could tell you apart already! You don't look quite so frowsy as Betty, and you've got a cute little quirk in the corners of your mouth. Maybe Betty would look like that too if she hadn't had to work so hard, and have such a lot of trouble."

"You're sweet!" said Marjórie, and suddenly reached up with a quick motion and kissed her new brother on his lean hard young cheek.

He blinked and the color went up in a great wave, and receding left it white, and his eyes shadowed and weary-looking.

"Okay with me!" he grinned. "If that's your line you better give warning next time. We don't have much time for mush and sob-stuff!"

Then he turned sharply away toward the window and she saw him brush his hand across his eyes, and swallow hard.

"Okay with me!" said Marjorie, trying to make her voice sound as much like his a minute before as she could. And suddenly he laughed.

"You're aw'right," he said grudgingly.

"Thanks awfully!" said Marjorie, trying to enter into his spirit. "But who is that coming in the door?"

"That's Bud," said Ted, peering through the crack into the hall. "Hey, Kid! Hush up there! Dad and Muth's asleep! They're sick and yer not ta make a noise! Come on out here an' shut the door carefully."

A boy about ten came panting into the room, so out of breath he could scarcely articulate.

"They—sent me—ta tell ya—!" he panted. "You gotta come right away an' get the kids. Bonnie's got a fever— an' she—wouldn't eat her cereal—an' she is crying for Betty—an' Sunny is yellin' his head off!"

"Good night!" said Ted. "Who told you that?"

"Miss Baker! She said we'd haveta take 'em home. She

said they couldn't do—a thing 'ith Sunny since Bonnie got sick. They said—" he was still puffing and panting from his run—"they said—they hadta—have the beds—fer the —little kids. They got too many—an' ours gotta come home now."

"Okay, you come with me, Kid. We'll get 'em," said Ted, "but I don't know what we'll do with 'em here. Gosh! Can you beat it?" He cast an apologetic eye at the new sister.

"What is it?" she asked puzzled. "Who are they?"

"The kids!" answered the brother in astonishment. "Didn't you know about them?"

"No!" said Marjorie. "Oh, I remember, Betty said something when I first came about taking the children somewhere, but I had forgotten about it. I didn't realize there were more of us."

"Two besides Bud!" said Ted lifting his chin maturely and sighing. "I don't know how we're going to make the grade with any more sick folks."

Marjorie gave a little gasp of amazement and then her soft lips set firmly.

"We'll manage!" she said. "I'll go with you to get them. I can carry one of them."

The boy Bud was standing now gazing at her in a kind of distress.

"Who's that?" he ejaculated pointing to Marjorie, his eyes wide with a kind of fear. "Where's Betty? That's not Betty."

"No," said Ted, "she's the new sister. Did you have any lunch, Bud?"

"Naw. They wouldn't give me any. They said I didn't belong. They said I was too big to be there and I couldn't come tamorra. And anyhow I hate 'em. They kep' tellin' me I oughtta be in school."

"Well, don't worry. You don't havta go again. We've got a fire now."

"Gee! It feels good!" said the child rubbing his red cold hands together. "I'm gonta stand over the register. Say, gimme a little piece of bread, can't ya? I'm holler!"

"You poor child!" exclaimed the new sister in horror. "Wait. I'll make him a sandwich before I go. It won't take a minute!"

"Who said sandridge?" said Bud. "Not honest? Gee! Where'dya get the ham? Real ham!"

He watched with shining eyes and grabbed the sandwich eagerly, too hungry to wait for an answer to his question, accepting the new sister quite casually, as being not nearly so important as the sandwich to his poor starving little stomach.

"Do you like ham?" smiled Marjorie as she buttered another generous slice of bread.

"I'll say!" said the urchin taking enormous bites of his sandwich.

"How about a glass of milk?" she asked.

"Got milk too? Okay with me!"

She laughed and poured out a brimming glass of milk, and then brought out an orange and some little cookies from a tin.

"Gosh!" he said eyeing the spread with genuine amazement, his jaws pausing for a second in their vigorous chewing. "All that!"

"Will that keep you busy till we get back?" asked Marjorie with another smile.

"I'll say!"

"Well, don't make any noise. You just stay here and keep the door and be ready to open it for us when we get back with the children!"

Then Marjorie flung on her coat, and put on her hat as she went out the door with Ted.

"Say, you don't needta come," said Ted with belated courtesy. "I can manage with the two kids. Sunny'll run along beside me, and Bonnie is nearly seven. She can walk all right."

"But if she has a fever she ought not to walk," said Marjorie. "Is she too heavy for you to carry? Couldn't we get a taxi?"

Ted grinned.

"Taxis don't grow around here," he said significantly. "Sure, I can carry her if it's necessary. It's only a little over three blocks."

They walked along almost a block before Marjorie spoke again and a great shyness was possessing Ted. Out in the sunshine with this strange new sister, who looked so much like Betty, and yet was different, who dressed like a "swell" and used scarcely any slang at all, he was deeply embarrassed. Conscious too of his shabby trousers, and torn old sweater, awfully conscious of that lovely squirrel coat she was wearing, and the chic little hat perched on her golden head. She seemed a strange lady from another world. In the house it had been comparatively easy to converse with another Betty, who was wearing Betty's apron, cleaning off pantry shelves and scrambling eggs. But out here it was different. He felt that everyone they met was staring at him, and comparing his shabbiness with his new sister's elegance.

Then Marjorie spoke.

"You said something about the beds, but I didn't take it in. Is there a place for the children? I expect the little girl with a fever ought to be put to bed at once. Where does she sleep? Will it disturb Father and Mother to put her to bed? I think it's important that they should not be disturbed."

"I was just wondering about that myself," said Ted in a troubled voice. "There's only three rooms upstairs. Bonnie has always had her little bed in Betty's room and Sunny's crib was in mine. But we had to sell their beds last week, to buy medicine for Mother. Bonnie's been sleeping on the mattress with Betty since, and Sunny with me."

He looked up half fearfully, almost defiantly, wondering what she would think of such poverty.

"I see," said Marjorie thoughtfully. "Well, we've got to do something else right away, I guess, if she really has a fever. She ought not to be down so near the floor. There are draughts on the floor."

Ted looked up thoughtfully.

"I could get Bonnie's bed," he said. "It's a light little thing made of bamboo. It was Betty's when she was a kid. I know where I could borrow a wheelbarrow. Two or three trips would do it."

"That's fine!" said Marjorie. "Suppose you do that as soon as we get them home. Has it a mattress?"

"Yes, and a pillow. Poor kid! She cried for her own pillow the first night it was gone. Funny little things, kids. They don't use their brains! Haveta have what they want."

Marjorie smiled at him.

"I guess we're a little like them, aren't we? Want what we want very badly. I know I am. That's why I came away off here hunting you all. I wanted a family badly!"

He grinned speculatively at that and didn't know what to say, but at last blurted out:

"I guess it would have made a lot of difference if we'd known you felt that way."

"Well, I'm sorry we didn't all understand sooner," said Marjorie, "but perhaps we can make up for lost time now."

Then they arrived at the neighborhood crèche and Ted led the way in.

V

ABOUT that time back at Marjorie's home in Chicago Evan Brower was standing at the front door impatiently ringing the doorbell.

He had been called away from the city on business the morning after his call upon Marjorie, returning about the middle of the next afternoon, and finding it a bit late for going to his office had decided to run in informally and see Marjorie.

Perhaps courtesy really demanded that he wait until she gave him the promised telephone call, but he had never stood on ceremony with the Wetherill household, and he had the excuse that he had been away and therefore did not know but she had called during his absence. So he drove directly to her home without waiting to inquire if she had called. It made a very good case for him, and also indirectly showed his devotion and eagerness to see her. So there he stood, and wondered why the faithful servants allowed him to wait so long for admittance.

Since he had left her, Evan Brower had been vaguely disturbed by Marjorie's attitude, and wished he had stayed, in spite of her request that he go and let her think things over. He should have reasoned with her right then and there. It was not like what he thought she was that she should have even considered such a romantic idea as running off after an unknown family, who would likely take instant advantage of her and her fortune.

He had never considered Marjorie Wetherill impulsive before, but now he recalled a certain look in her eyes as she had spoken of her own people, that smacked of fanaticism. Of course when he had tried to warn her gently he had used the phrase "over-conscientiousness," but to himself he called it by what he felt was its true name He reasoned that sentimentality often developed into fanaticism, and it had certainly seemed as if Marjorie was sentimental toward her real parents Though she had always seemed sweet and sane in everything it was quite possible that in her present lonely state she might go off at a tangent, aided by an over strong conscience, and commit herself to these strangers in some way that would hamper her all her life, unless she was restrained He blamed himself that he hadn't exerted his utmost to restrain her before he allowed her to cut short the interview.

Also, she was young and utterly without experience in financial affairs, and here she was suddenly left with a fairly large fortune, and menaced by a family of unknown quantity and quality There was no telling to what lengths of generosity these people might lead her before her friends could rescue her And of course if he was going to marry her, as he had about come to the conclusion he would, he certainly did not want a lot of impecunious in-laws hanging around his neck. Neither did he want his future wife's ample inheritance divided with people who had no right to a cent of it. They had probably been well paid for giving up their baby and they had no right whatever, according to the adoption contract, to bother her in any way at any time He felt surprised and annoyed that Mrs. Wetherill should have been so weak as to leave a hint of their whereabouts. Probably in her last hours she was suddenly attacked by a morbid conscience, but it was most ungenerous in her to have cast the whole matter off onto Marjorie. She must have known of course that it would trouble her.

These thoughts had been milling about in his brain all day as he drove from one appointment to the other and then back to his home city, coming straight out to Wetherill's instead of going to the office first.

But after the third ringing of the bell he grew alarmed. What could have happened? Surely they would not leave the house with no one to answer the door!

He walked around the house to the garage where he found the chauffeur out washing the car.

"What is the reason I cannot get any answer to my ring?" he asked severely. He was the kind of young man who always required perfect service, and usually got it.

The chauffeur looked up from his work deferentially, recognizing a friend of the family.

"Why, sir, they're all away for the holidays. Miss Wetherill went last night and gave all the servants a holiday while she is gone. Very kind of her, sir. She's always kind."

"Indeed!" said Evan Brower as if it were somehow the chauffeur's fault. "It must have been a sudden decision. I'm sure she had no idea of going away immediately when I was here night before last. Nothing happened, did it? I mean, like a funeral, sudden death of a friend, or something? She didn't get a telegram that sent her off so soon?"

"I wouldn't be supposed to know, sir," said the chauffeur. "I'm not a house servant, you know, and I didn't happen to hear the others say."

"You don't know where she's gone? Haven't you her address?"

"No, sir, I haven't. She said she'd write me a day or so before she returned so I'd know to start up the heater, and expect the other servants. She only said she was away for the holidays, and that she might be visiting relatives. She wasn't sure how long she would stay. Probably till after the New Year."

Evan Brower frowned. This was really serious. What a fool he had been not to make Marjorie sit down and listen to him the other night!

"But don't you know where she went? What city? Whether she went east or west?"

"No, sir, I don't. She sent me to take the servants to their trains. She said she would take a taxi. When I got back she was gone and the house locked. She left the key with Martha, my wife."

An interview with Martha brought no further information, except that Martha was sure she did not take a trunk.

"Only a couple of suitcases, or bags. I couldn't rightly see which from here," said Martha. "I'm not one to be snooping. I just happened to be out in the side yard hanging up a couple of pieces I had washed out when the taxi drove in. I can just see the front door from where the line hangs. The driver brought out her things and she got in and drove off. That's all."

Evan Brower got into his car and drove away in much dissatisfaction. It was good, of course, to know that she had probably not taken a trunk, and therefore could not have gone for long, but she had gone, and left no clues behind her, and a great deal of damage can be done to a fortune in a very few days, or even hours. In much perturbation he went to his office and then to his home inquiring for telephone calls, but there had been none from Marjorie. Then he opened his mail and found her brief note.

So! She had gone. Headstrong little girl! Impetuous! He hadn't thought she was like that. If he married her, and he had practically committed himself to that course, he would certainly have to train that out of her.

After some hard thinking he finally called up the Wetherill lawyer, and was fortunate enough to find him still in his office.

"Good afternoon, Mr. Melbourne, this is Evan Brower. Sorry to have interrupted you, but I won't keep you but a minute."

"Oh, that's all right, Brower, I was just leaving for home anyway. Work all done for the day, I'm happy to say. What can I do for you?"

"Why, I am just wondering whether Marjorie Wetherill happened to leave her address with you? She spoke of the possibility of her being away for the holidays, but I don't think she expected to go so soon. I've been away for a day and I find she's already gone. I wondered if she left her address with you? I am sending her a remembrance for Christmas and want to give the address when I order it."

"Well, now that's too bad!" said the kindly old lawyer. "I had a telephone message from Miss Wetherill saying she was to be away during the holidays, and would send me an address later. But I fancy if you just address it to her home here the post office will forward it. She likely left her address with the carrier. However, I'll be glad to send it to you as soon as I get it."

Evan Brower thanked the lawyer and hung up, frowning. So that was that, and he couldn't do a thing about it. Marjorie had slipped neatly through his fingers and gone her own way in spite of his protests. He would try the letter carrier and post office of course, though they were not supposed to give such information. Well, she would have to learn her own lesson by the hardest. But, would she learn it before it was too late? There was no reason why she should let her property drift through her fingers to a lot of unprincipled relatives, just because she was sorry for them.

But the post office when consulted said they were to hold all mail for further orders. She had left no address.

Well somehow he must get in touch with her. Perhaps Melbourne would hear from her in a few days and then he would make a little trip out to wherever she was and bring her back She would likely be good and sick of her new family by that time and be glad to be rescued. Also it would give him a good chance to look this family over and see what were the possibilities before he put his head into the noose of marriage One had to be careful, of course for the future. Though if he really decided to marry Marjorie he would trust himself to get rid of any objectionable relatives. Perhaps it would be as well for someone from her home to meet them and freeze them out right at the start Marjorie might not like that, but what she didn't know wouldn't need to trouble her, and if it were wisely done. and if they had any shame at all a hint or two quietly given would subdue them. He flattered himself he could deal with them right at the start. Mrs. Wetherill had been able to hold them off for years, hadn't she? Well he could do at least as well as a woman.

So he went his way. and made his plans for going after Marjorie when the right moment should come, and that would be the first minute he knew where to find her.

He went out and bought a delightful Christmas gift for her. He even went so far as to look at engagement rings. And he called up Mr. Melbourne at frequent intervals to know if he had heard from Marjorie yet.

The more he thought about it the more his thoughts became intrigued with the girl who was so sweet and unspoiled How easily she could be molded to fit the environment in which she would live if she were his wife. He spent a good deal of his leisure time planning how he would mold her. The more he planned the more sure he was that he was going to ask her to marry him. And of course she would accept him There wasn't any question about that. Not that Evan Brower was conceited. But he was strong in the knowledge that his was an old family, that his family and the Wetherills had been friends for years, that he had been fairly successful even so early in his business career, and he was popular and good-looking. He couldn't help knowing the latter, although he hoped he had never let it make him vain. He despised men who were vain of their looks. One couldn't help one's looks. They were merely an asset.

Then, he reflected, Marjorie had always been fond of his company, had been ready to accept his invitations always, although until recently he had taken her out very little. There was no reason thinkable why she should not want to marry him. He was sure he had seen genuine admiration in her eyes. Yes, and her hand surely lingered in his the first time he came to see her after Mrs. Wetherill's death, as if she naturally turned to him in her sorrow. Of course, why shouldn't she? He was one of the closest friends of the family.

And it was quite the appropriate thing for him to marry her. More and more as he turned it over in his mind his common sense as well as his inclination approved the plan. And it was comfortable to think of the girl of his choice as being utterly unspoiled by contact with the world. She had been guarded so carefully all her life, surrounded with just the right environment, just the right companions. None of the noisy ill-bred ways of the social life of the day had touched her. There had been no other man in her life, he was sure of that. He would not have to worry about any youthful indiscretions. Innocent and lovely, that was what she was, and very likely he had been the ideal man in her eyes. It was most desirable to have a wife who adored one and had never turned her thoughts toward another. Not that he had always had one ideal of womanhood, himself; but of course men were different. It was man's part to choose, and naturally, he had considered other girls, but had never been quite satisfied.

Of course, there were things about Marjorie that might be changed. But he could change them, he had no doubt. Take, for instance, her conscience, which seemed to work a little too easily where others were concerned. She was almost too self-sacrificing. True, that might be a good thing in a wife toward her husband, but not toward the world in general. However, that could be easily remedied. And of course it would be different when she had a man of her own to think about and consider first.

He began to think back to his first consciousness of

Marjorie, when she had come home from college after graduation. Of course he had seen and known her before that, in fact nearly all her life. But he had then become conscious of her as a woman. He remembered her as she sat in church, across the aisle, a row in front of where he was sitting with his mother. He had never noticed her beauty till then. She was wearing a little spring suit of gray tweed, and a small round hat that showed her gold hair, and the delicate oval of her rounded cheek. He had been struck with her beauty then, and wondered that he had never seen it before, wondered that here was a lovely person right at hand, who seemed somehow to have been kept from the common trend of modernism. He had glanced from her to Mrs. Wetherill, patrician in every line of her tall body and every feature of her handsome face, and wondered that she had been able to put the imprint of herself so unmistakably upon the girl whom she had taken in babyhood and brought up as her own. Whatever was behind the girl's early life that might have been undesirable was surely obliterated The girl had conformed utterly to the model of a well-balanced, sane, conservative life of culture and refinement, and, to a degree, of religious belief. She would be an ornament anywhere, one of whom to be proud.

He had watched her during the service, as she gave attention to the sermon; her sweet seriousness attracted him strongly From that time he played more or less with the thought of her as a life companion He began to take her out, cautiously, as was his nature, studying her from every angle, exploring the ways of her keen young mind, probing to the depths of her nature. He marveled at her quick clear judgment in most things, her willingness to be taught her yielding nature, so free from selfish aims, so utterly free from self-consciousness and self-esteem.

This difference they had had the last time he had talked with her, about hunting up her own people, had been the first unwise decision he had ever seen her make. Doubtless harking back to something primitive in her nature, he told himself But as such it should be dealt with at once and summarily, for the sake of her future and his own.

Restlessly he argued these things over and over in his mind as the days went by and he heard nothing from Marjorie, yet he could think of no way to get into touch with her that would not cause publicity and comment.

In the meantime his mind was making itself up very definitely that Marjorie was desirable. The more so as he discovered through an old friend and confidante of the Wetherill family that an unusually large number of shares of a very valuable stock were a part of the Wetherill estate which Marjorie had inherited. Marjorie had a lot of money and needed the right man to look after it. And he was convinced that he was the right man.

That was the day he selected the great blue diamond engagement ring.

VI

But Marjorie was walking along a sordid back street holding the thin cold hand of a little new brother who was crying.

The child looked anything but sunny as he dragged his reluctant young feet along, trying to pull away from this strange new sister who looked just enough like the familiar sister Betty to frighten him. There were tears running down his thin cheeks, tears freezing on his chin and nose.

Some benighted visitor to the day nursery had administered a square of cheap chocolate as an antidote to fright and homesickness and hunger, and the recipient while devouring it had not ceased to wail, thus mingling the chocolate with the tears, and applying most of it externally.

The baby-gold of his curls was matted in a tangle, the curls that had given him his happy little name of Sunny, and the faded red cap was awry on them. The small threadbare coat that had seen several steps of the Gay family through the baby stage had lost most of its buttons and was dragging open showing a mended blouse much the worse for chocolate and the wear and tear of the day. One stocking had come down around Sunny's ankle showing a bare little knee rough and red with cold.

"I—d-d-don't—vantta—valk—vif—her!" he was wailing in a voice halfway between a howl and hysteria. "I vants—my—B-B-Bet-ty! I vants my—muvver!"

The passersby stared after them, the beautiful girl in

the expensive fur coat and the smart hat and gloves, dragging the howling dirty child; the shabby young fellow carrying a little girl in his arms, a little girl with scarlet cheeks, who lay back unresisting, one arm hanging down limply, one little bare hand sticking forth from a too-short sleeve. It made a queer procession, and people stopped amused.

"Shut up, Sunny!" growled Ted, plodding along behind. His own strength was none too great in spite of his recent meal, and Bonnie was a dead weight, even though she looked frail.

Instantly the indignant baby turned back and dragged at his captive hand.

"I d-d-don't vantta—go vif her! I vants *you* to tarry me, Teddy!"

"Aw, be a man, Sunny boy!" implored Ted desperately. "Can't you see I've got to carry Bonnie? Bonnie's sick! Be a good kid and walk along with your new sister. She's okay, Sunny. We're almost home."

"Naw! I von't valk vif her! I vants *you* to tarry me!"

Marjorie suddenly stooped down and swept the youngster into her arms. She had never had much to do with children before, but she was quite strong and held him firmly.

"*I'll* carry you," she said brightly, struggling with the frantic child. "There! There, you're cold. See, I'll tuck you inside this nice kitty-coat!"

She unbuttoned her coat and put him within its folds.

"There! There! Poor little boy! You are cold and tired, aren't you? Sister will wipe your face nice and dry!"

She fumbled for her handkerchief with one free hand, and the young man dealt her a few futile kicks.

It wasn't an easy trip, that, but Marjorie was very determined when she started a thing, and at last, breathless and aching in every muscle, she arrived at the house, a little behind Ted and his burden.

Bud opened the door for them, a large piece of bread and butter in one hand. Betty stood on the stairs, her eyes wide with anxiety at this new catastrophe as the little procession filed in.

Sunny, standing on his own feet in the hallway, went with a howl to Betty, and was promptly hushed with a promise of bread and jelly and a glass of milk. Her glance went anxiously toward the inert Bonnie, who opened indif-

ferent eyes, took in that she was at home, sighed and lay
back in Ted's arms.

"What am I going to do with her, Betts? Take her upstairs to your bed?" asked Ted leaning against the wall for
support as he held the child still in his arms.

"No, you can't do that. Father's asleep there, and we
mustn't disturb either of them " said Betty in distress.

"Let's go into the kitchen where they can't hear us,"
suggested Marjorie. "And, Ted, you give her to me and
you go for her bed. I'll sit down and hold her till we get a
place to put her."

They adjourned to the kitchen where Betty stopped
Sunny's mouth with a plentiful slice of bread and jelly and
seated him on a box to enjoy it.

"I'll get a couple of comforters and make a place for
her on the floor," said Betty. "You can't sit and hold her.
She's heavy."

"She's not heavy," said Marjorie gathering the unresisting Bonnie into her arms. "Get me her nightie and I'll fix
her comfortably. My! She's hot. I wish I had my thermometer here Ted. you'd better stop at the drugstore and
get me a clinical thermometer Get the best one they have.
Then we'll know what we're about. If she has much of a
fever we'd better send for the doctor again. But hurry
back with the bed as fast as you can. What if you took
Bud with you and sent him back with the thermometer?"
said Marjorie. all business now, as she held the little sick
girl gently and began to slip off her little coat and unfasten
her shoes. "She's pretty hot," she went on. "Bud could
come right back couldn't he?"

"Sure!" said Bud importantly, ruffling his sticky fingers
through his red curls.

"And Ted." said Marjorie as Ted was about to go out
the door "I think you'd better see about getting that truck
right away and get the rest of the things here as soon as
possible There ought to be some place for the rest of you
to be comfortable. Don't wait till dark. What does it matter about the neighbors?"

"Okay " said Ted with a glance out the window, "but it
won't be long before it's dark now, anyhow. It's gonta
snow and the sky is heavy. I'll bring Bonnie's bed in a
hand cart and then I'll go right over for the truck. Come
on, Bud Let's go!"

Betty appeared with her arms full of ragged quilts.

"These are all there are left except the ones over Mother and Father," she said anxiously. "Do you think she's very sick? I don't know the first thing about doctoring. Mother always did that. I've always been in school or the office since I was old enough."

"I know a lot about sickness," said Marjorie comfortingly. "You know Moth—that is, Mrs. Wetherill, was sick for several months before she died, and I helped take care of her. until toward the end when we had to have two nurses Besides. I took a short course in the hospital. Mrs. Wetherill thought it was a good thing for everybody to know at least a little about nursing. I can't be sure how sick she is till I take her temperature. But we'd better get her into a comfortable position as quickly as possible. Has she been sick at all before this? How was she this morning?"

"Why, I didn't notice much," said the troubled Betty. "She complained of a stomach ache last night, and I thought it was just emptiness. because she'd had so little to eat, but she didn't say anything about it this morning. She didn't even ask for breakfast, and so I let her go without it because I knew they always gave the children milk at the nursery about half past ten."

"Her vouldn't dink her mi'k," volunteered Sunny, suddenly emerging from his bread and jelly.

The sisters exchanged troubled glances.

Then Sunny vouchsafed more information.

"Her eated hot dogs. 'esterday!" he announced.

"Hot dogs?" said Betty sharply. "Where did she get hot dogs?"

"They vas cold," said the newsmonger. "Ole Sam frowed 'em out from th'back vindow of th'lunch car fer his dog only Bonnie picked 'em up 'afore the dog could get there! I telled her not!" he added virtuously "I didn't eat 'em. *I'm a good boy!* I only eated one little teeny bitta bite But it didn't hurt me! I'm stwong!" He swelled his little chest out boastfully.

Betty looked at him aghast.

"You mean our Bonnie ate sausages that Old Sam threw away? Oh. Sunny! Do you know what you are saying?"

"Wes'" said Sunny firmly.

"Oh!" groaned Betty, "that must be it! She's got ptomaine poisoning. I've heard spoiled sausages are awful! And Sam's place is a terrible little joint. Oh, I ought not to

have trusted them to go alone with Bud, but Mother was
so sick then, and Ted was gone, and Father too, and the
house was so terribly cold I didn't dare let them stay here
any longer, so I let them go with Bud. He promised me he
would walk right straight there and not let them out of his
sight!"

"Bud was chasin' a alley cat!" said Sunny with a spice
of relish in his voice.

"Well, if it's just a stomach upset, perhaps it won't
amount to much," said Marjorie. "She's pretty hot, but if
it's stomach I know what to do. The doctor said he
wouldn't be back in his office till half past five, didn't he?
We'll do our best till then, and if she doesn't seem better
we'll have him come right away. Now don't you cry,
Betty! It wasn't your fault. And I don't believe she's going
to be very sick. Let's just get busy planning what to do,
and then there won't be time to feel worried. How about
dinner? Do we need anything else? And can you cook
steak?"

"Steak!" said Betty. "Did you bring steak? Of course I
can cook steak. That is if I haven't forgotten how. It's
ages since we had a real steak in the house."

"There are potatoes to roast, too," said Marjorie. "And
some vegetables, cans of things, you know. I didn't think
we'd have much time to cook fresh ones today while everybody was sick. But I got some lean beef. I thought the
sick people would need beef tea perhaps, and I know how
to make that. As soon as we get this little sister fixed comfortably in bed I'll start some, and then it will have time to
get cool and be thoroughly skimmed from grease before it
is needed."

All the time she was talking Marjorie was gently un-
dressing her little sister, marveling at the touch of the soft
childish flesh, thrilling to think that it was her own little
sister to whom she was ministering.

Betty was spreading the comforters down on the floor,
plumping a pitiful tiny pillow.

Then Bud arrived with the thermometer.

While Marjorie was taking the child's temperature Betty
put on a kettle of water to heat, and got out some potatoes
to wash. It was five o'clock. Supper would have to get itself done somehow while everything else was going on.
Betty had a frightened sinking feeling. Her own head was

dizzy and her eyes heavy with sleep. If Bonnie was going to be sick what would they do? They never could carry on with another patient in the house, and oh, they couldn't let dear little Bonnie go off alone to the hospital. Bonnie who was so shy of strangers! The tears were slipping softly down Betty's white cheeks.

And there sat that new sister-interloper, holding a thermometer and watching Bonnie with her heart in her eyes. A pang of jealousy went through poor tired Betty's heart. She ought to be caring for Bonnie, not a stranger, even though she was a kind stranger who had furnished money for coal and bread and oranges and gas and light and a doctor!

But just then Sunny, having finished his bread and jelly, created a quick diversion by climbing to the pantry shelf and bringing down the tin can of sand tarts to the floor with a bang. tin can, sand tarts. Sunny and all. The cover rolled off with a tinny cry of triumph, and Sunny came upright with a howl that Betty had to rush to suppress quickly lest it should waken the invalids upstairs.

When she had quieted him by washing his exceedingly dirty face and telling him he must be a man because Father and Mother and little sister were so sick. Marjorie was holding up the thermometer to the light to read it.

"It's only a little over a hundred and one, just barely a shade," she said triumphantly. "Our doctor used to say that unless a temperature went above a hundred and one there was no need to worry. Now, we'll get to work and see if we can't bring this fever down. Is that water hot yet? You'll have to help me. Sunny, how about your going into the other room and drawing pictures? I've got a note book and little pencil in my handbag. and I'll lend them to you if you'll be a good boy and stay in the other room and draw until we get sister in bed and comfortable."

"Okay!" said the subdued baby gulping the last sob.

By the time Ted arrived with the hand cart the sisters had Bonnie established on a hard little bed on the floor in the kitchen.

"I believe she's getting a little cooler already," said Betty stooping to lay her hand lightly on the little forehead that had been so very hot but a few minutes before. "You don't think we need to call the doctor again, do you?"

"We'll see," said Marjorie. "I'll take her temperature again in a little while, and we'll call him if necessary. I don't believe in wasting time if there is any doubt."

"But there will be so much to pay," protested Betty. "You've done so much already. You don't realize how quickly bills mount up, and I do."

Marjorie smiled.

"It's all right, dear," she said slipping an arm around her new sister. "There's money enough for this and a lot of other things, and what's mine is yours, you know. Now don't think anything more about it. Isn't that Ted with the things? We ought to manage not to have the door open much to cool off the house. Perhaps Bud would stand there by the door and open and shut it softly. We mustn't let them make a noise."

"Of course not," said Betty alertly. "I'll see to that. I'll go talk to Ted. Mother would get so excited if she knew what was going on. What has Ted been after, anyway? Bonnie's bed?"

"I told him to bring that first and then go get a truck and bring all the rest of the things."

"Oh!" said Betty breathless with relief. "Oh! Won't that be wonderful! But—what a lot we'll owe you."

"Don't, please!" said Marjorie sharply. "You hurt me! I'm your sister! You don't owe me a thing."

Then they heard the front door open and heavy footsteps tramping in, and the girls flew to caution Ted, and set Bud to watch the door.

"I found Bill hanging round with nothing to do, so we brought everything," explained Ted in a low mumble to Marjorie, as he measured his step to suit the step of Bill, the rough truck driver in a sheepskin coat with a greasy cap on the back of his head.

It proved a bit hard to subdue Bill's voice and step, but Betty was vigilant, and Bud was delighted with his office of doorkeeper, and it didn't take long after all to marshal in the poor bits of household comfort that had gone out one by one to supply necessities. When the door shut at last on Bill, and they heard his truck drive away, the brothers and sisters looked at one another in the garish light of a single stark electric bulb swinging from a long wire in the parlor ceiling and drew breaths of relief. Suddenly Betty dropped down in a big shabby faded chair, buried her face in her hands, her weary slender young shoulders shaking with the sobs she would not allow to become audible.

Marjorie was by her side instantly, her arms about her.

"There dear! Don't cry. Poor dear! You're so tired, aren't you? But listen! We're going to have a nice supper now and a good time getting things to rights. Come, cheer up! You'll have to put things in their places because I don't know where they belong."

Betty raised tearstained eyes and began to laugh softly, hysterically.

"I'm—only crying—because it's so wonderful—to see our old things back again!" she gurgled. "I used to hate them all so. this faded chair, and couch, and those ugly tables. but now I'm so glad to see them!"

Marjorie smiled.

"Well, it does seem more homelike, doesn't it? My! That couch looks good to me. I'm going to try it after a while, but now I'm going to take Bonnie's temperature again and see whether we need the doctor."

But while she was taking the temperature, the doctor arrived.

"I've had a call out into the country," he explained as Betty opened the door for him, "and I might have to be gone all night. I thought I'd better just step in and see how the patients are before I leave. I want to make sure your mother's lungs are not involved before I go so far away!"

Betty went with him upstairs, hurrying to close the doors into the other empty rooms so that he would not see their bareness. resolving not to let him disturb her father if she could help it. She knew he would be terribly mortified to have the doctor see him asleep on a mattress on the floor.

Ted came in the back door just as the doctor went upstairs, and Marjorie turned to him with troubled eyes.

"Ted, could you help me put Bonnie in on the couch?" she asked. "The doctor is upstairs and I think he ought to see her. Her temperature is going up in spite of all I've done, and she ought to have some medicine. It looks better in there than here."

Ted turned and glanced down at the hot little face on the pillow with new dismay in his eyes.

"Good night!" he said sorrowfully. "Can you beat it? Everything comes at once. Sure we can move her. I'll carry her and you fix the covers."

He stooped and lifted the little girl gently. Marjorie hurried ahead with the quilts and pillow, and in a moment the child was comfortably established on the old couch.

"I'm glad I laid down the rug first," said Ted standing back and casting a critical glance around. "It doesn't look so bad here, does it?"

"No," said Marjorie with a bright smile, covering a sinking at heart. "It just looks homey, as if it was lived in, you know."

She straightened a chair, and wiped the dust from the table. Then went over to the bookcase and took out two or three books, laying them on the table as if they had been recently read.

"I'm glad you brought the books," she said with satisfaction. "It never looks like home without books."

"I guess that's so," said the boy seriously. "I brought them because Mother loves them so much. I didn't know whether I ought to or not. We can't sleep on books, nor wear them. Maybe I should have saved the money, but he didn't allow but three cents apiece on them, so I thought I'd bring them."

"Of course. That was right! I wanted you to bring everything back. Are you sure there aren't any more?"

"Clothes!" said Ted laconically. "But we sold them out and out. Betts thought we wouldn't want to wear them anyway after they'd hung up in the window of that junk shop for everybody to stare at and recognize."

"Of course not!" said Marjorie suppressing a little shudder of horror. "Well, we'll look after those things later when everyone gets well and things are going comfortably here. Oh, we'll have things all right by Christmas."

"Christmas!" said Ted a trifle bitterly. "It'll be Christmas enough for me just to have our things back, and enough to eat and have it warm here!"

And then they heard the doctor coming down the stairs and the talk was cut short.

"All going well above stairs," he announced cheerfully. "Mother's breaking into a nice perspiration, and her lungs are clear so far. I don't expect her fever to go up tonight at all."

He glanced down at Marjorie.

"You're the sister, aren't you? You two are very much alike. Well, I think you can be easy in your mind. I didn't go in to look at your father. Your sister said he was sleeping quietly, and that was all he needed, rest. He's been worried of course, like everybody else in these days of depression, but if he gets rested up he'll take hold of things with new zest. So you girls needn't worry. Anyhow, I'll be back in the morning and if you need anything early you can call me."

"But we have another patient in here," said Marjorie. "I think you'd better look at her before you go. I've done all I know how to do but her temperature seems to be going up in spite of it."

She led the way to the couch.

"We put her down here so we wouldn't disturb Mother," she explained.

The doctor bent over the little girl, touched the hot forehead, the limp wrist, counting the pulse, then he straightened up, asked a few keen questions, and called for glasses of water and teaspoons.

"I'll get them," said Ted, and hurried to the kitchen terribly glad that the teaspoons were back from the pawn shop.

Betty came downstairs while the doctor was giving directions She stood by the doorway looking anxiously at the little sick sister.

"I don't anticipate anything serious," said the doctor with a smile toward Betty, and another at Marjorie. "Her fever may go up a trifle until midnight, but there's nothing to be alarmed about. Give the medicine regularly and I think you'll see the fever go down before morning. Thanks to your prompt treatment I think the worst is over. It's her stomach, of course. Children will eat all sorts of things, you know It looks like a light case of ptomaine, but I think she'll come out all right."

Betty and Marjorie exchanged glances, and then Betty spoke up, telling about the "hot-dogs-that-were-cold," that Sunny had said Bonnie had eaten. Betty's face was crimson with shame lest the doctor would wonder why a child would be so hungry that she would pick up cast out food, but the doctor took it in a very matter-of-fact way, twinkling his nice kind brown eyes at Betty, and grinning.

"The little reprobate!" he said, patting Bonnie's thin little hand. "Isn't it a wonder that any of us survive? My mother used to tell a tale of finding me at the age of two seated on the back steps devouring the skins of baked potatoes that I had snitched out of the garbage pail! Well, we all have to learn by the hardest. I remember I got a very effectual spanking before I learned my lesson. I guess she'll be all right. Give her the medicine every hour, and orange juice if she wants it. Nothing else. I'll come in the first thing in the morning and see how you girls are getting on. You look young to run a hospital, but I guess you'll make a go of it."

There was a sudden dismay in Betty's face as the doctor opened the door, and perhaps he saw it, for he reached over and patted her shoulder before he put on his glove.

"Don't you worry," he said comfortingly, "everybody's going to be all right. They'll all be decidedly better in the morning, I'm sure."

Betty looked up and met his eyes wistfully, and Marjorie, watching, saw the glance, and thought what nice eyes the doctor had. Nice brown eyes.

VII

WHEN the doctor was gone Betty turned to her new sister.

"You ought to go now," she said sharply. "It's getting dark, and you ought to go back to your hotel. You can' stay here tonight in a mess like this."

Marjorie looked at her sister with a startled glance. Was Betty anxious to get her away?

"Oh, my *dear!*" she said aghast. "You don't think a mess like this is any worse for me than it is for you, do you?"

"You're not used to it," said Betty sullenly. "I can manage. And you've done a lot. You ought to get a good night's rest and not be burdened with things that don't belong to you."

"But they do belong to me!" said Marjorie. "It's my father and mother who are sick upstairs, isn't it? The father and mother God gave to me as much as to you? And it's my little sister who is sick down here! And how could you possibly think you could manage alone? You are half sick yourself. And even if Ted helped you he is just about ready to drop. You know you are all weakened with cold and hunger and anxiety. Please, my dear, don't shove me out! After everybody is well I'll go away and give you a chance to talk it all over and if you decide you don't want me I won't trouble you any more. But I couldn't leave you now. I haven't even seen my mother yet."

There was a sob in her voice that went to Betty's heart.

"I didn't mean that!" she said almost fiercely. "I don't want you to go. Goodness knows how I'll get along if you do, but I'll do it, somehow, or die in the attempt. But— well, how *could* you stay here? The only bed there is for you would be my mattress on the floor upstairs, and Father's asleep there. Maybe he'll wake up after a while, but I don't think I ought to disturb him till he does, do you?"

"Certainly not," said Marjorie, "and in any case I would want to stay beside Bonnie—that is, if you would let me, tonight, and you get some sleep. You look sick yourself. But where were you planning to sleep yourself, even if I weren't here?"

"I hadn't planned," said Betty with a toss of her head and a weary sigh. "I can sleep anywhere if I get a chance. The floor is plenty good enough for me. I could sleep down cellar if I had to."

"I haven't a doubt but that you could," said Marjorie seriously, "anybody probably could if they were tired enough. But it wouldn't be good for you, even if you could. As for me, I'm quite rested. I haven't done anything for the last four or five weeks. I certainly can stand more hardship than you can. You look as if you were ready to drop. I fully realize that you have nerve enough to keep you going if you were dead on your feet, but I don't intend you shall. Not unless you would rather have me get a trained nurse! Or unless you deliberately turn me out of the house. Of course I know I haven't any right here at all. I haven't a right to say what you shall do or shall not, unless you give it to me. But I wish you would understand that I want to help and make things as easy for you as I can. Now, suppose we put aside hostilities and talk it over quietly together, find out what is best to be done. I had thought that perhaps you would trust me to look after Bonnie tonight and let you get a good rest. She is the only one of the sick who seems to be in a condition that won't be hurt by the presence of a stranger. I thought perhaps Ted could put her little bed in here where if she woke she wouldn't make any noise upstairs to disturb the others, and I would just lie down here on the couch beside her and keep watch. Then you could get a good sleep for you certainly need it. It wouldn't hurt me in the least for I'm used to night nursing. I did it for several weeks at a time while Moth—while Mrs. Wetherill was so sick. But, you see, what I didn't realize was that there wouldn't be a good comfortable bed for you. You know I haven't been upstairs. It isn't my fault that I didn't know that. I was only trying to plan to have you comfortable."

"Well, and I was planning to have you comfortable for the night when I suggested you go back to your hotel," said Betty with an apology in her voice. "I didn't mean to be disagreeable. I was just worried."

"Well, there, let's sit down in the dining room and talk it over. There is surely something we can do to make us all comfortable for the night. Where does Sunny sleep?"

"He sleeps in the room with Ted and Bud. He has a little crib. Why, where is Sunny? Ted didn't take him with him, did he? Where did Ted go, anyway? Do you know?"

"He said something about going back for another load. But I don't think Sunny went with him. At least if he did Ted didn't know it. Bud went along, but I didn't see Sunny anywhere. He was eating bread and jelly the last I saw of him. Maybe he's in the kitchen."

The girls hurried into the kitchen, but Sunny was not there. Betty swung open the back door and called softly, fearing to waken the sleepers upstairs, and then rushed out into the little side yard calling.

"He isn't anywhere!" said Betty coming back with terror in her eyes, "and it's awfully dark and cold. And he didn't have his coat on, either. Now *he'll* be sick. I suppose. And where shall I look for him? I guess I'll have to go to the police station. He might be lost or kidnaped or something."

But Marjorie suddenly swung open the pantry door and switched on the light, and there lay Sunny on the floor in a corner with a tin can of graham crackers clasped in his arms, crumbs all over his baby face, sound asleep, a half eaten sand tart in one hand, dead to the world!

The girls sat down and laughed till they cried.

"What shall we do with him?" asked Marjorie suddenly sobering.

"Leave him there for the present," said Betty. "I'll get Father's old coat and put under his head. If we wake him up he may cry, and we haven't any other place to put him, not till his crib is up. He probably won't sleep long anyway. I wonder where Ted is."

"Couldn't we put up the crib?" asked Marjorie looking at the unassembled parts that stood against the dining room wall.

"Perhaps we could," said Betty. "I never tried. Father always did things like that. This is the headboard. And those are the sides."

Marjorie got down on her knees and examined the side pieces.

"These must hook into those sockets in the headboard," she said briskly. "You hold the headboard and I'll see what I can do."

"You ought not to be doing that," said Betty coming forward and setting up the headboard of the crib. "You'll get your pretty dress all dust."

"It will clean," said Marjorie indifferently. "There, see how easily that slides into place. Now, the other. Why this is no trouble at all. Now, which is the head of these springs?"

They had it all together when Ted came in carrying a heavy load, and putting it down he began to open it out, and it proved to be an army cot.

"Where in the world did you get that?" asked Betty, wide-eyed.

"Over at the Army and Navy store," said Ted laconically. "Bought it. Fifty cents. They were having a sale. I knew we hadta have something."

"For pity's sake!" said Betty eyeing Ted in astonishment. "But where did you get the fifty cents? Not out of that I gave you to pay the grocery bill, Ted Gay?"

"No. Guess again!" grinned Ted, and he hauled the roll of bills out of his pocket that Marjorie had given him and grinned at her.

Betty looked from one to the other understandingly. Then she said to Marjorie:

"If you stay here another day we'll have you fleeced."

"Suits me," said Marjorie with another grin. "Now, where is that Sunny boy? Will he howl if I pick him up?"

"Go get him, Ted," said Betty. "He's asleep in the pantry."

"Good night!" said Ted standing in the pantry door laughing. "Where'd he get all the grub? Poor little kid, he's been half starved for days!"

Ted put Sunny in the crib, and then turned on the girls.

"Now, what do you want done first?"

Betty looked at her new sister.

"I'll get dinner," she said, "and you show Ted where you want Bonnie's bed put."

"I thought you girls could have my room," said Ted, "and Bud can have the cot, and I'll park beside Dad."

"That will be fine for Betty tonight," said Marjorie, "but as for me, I'm going to watch Bonnie and lie down on the couch between times."

"You think she ought to do that, Betts?" asked Ted. "She isn't usedta roughing it."

"Indeed I am," laughed Marjorie, "at least I'm used to being up nights and caring for sick folks."

"Well, she wants to," said Betty with a troubled sigh, "and I'm sure I wouldn't be much good at nursing. For Bonnie's sake I guess we've got to let her have her way."

"Okay!" said Ted. "Well, where do we go from here? What do I do next? Peel potatoes or what?"

"We're not going to peel the potatoes," said Betty. "We're roasting them. You can light the oven. We're not doing any fancy cooking, just beefsteak and potatoes and a can of tomatoes. You can open the can. I'll do the rest."

"All right," said Marjorie, "I'll cut the bread and get the butter and the pickles, and wash some celery. Open a glass of currant jelly too, Ted. That will be for dessert."

Dinner was ready in a surprisingly short time, and the starved young appetites were ready too.

Bonnie was still sleeping, and Marjorie fancied that she was not quite so hot as an hour ago.

They were just about to sit down when Sunny woke up making an outcry and had to be hushed and brought in to the kitchen to quiet him.

Then Bud burst in, his eyes wide with wonder at the unusual dinner.

"Gee! Where'd'ya get the meat! Real meat! Can I have a piece too, or do we have ta save it for Mother 'cause she's sick?"

"No, you don't have to save it," smiled Marjorie, "there's plenty for everybody. Mother couldn't eat meat tonight anyway, but maybe she can have some soon."

Marjorie went out to the kitchen to get Bud his glass of milk, while Ted attacked the big beefsteak with the carving knife which had just been recovered from the pawn shop.

"It's almost too pretty to cut, isn't it?" he said. And then he heard a step behind him. They all turned and there stood their father staring at them all in wonder, and sniffing the air.

"I smelled something so heavenly," he said, and he smiled a tired little smile that made him look like Bud. "Where did you get the meat, Ted?" he asked, his eyes resting on the laden table. "It appears that you are having a feast. Did you succeed in getting any subscriptions, lad? They surely didn't pay you enough commission on a few subscriptions to buy all this?"

"Sit down, Dad," said Ted laying down the knife and springing to draw up a chair for his father. "You aren't fit to stand up."

"Oh, I'm all right," he said, passing a hand over his forehead. "I just had a little dizzy spell, but Betty gave me some coffee, and I had a good sleep, and feel better. I thought I'd go out and see if I couldn't get an evening's work. It might bring in a few cents and help to buy another bag of coal. You know some of the stores are keeping open evenings until Christmas and they need extra help. I've heard they pay pretty well, too. I'll just take a bite and go out. I might get a job for evenings for all this week."

"My eye, you will!" said Ted. "You sit down and eat your dinner, that is, if you feel able to sit up. We were just going to bring you up a tray, but now you're down you might as well eat in style. Shove over there, Bud, and give Dad more room. But you might as well understand right now, Dad, that you are under the doctor's orders. You don't stir a step out of this house till he says you can. See? And not then till I've gone and got your overcoat back. Where's that pawn ticket, Dad? Hand it over. No, you don't need to cut this steak. I can do it as well as you can. Not that I've seen any recently of course, but I remember how you've cut it for years. I used to think I would really be grown up when I could cut the meat for the family, and this is about the first time I've had a chance to try. Get him a plate, Betts, and pour him a cup of coffee quick while I manipulate this beefsteak."

The father sank back in the chair under Ted's powerful young handling, and looked about dazed.

"But you haven't told me yet where you got all this dinner? Am I dreaming or is this a real dinner on the table? Betty, you don't mean that you allowed the Welfare to furnish this, do you? I couldn't bear to think we had come to that!"

"No, Father," said Betty with a twinkle in her eyes.

"We didn't have to go out and beg, either." And then as she heard Marjorie's step in the pantry, Betty suddenly grew sober.

"Father, I'd better tell you right off quick. It's all in the family. You don't need to be troubled. My twin sister has come and she got all these things!"

The father looked up with great startled eyes, and turned perfectly white.

"Your sister has come? What do you mean, Elizabeth? Do you mean the little sister who was adopted? Do you mean that she has come and gone and your mother and I did not see her?"

"No. Oh no, Father," said Betty, half frightened at what her revelation had done to her father. "She hasn't gone. She's right here in the house. Here she comes now!"

Marjorie stood there smiling with a plate of bread in one hand and the glass of milk in the other, looking so at home, and so sweet and domesticated that he had to look twice to be sure she wasn't Betty. And Marjorie met her own father's eyes for the first time in her young life, and loved him at once.

Suddenly she put down on the corner of the table the things she was carrying and went to meet the father, who had risen to his feet and was staring at her, went sweetly across the years into his arms and laid her golden head on his shoulder looking up into his face.

"Father, I've come home! Do you mind?" she said shyly.

Hungrily his arms went round her, and his face came down softly and touched hers.

"Do I mind?" he said wonderingly. "Do I mind? Oh, my little girl, whom I have never seen before! My other little Betty. Do I *mind?*"

He touched her forehead with his lips, almost as if he felt she was not real, and then he looked up again, while all the other children sat and looked on in wonder. A sadness had come over that sudden radiance of his face.

"But what a home you have come to, my child! What a home! All the comforts gone!" Then suddenly he looked around and saw the familiar sideboard and chairs and table, and bewilderment came into his eyes.

"Am I dreaming, Ted? Or is all this real?" He turned troubled eyes on his boy.

Ted gave him a sharp look.

"It's real all right, Dad, but you won't be long if you don't sit down and eat some of this beefsteak pretty quick, and I mean it. Time enough to satisfy your curiosity after you have eaten this dinner. This is some dinner, I'm telling you!"

Ted pushed his father down in his chair summarily, and handed over a plate with a fine juicy piece of steak on it.

"There! Get on the outside of that as quick as you can. Betts, pass the potatoes, and get Dad going, or we'll have to put him back in bed again."

They laughed and kept passing him things, quite confusing him, but succeeding in turning his thoughts away from the new child for the moment, till he really got a bite or two swallowed.

But he came back to realities presently.

"But I don't understand," he said looking keenly at Ted, "how did you get such a dinner as this? You didn't go somewhere and charge all these things, did you?"

"No, Dad. They are every one of them paid for," said Ted as he handed out the last plate and sat down to enjoy his own dinner.

"You—didn't do anything—that I wouldn't—approve —did you, son?"

"Not a thing, Dad. Everything aboveboard and honorable. All the bills paid and everything going slick. Coal in the cellar, fire in the heater, gas in the range, water in the pipes, light in the wires and the pantry full of food. Have some celery, Dad, and just be thankful."

"But, my son, I cannot eat until I understand."

"All right, tell him, Betts!" said the boy.

"Why, Father, it's just that we have a fairy sister with pockets full of money, and she insisted on paying for everything," said Betty.

"Do you mean," asked the father, laying his fork down beside his plate with a look of finality, "that we are feasting on Mrs. Wetherill's money? I could not possibly do that, my dear."

There was such pain and pride in his voice that Marjorie's heart was thrown into a panic. Was pride after all to put an end to her new hopes and plans?

"Father—" she said earnestly, and did not realize how naturally she had called him that, "it isn't her money at all. It is my money. It was left to me to do just as I liked

with it. She even left me a letter suggesting that I would
like to hunt you up and use my money in making you
happy. I came here at once as soon as I heard about you.
At least I didn't hear very much about you, only the address, and the fact that I was one of twins, and that
Mother wanted very much to see me, and came after me
once not so very long ago. That was about all Mrs. Wetherill knew. It was all she ever told me. And as soon as I
knew I had a living own mother I came to find her. I
didn't know whether you wanted me or not, or whether
anybody was alive or not, but I had to come and see. I
had to find out if there was anybody who really loved me
a little bit."

There was the catch of a sob in her voice as she finished, and a mist in her eyes. Even young Bud paused in
his chewing for an instant and looked at her sympathetically.

"Tourse ve vants you," piped up Sunny with his mouth
full of baked potato and butter.

Then the father came out of his sorrowful daze.

"Want you?" said he tenderly. "How we have wanted
you! How we have longed for you, and talked about you,
and tried not to blame one another, your mother and I,
for having let you go! You will never know how we have
suffered. How each of us has blamed ourselves! Your
mother found out that I was desperately ill, and ought not
to work for a year or two, and she was weak and ill herself, and was over-influenced by Mr. Wetherill. He was
kindness itself and very generous, but he was quite determined to have you. And when they came to me it was represented to me as a necessity that Betty have the care of
an expensive specialist or she could not live the life of a
normal healthy child. So in a moment of weakness we
both gave our consent and signed the necessary papers.
But oh, how we have regretted it all the years, and we did
our best to have the papers revoked and get you back."

"Oh, dear Father!" said Marjorie deeply stirred, and
putting out a shy hand to lay upon his. "I'm so glad it is
not too late for me to try to make up just a little for your
suffering!"

He gathered her hand into his thin nervous one and
clasped it close.

"Does your mother know?" he asked of Betty.

"Not yet. I thought she ought to get a good sleep first before we excited her. Besides there was so much to do to get things going right again," explained Betty.

"Well, this will be meat and drink to your mother," said the father, gazing intently at the new unknown daughter. "I'd better go right up and tell her."

"No, Dad! You sit still and eat your dinner. Mother's asleep. You'll have to wait till she wakes up. You don't want to make her sick, you know. Come now, you've got to be sensible." It was Ted who set up authority, talking as much like his father's voice as he could, till they all laughed, even Mr. Gay.

Then there came a moan from Bonnie in the other room and Marjorie with a quick glance at Betty slipped out and went to her.

They heard the clink of a spoon and a glass, as Marjorie coaxed the medicine into the child's lips, and then she was back almost immediately.

"I don't think she's quite so hot," she said happily.

And then they had to tell the father about Bonnie, and the pleasant homely talk of everyday matters helped them to eat more quietly and normally than if they had had a great scene of excitement over the new-found sister.

"Well, I'd better run down and look at the heater," said Mr. Gay when at last the delicious supper was finished and he drew back from the table. "I didn't put much coal on, and I wouldn't have it go out because we haven't much coal, you know, nor any more kindling."

"That's all right, Dad," said Ted putting a detaining hand on his father's arm. "Me for the heater from now on. There's a whole lot of kindling down cellar, besides two tons of coal, and the fire is going for all she's worth. Don't you feel how warm it is here?"

The father looked at his boy, and then across to the new-found daughter. Then his eyes traveled around the rest of the group, and suddenly he bowed his head in a kind of shame.

"I've failed!" he said sadly. "And my little girl had to come and put us all on our feet again."

"Okay, dad. She's put us on our feet, but you didn't fail. It wasn't your fault that you nearly got your death in the world war and haven't had half your health since. It wasn't your fault that Mr. Matthews died and the firm went to the wall and there wasn't any job for you to keep.

It wasn't your fault that the bank went flooey and took all your savings. And it wasn't your fault that there weren't any more positions waiting for anyone just then when you needed one."

"No, it wasn't my fault, perhaps, but if I'd been half a man I would have been able to do something." There was dejection and bitterness in his tone. But Ted put in eagerly.

"Look here, Dad. None of that! Look at the family you've raised. Wasn't that an achievement? Aren't we something to be proud of? Now quit your glooming and let's be glad. We're all here together, new sister and all, and we have a fire, and plenty to eat, and no bills anywhere. Isn't that enough to smile about for one night?"

"It is," said the father heartily, "it is. And not the least of all that we have our other little girl here." He gave Marjorie a loving smile, as if he was afraid even yet to let himself be happy!

"Now, Dad," said Ted pushing back his chair and getting up. "You go upstairs and get to bed, see? And you're to sleep in Betty's bed. We've got things all arranged, and you can trust the whole thing to us."

"Oh," said the father firmly, "I can't go to bed yet. I want to be awake when your mother wakes up and tell her our little girl has come back."

"Sure, you can tell her. You ought to be the one to tell her. But we've all agreed it would better not be tonight. Mother needs to be perfectly quiet tonight or her fever will come up again, and you don't want her to get pneumonia, do you, just because she gets excited? Now you go and get to bed. There isn't a thing you can do tonight. Positively. Tomorrow we'll talk things over, and have a good time, but tonight you're getting a good rest. Perhaps you don't know that was the doctor's orders. Now, scram!" and Ted led his reluctant parent toward the stairs again, and himself saw him up to bed.

When he came down the girls were washing the dishes together and chattering as happily as if they had always done it every night of their lives.

"Betts, what shall I put on that cot to make it up for Bud?" said Ted.

"You put that cot down here in the dining room," said Betty, "over there beside Sunny's crib. I'm sleeping on it tonight to keep our new sister company, and besides, we don't want to bother to take Sunny's crib upstairs tonight. It might wake Mother. So you just keep Bud with you tonight, and we'll see about it in the morning. Don't worry about bedclothes, I'll find something that will do for tonight."

Ted looked at Betty, opened his lips to object, and then closed them meaningfully. And just as plainly as if he had spoken and Betty had assented, Marjorie knew that he had been about to say to Betty that there weren't any bedclothes at all for that cot.

Marjorie went into the dark parlor and looked out of the window and off toward the city where the sky was lit up like a distant garden of bright flowers, lights everywhere. Presently she turned and went over to the little sick girl, touched her lightly with an experienced hand, then she came back to the kitchen where Ted and Betty were persuading the two boys that it was bedtime.

"Is there a place near here where I could get a taxi?" she asked.

"A taxi?" said Betty looking up in dismay. "I thought you said you were going to stay all night."

"Why, I am, of course," said Marjorie brightly, "but I was thinking perhaps I could run back to my hotel and get my baggage. It wouldn't take me long and I'd like to have my toothbrush and things. If you thought you could lie down beside Bonnie for a little while I'd hurry right back. It doesn't take so long to go places in taxis, you know."

"Of course," said Betty. "I can manage nicely. Only you mustn't go alone. It's pretty dark and you might get lost."

"Couldn't I go for you?" asked Ted.

"No," said Marjorie quickly. "I'd better go myself and pay the bill and tell them I'm checking out."

"Well, then, Ted had better go with you," said Betty decidedly. "It isn't a very nice neighborhood you would have to pass through in going to the taxi stand."

"You go that way when you go to the office," put in Bud officiously.

"Oh well, I'm used to it. Besides, it's night," said Betty.

"It isn't very late," said Marjorie looking at her watch. "It's only quarter past seven. We had dinner early, remember, and besides it's winter. It gets dark early. I'm not afraid. Ted, aren't you awfully tired? I hate to take you out in the cold again."

"Tired nothing. Of course I'll go. I wouldn't let you go

alone. What do you think I am? Only, maybe you'll be ashamed of me. I haven't anything to doll up in."

Marjorie laughed.

"What do you think I am? Well, come on then. I'll be ready in half a second. Betty, if Bonnie stirs just give her a spoonful of the medicine at the right hand. She'll probably sleep all right. If she wakes up have some orange juice ready and give her a few spoonfuls. Don't you want me to fix some before I go? Mother might need some too. You must be awfully tired."

"No, I'll fix it. It will be such a pleasure to have oranges to fix, that it will be a real treat."

So Marjorie and her new brother started off together into the dark little street. Marjorie tucked her arm inside Ted's and fell into step with him chummily.

"My, but it's nice to have a brother of my own!" she said. "I've always wanted a brother and a sister."

"Well, you've got plenty of them now," said Ted, both pleased and embarrassed.

The night was cold and little lazy flakes of snow were floating down. Marjorie wondered if Ted was warmly enough clad, but she did not dare to ask about it. She was glad when they found a taxi and got in, glad that it had a heater. So they rode down to the city together, Marjorie skillfully questioning, finding out little things about her family without seeming to do so.

Just before they reached the hotel Marjorie asked:

"Ted, aren't there stores somewhere that would be open at this hour? I would like to get a few things."

"Sure. All kinds of stores if you know where to find them. Not the swell places, of course. They close at five o'clock, though I remember some of even those are open this week till nine o'clock. It's Christmas week, you know."

"Oh, that's so! That's nice. Well, then, before we get my baggage, let's drive to a department store. I won't be long getting what I want, and we can take another taxi from there to the hotel."

So presently they got out at a large department store.

Ted watched his pretty sister with admiration as she went her way, asking directions to the department she wanted. He was proud to be with her, yet ashamed of his own shabbiness.

But he was amazed when they brought up in the blanket section and Marjorie purchased three great warm double blankets and three of single bed size. They were soft and bright, and Ted stared in amazement.

Suddenly he stepped to her side and said in a low tone:

"What's the big idea? You don't need to get all those. We are used to getting along with what we have. Get one for yourself maybe, but we'll be all right with any old thing."

Marjorie turned to him lovingly.

"Ted, look here, I thought you and I were partners in trying to get our family comfortable as quickly as possible. Please don't try to hinder me. I knew by the look in Betty's eyes when you talked about the cot that she was hard put to it to find any bedding for it at all. She told me a little about things, and I know these things are needed. Don't try to hinder me. Help all you can. And if you don't say anything about it nobody is going to notice a blanket or two more or less."

Then Marjorie bought some sheets and pillow cases and a few towels, and they started for the street door accompanied by two cash boys carrying their big boxes.

"We travel in style," said Ted with a grin as he hailed another taxi, helped his sister in, and stowed the big boxes around them. "The beggar and the maid."

Marjorie laughed.

"I'm having fun," she said.

"Here too," said Ted.

At the hotel Ted stayed in the taxi while Marjorie went in to pay her bill. She came out with a porter carrying her suitcases. But when they reached the little house on Aster Street again, Ted's spirits arose to the top notch.

"I'm the advance guard of Santa Claus!" he announced in a subdued jubilance as he bore the big boxes into the hall and put them carefully down.

Betty stared in growing amazement as the soft blankets and smooth sheets came to light, and finally sat down on the lowest step of the stairs and cried into a pink blanket for sheer joy in its lovely woolliness.

She looked up at last and smiled wearily.

"I never thought this morning that we would be as happy as this by night," she said.

Ted grinned.

"I told ya," he said, "I told ya God wasn't dead!" and then he went off down cellar to fix the furnace for the night, and his new sister stared after him, and wondered how a boy like Ted came to say a thing like that. He had said it half sheepishly, but as if he meant it.

Then she turned and asked after the patients.

"Father's sound asleep," said Betty. "He didn't even rouse when Mother woke. I gave her the medicine and some orange juice and she went right off to sleep again. Bonnie has talked in her sleep a little, but she often does that. I don't think she is nearly as hot as she was when you went away. You go feel of her."

And so presently Marjorie had them all tucked away to sleep under the new blankets and sheets, and she was thankful to lie down. It had been a long day, but it had been an interesting one. There was a good deal to think over, but instead she went to sleep as quick as her head touched the pillow, and none of the questions she wanted to think over and decide got even a passing thought.

Just as she was sinking away to sleep she wondered dreamily: "What would I have thought if I had known I was coming into a situation like this?" And the answer came quickly from her loving heart, "Oh, I'm glad I came!"

And still she had not seen her own mother.

VIII

MARJORIE was awakened the next morning by soft wet little lips on her cheek, and soft experimenting little fingers trying to pull open her eyes.

" 'Nother Betty, will there be bretsus again this morning?" a little voice whispered in her ear.

And there was Sunny in his ragged little pajamas standing beside her couch. He had somehow managed to climb out of his crib and find her. The rest of the house was still very silent. Perhaps nobody else was awake yet.

Marjorie laughed softly and looked at her wrist watch. It was five minutes after eight! She glanced over at Bonnie's bed, and there was Bonnie very pale and washed-out, sitting bolt upright in her small bed staring at her.

"Oh, lie down, darling," said Marjorie quickly, "the house isn't very warm yet, and you will catch a cold. You've been sick, you know."

Bonnie's eyes got larger and sought her little brother's face in question.

"Who is that?" she asked in a small trembling voice, her lip quivering. "That's not our Betty!"

"Her's 'nother Betty!" asserted Sunny, round-eyed. "Her has bretsuses. Bwed an' jelly!"

"You'd like some nice orange juice, wouldn't you, Bonnie?" asked Marjorie, springing up and flinging her pretty kimono about her.

Bonnie slumped down on her pillow weakly and continued to stare. Marjorie went over and laid her hand on the little forehead that had been so hot in the night.

"Why, it's nice and cool, isn't it?" she said delightedly. "Now, suppose we take your temperature, and then I'll fix your orange juice."

Bonnie lay and looked at her solemnly.

"Now, Sunny boy, back into your bed you go till somebody has time to dress you. I'll give you a cracker to nibble on. How is that?"

"Nice," said Sunny, putting up a confiding hand to be led away, and Bonnie lay solemnly with the thermometer in her mouth and stared at this new sister who was so like Betty and yet wasn't Betty.

Then Betty appeared on the scene, heavy-eyed with sleep.

"Oh, there you are!" said Marjorie cheerily. "How are the patients upstairs? Did you have to be awake with them much?"

"Not once!" declared Betty. "They seem to be better this morning. Father says he's all right and is going out to hunt a job. Mother wants some hot cereal. She asked for it herself. I don't know where she thought it was coming from, but she wanted it."

"Well, we'll fix her a nice tray. You go and get dressed. Should I do something to the furnace? I don't know much about draughts and things."

"No, I heard Ted fix it before he went out."

"Oh, he hasn't gone out without any breakfast again, has he?" cried Marjorie.

"Oh, he probably took a sandwich with him or something. He goes on his paper route. He told me last night the fellow that bought it wants to sell it back, and will go shares till it's paid for. He goes out for the papers about four o'clock."

Marjorie put Sunny in his crib thoughtfully, reflecting on how easily she had always gone to the front door to pick up the morning paper, without ever realizing that somebody had to get up at four o'clock to make it possible for it to be there on the porch when she wanted it. Life had in one short day taken on a different aspect. She was thinking of things she had never noticed before.

Bonnie proved to be a little below normal.

"That's all right," said Marjorie out of her superior experience. "It usually does that the first day after a fever.

Now we must keep her very quiet today so it won't go up again tonight, and then she'll probably be all right." She smiled cheerfully at the little girl, who managed a wan quiver of her thin little lips in reply. Perhaps she thought it was a smile.

Marjorie gave the children orange juice and fixed a tray for her mother. Betty came down when the cereal was ready and took it up.

"She'll know something's happened with a tray looking like that," she said as she noticed the daintiness of everything. Even without an array of silver and linen Majorie had managed to make everything look inviting.

When Betty came down Marjorie was setting the table. She had cut the bread and laid out the eggs and bacon.

"You'd better make the coffee," she said to her sister. "I don't know how without a percolator. I'm afraid I would spoil it."

"We used to have a percolator when we were at Brentwood, but it got broken in the moving " sighed Betty.

"Brentwood? What's Brentwood? Was that where you lived before you came here?"

"Yes," said Betty sadly. "It was swell! It was an old farm house that had got caught on the edge of a new suburb when the city grew out there, and it had been fixed up with a great big porch across the front, and the grass growing up close to it. It was built of rugged old stone, and they paved the porch with big thin flat ones. It was ducky. We had a hammock and big rocking chairs out there, and a dear little tiled table Mother used to bring her sewing out and stay hours at a time Mother loved it. There was a view out across a valley, looking away from the city, and a little brook in a meadow next to our place. It had a garage in an old barn, and Father had a little car to go to business in. We were just getting it pretty nicely furnished too. That was when Mother was getting ready for you to come to visit us. She just lived on the thought of it. And then she went out to see Mrs Wetherill, and she turned us down, and Mother came home just crushed! A little while after that the crash came and Dad's money went in a bank failure. Then the man Dad worked for died, and the firm closed up, and here we are!"

Betty's tone was almost hopeless as she finished. Then after a minute she went on again.

"Can you blame Mother for getting sick and going all

to pieces? It just seemed too hopeless. And I was thinking last night. You've been wonderful of course, and you've pulled us out of starvation, but what is it all going to amount to? You'll get tired of us and go back to Chicago, of course. You couldn't be expected to want to stick around a place like this. And we'll all slump again. Of course you've brought back our furniture, and you've paid our bills, and we've had something to eat, but Dad hasn't any job, and mine's gone too, and how can I ever hope to get another job looking like this? Of course we can't go on living on you, grateful as we are for what you've done for us so far."

"Look here, Betty, you just stop that sob stuff. That's no way to act. We're all here, the sick ones are better, and we'll get straightened out after a little and think things out bit by bit. There's no point in trying to swallow the whole future in one bite when you haven't had your breakfast yet. Come, let's get everybody fed before we tackle the next things!"

Then the father's voice was heard calling:
"Betty!"

Betty turned and flew up the stairs. In a moment she was down again, her eyes full of excitement.

"Father's told Mother, and she wants you to come right up!"

Marjorie turned on her eager sister and kissed her.

"Don't worry," she said softly, "it's all going to come right."

Then she hurried off upstairs.

Afterward Marjorie couldn't quite remember everything that happened, or what they all said. It was just a memory of being folded in tender frail arms, gentle hands upon her head, the softest lips in all the world upon her own, kisses on her lips and forehead and eyes. A voice saying softly:

"My little, little baby. My lost darling!"

Mrs. Wetherill had loved her. She had never had any doubt about that. And when Mrs. Wetherill had died she was stricken and forlorn. She had felt bereft of mother love. It was all the love she had ever known. But this was different! This was her very own, and was something sweeter and tenderer than anything she had ever known.

When she came downstairs at last she had a look upon her as if she had been crowned.

Betty cast a curious questioning glance toward her and she smiled.

"It's wonderful to have a real mother," she said. "That's something you've had all these years that I didn't quite have. Of course Mrs. Wetherill was sweet and dear to me. She loved me very much, and I loved her dearly. But as I grew older I thought a great deal about what an own mother would be like, and now I know. I can't just put into words what I mean, but it is sweet and satisfying and it makes me very happy. She's beautiful, isn't she?"

Betty's tense expression relaxed.

"Yes, she is. I'm glad you can see it. I thought if you didn't think so it would be just too bad!"

Marjorie flashed a look at her.

"How could I help seeing how lovely she is? She is like an exquisite flower! Mrs. Wetherill was a handsome woman, everybody said, and I was proud of her looks and bearing, but she wasn't anything like this. Mother is wonderful, beyond anything I ever dreamed. Just seeing her for that minute I know she is just what I've longed for."

She hesitated and looked at Betty half shyly, as if she wasn't sure just how this tense belligerent sister would take what she was about to say.

"You are very like her, do you know it?"

The color swept up like a flood into the other girl's pale cheeks.

"They used to say I was when I was younger," she said, "but I've got awfully skinny and sickly looking. You're more like Mother, yourself."

"Why, we're just twins, my dear, and how could one be more like her than the other. I can see myself how much alike we are. I'm proud of it and delighted about it."

"Well, I guess I must have been awfully mistaken about you," admitted Betty grudgingly for the third or fourth time since Marjorie had arrived. "I can see you're real. If you'd been like what I thought you were you would have been ashamed of us all in these old ragged things. You wouldn't have recognized the beauty in Mother up there in her tumbled bed with her patched old flannelette nightie on. You would have flung us a five dollar bill maybe, and then gone off to your nice luxurious life. That's what I thought you were."

"Well," said Marjorie thoughtfully, "when I've passed

my probation, if I do, perhaps you'll decide to love me like a sister and then won't we have fun?"

Betty looked at her hungrily.

"I haven't had much fun in a long time. I've about got used to not having any."

"Well, we'll see about that later. Now, breakfast is ready, isn't it? Here they come."

There was a new spring in the father's step as he came downstairs.

"Your mother says she's well," he said as he came into the room. "She says she wants to come down to breakfast and see her family all together!"

His face was radiant.

"You didn't let her get up, did you?" asked Betty anxiously.

"Certainly not," said the father. "She turned right over and went to sleep. She was more tired than she realized. That's why I didn't let our new girl stay in the room but a minute. I told her the doctor wouldn't let her have excitement. Isn't that right?"

"It certainly is!" said Betty. "The doctor was very particular about her not being tired or excited."

"Well, I think she's going to get well, now," said the father. "Where is Ted?"

"Out on his paper route. He's bought it back on time," said Betty.

"But won't he get back to get some of this nice breakfast, at all?" asked Marjorie. "You certainly are a good cook, new sister."

"Yes, he ought to be here any minute now unless he's found another job somewhere, in which case he may stay all day."

Then Bud arrived on the scene with tousled head and an eager hungry look.

"Gee! That breakfast smells awful good!" he declared. "Oh great cats! Lookit! Orange juice an' cereal an' bacum 'n' eggs! Do we haveta choose, ur do we get all three?"

"All three!" smiled Marjorie pushing out the chair beside her for him.

Sunny looked up with a face beaming in egg from ear to ear.

"It's 'licious, Buddie," he said with a comical grin, and then they all laughed.

"I wantta come out, too!" wailed Bonnie from the other room.

Marjorie flew to her charge.

"Not just this morning, Kitten dear," she said smiling down at her. "We'll have to wait till the doctor comes to see when you can get up. But don't you worry. We're going to have a nice time. When Betty and I get the work done we're coming in here and fix you up nice and clean and then we'll have a story or something. Now, suppose you take another little nap till I get done my work."

Bonnie obediently turned over and shut her eyes, and Marjorie stole back to the table. It gave her a thrill to realize that this family was all hers. They hadn't really taken her in yet, or at least she felt that they hadn't had time to think her over and decide about her, and they would probably prove to have faults themselves, but they were dear already.

Then in came Ted, giving a little shiver, and rubbing his bare red hands together.

"Gosh, it feels great in here! Nice and warm!" he said, and flashed a smile at Marjorie that made her feel warm around her heart.

"Say, Dad, you look fine!" he said looking keenly at his father.

"I feel fine, son," said Mr. Gay. "I'm going out this morning and get a new job and set the world on fire."

"Oh, yeah?" said Ted shutting his lips in a thin line. "Not this morning you aren't! Not on your life! There's going to be a big snow storm if I don't miss my guess, and you're staying in till the doctor says you can go out. Besides you're not sticking even your nose out the door till I get your overcoat back. Where's that pawn ticket, Dad? Hand it over."

The father grinned and put his hand in his pocket bringing out the ticket.

"All right! I guess you're right about the overcoat. I did get a little chilled yesterday, but it seemed necessary. However, since we have a Santa Claus in the house, perhaps it will pay in the long run to get that overcoat back, for I couldn't reasonably expect to get a job going out in a day like this without an overcoat. That overcoat was one of my greatest assets, so if you'll run around and get it for me, Ted, I'll be obliged."

"I'll get it, Dad, but I'll hide it well, until you're fit to wear it again. We can't afford to have any more sick people around just now. Christmas is coming."

"Yes!" said the father, a sudden sharp pain in his voice. "Not much of a Christmas, I'm afraid, for a little new sister who has just come to us, but we've a lot to be thankful for!"

Ted cast another keen look at his father.

"Mother know about her?"

"Yes," said the father with a quick radiant look. "She's overjoyed. I wouldn't let her stay up there but a minute, told her the doctor forbade it, but she looked perfectly satisfied. I think perhaps in spite of everything that this is the happiest day of her life."

"Now," said Marjorie when the girls had finished the dishes, and Sunny was established by the dining room table making a fence of pins from Marjorie's pin ball around a cake of soap, "it's time you and I had a consultation."

Bonnie was still asleep and her father was sitting upstairs near his sleeping wife, reading the paper that Ted had brought him, carefully going over the want ads.

The girls sat down in the kitchen for a minute. Bud had gone with Ted after the overcoat and a few things from the store Betty said they needed, and the house was very quiet.

"You'll want to fix Mother's room before the doctor comes, that is, if she wakes up in time. If she doesn't we'll just have to let it go as it is. Doctors always understand."

"Oh, I'll straighten it a little. I can do it without waking her. She's used to my step. But I wish you would go up with him this time. I hate to meet him looking this way. I ripped the sleeve half out of my dress last night when I stooped over to pick up Sunny, and I've just spilled some grease down the front of it. I'm a sight! And this is the only dress I have. I couldn't possibly get it washed out and ironed and on before he comes."

"Oh, I can fix that," said Marjorie smiling, "you'll wear one of my dresses, of course. We're just the same size, so it's sure to fit you. Let's open my suitcases and rummage."

Betty's eyes lighted with sudden longing, but her lips set in a thin line.

"Indeed I couldn't deck myself out in your wonderful clothes. I couldn't do that!"

"No?" said Marjorie teasingly. "Suppose *I* deck you

then? Come on, let's see what I've got that will be suitable."

She dashed into the front hall, brought back her airplane baggage and opened it right there in the kitchen before the ravished eyes of her beauty-starved sister.

Marjorie reached under the neat muslin packing bags that contained frivolous evening things and pulled out two knitted dresses, simple of line, lovely of quality, and rich of color. A brown one and a green one. Hand-knit and expensive of course, since Mrs. Wetherill had picked them out for her beloved child. But they were so beautifully simple that they did not look out of place for morning attire, though they might have graced almost any occasion.

"There!" said Marjorie happily, "take your pick. I think there's a blue one here somewhere, too. Yes, here it is," and she flung it across a chair. "Put them all on and see which you like the best!"

Betty stood spellbound.

"Oh! I couldn't wear those lovely things. It wouldn't seem right!"

"Now, please, Betty, don't spoil things by objections. Put them on one at a time and let me see which is the most becoming."

Betty finally chose the dark blue.

"It is less dressy than the others," she said gravely, "though it's awfully smart. I couldn't ask anything handsomer on this earth. I never thought I'd have a chance to even try on one of those wonderful hand-knit costumes. I thought about trying to knit one for myself just before we left Brentwood, and then the crash came and I couldn't even afford to get common string to knit it with, so I gave it up. But I oughtn't to put this on in the morning! It's too fine."

"Nonsense!" said Marjorie. "Put it on. I like to see you in it. It makes your eyes bluer, and how well it hangs! What a pretty figure you have!"

"Well, I'll be awfully careful of it," compromised Betty, "and I'll take it off as soon as the doctor has gone."

"Nonsense! You'll do no such thing!" said Marjorie. "You'll wear it whenever you like. Here, I've got a couple of little cotton house gowns, sort of aprons they are, to slip over another dress when you're actually working. You take the blue one and I'll take the pink, and then we can tell each other apart. We'll put those on for kitchen work."

Then they heard Bonnie stirring.

"I'll go and fix her up, give her a little sponging off and make her nice for the doctor, and you slip up and fix Mother. Then we'll be ready for the doctor whenever he comes, and after that we'd better plan the meals and see if we have everything we need. Here, put on this apron thing. If Mother wakes up she'll like to see you in something different."

"You make life like a kind of play," said Betty as she wonderingly obeyed. "It doesn't seem right to be dolled up like this to make a bed."

But she put it on, and Marjorie slipped into the other one and went to Bonnie.

"You've got a new dress," said Bonnie astonishingly, out of her long silence.

"Yes, do you like it?"

"Yes, it's pretty. Have you got two dresses?"

"Oh, yes."

"Betty hasn't got but one," said Bonnie irrelevantly.

"Well, we're fixing that all up now," said Marjorie. "How about you? How many dresses have you got?"

"Just two," said Bonnie. "One white one, only it's too short and Muvver won't let me wear it in the winter, and one nasty bwown one. I don't like it. I want a plaid one."

"Well, Christmas is coming pretty soon. We'll see what can be done about that, too."

"Oh, but we aren't going to have any Chwistmas at our house," said the little girl sadly. "Betty said we wouldn't. Muvver was going to do sompin about it but she got sick, and so she can't. So we won't have any."

"Well, perhaps Betty will find she was mistaken," said Marjorie. "Besides, Muvver is getting better, we hope."

"Oh, is she?" The little girl raised her head with a light of hope in her eyes. And then suddenly her face clouded again.

"Do Sunny and I haveta go to the nursewy today?"

"Oh, no," said Marjorie, "we have a nice fire here now and you can stay at home."

"We don't liketa go ta the nursewy," said Bonnie wearily. "It smells of onions and they said my muvver was high-hat because we had wubbers on to keep our feet dwy."

"Well, now, shall we have our face washed and get fixed up nicely for the doctor?"

And so Marjorie made the little girl fresh and sweet, brushed out the pretty curls and put her own pretty pink dressing sack about the child's shoulders to her infinite delight. Then she made the room somehow look lovely, even with the old shabby furniture, and the faded wall paper. Marjorie had a knack at doing things like that. Presently they heard the doctor coming up on the porch, and Betty in the slim blue dress went to open the door, her hair a little gold flame of light about her shapely head. Marjorie, standing back in the tiny parlor almost out of view had time to notice the quick look of interest in the doctor's face as he took account of the exceedingly pretty girl who was meeting him, and the little flush of rose that crept up into Betty's cheeks as she met his gaze.

Mr. Gay came down the stairs himself with the doctor, walking straight and a bit proudly.

"Yes, I think she's decidedly better," the doctor was saying. "I think another day or so will clear up that fever and then she can begin to sit up a little, but I would be exceedingly careful. If you want her down for Christmas she'd better go slowly. And I'll say the same thing for you, Mr. Gay. You know you are a bit run down, and in a condition like that a man is open to anything that is going about. If I were you I'd keep in the house for two or three days yet. It's beginning to snow, and I think we're in for a big storm. The atmosphere is too damp for you to be out in it till that soreness in your chest is all gone."

Then the doctor turned and looked keenly at Marjorie.

"Oh, you're the new sister, aren't you?" he said pleasantly. "Aren't you twins? You look so very much alike. I doubt if I could have told you apart if I hadn't met Miss Betty before several times."

Marjorie looking up caught a bright flame of color on Betty's face and thought how pretty she looked in the new dress. She wondered in passing if this nice pleasant doctor was interested in her sister?

Then she turned to answer the questions about Bonnie.

It was when the doctor had closed his medicine case and was just going toward the door that silent little Bonnie suddenly sat up and spoke.

"They're having awful good things to eat. Can't I have any of them? I'm awful hungwy!"

They all laughed and the doctor turned sympathetically toward the little girl.

"You surely can," he said. "You tell those two sisters of yours to feed you well. How about some cereal? Do you like cereal?"

Bonnie nodded.

"Wif cweam," she said aggrievedly. "They had it for bweakfast and they didn't give me any. Just owange juice. It was good, but I wanted ceweal too, wif cweam and sugar."

"I guess you are really better, young lady. All right. Give her some cereal, and if she continues to improve she might have a baked potato for dinner, and a poached egg. Tomorrow she can have chops."

"A whole chop for me?" said Bonnie with wide eyes. "Won't that be too 'spensive?"

"Of course not," spoke up Marjorie. "Oh, we're going to have a good time, girlie."

Betty lingered a moment at the door talking with the doctor, asking him particularly about her mother's diet and medicine, and the young doctor looked at her approvingly and smiled as he finally went out.

Then came Ted with a big basket from the store, and the overcoat over his arm.

"It's a chicken," said Ted succinctly as he handed over the basket. "There's two of them. I thought Mother ought to have chicken broth."

"Oh, you extravagant boy!" said Betty aghast.

"That's nice, Ted," said Marjorie, "be just as extravagant as you want to. Mother needs everything nice, and so do the rest of you, and chicken will be good for the children, too. I'm so glad you got it!"

Then the real business of the day began, Betty and Marjorie settling down to plan the meals, Betty trying to save, and Marjorie determined to spend for her dear new family.

IX

For two days the girls had their hands full caring for the invalids, getting the house in some sort of order, and doing the necessary cooking and cleaning in a household that had been near to being cleaned out entirely. But the third day the invalids were decidedly better. Bonnie was dressed and playing about with Sunny, or tagging after her two sisters, pretending to help a little.

The mother was allowed to sit up against her pillows for an hour at a time, and to have gay little visits from her family a few minutes at a time, while the father hovered over her and called time up so that she wouldn't get exhausted. It was rare, his care of her. They were like two lovers, Marjorie thought as she watched them shyly, and tried to work out her new relationship and understand just what her absence had meant to them. Precious little times together, Marjorie and her mother had, too, although both of them were shy, and though they felt deeply, they could not yet bring themselves to tell out all they had felt.

Meantime it had been snowing hard for two days, and Ted had been absent most of the time. He came home the first night with a new snow shovel. Snow was a windfall for Ted. He shoveled snow early and late, and was proud to bring home a pocket full of dollars all his own. But he said very little about it. He wasn't a boy who talked much about himself or his doings. It was only by chance that they found out he had been shoveling snow. It was Bud as usual who let it out.

They discovered Bud working away at their own walk with the heavy coal shovel from the cellar, and Marjorie gave him some money and sent him to the store to buy a snow shovel suited to his years. He came back triumphantly and not only polished off the family paths elaborately, but afterwards shouldered his new shovel and started out on a business enterprise of his own, coming home proudly with a dollar and a quarter in silver jingling in his pocket.

"Chrismus money," he told Betty with shining eyes. "Don'tcha guess we all can have Chrismus now, seein' Muth is gettin' well?"

And Christmas was only a week off!

"Why, of course!" said Marjorie coming into the room just then "That's what I came here for in the first place, to spend Christmas with you all. Certainly we've got to have a Christmas. Where do you put the tree, Betty?"

"Tree!" said Betty with a sudden scorn. "We haven't had a tree since we left Brentwood. I don't even know if Bud remembers our last one, and I'm sure Sunny doesn't."

"Sure I remember it," said Bud indignantly. "Whaddaya think I am?"

"We could put it over there by the window," said Bonnie thoughtfully, "if we weally had a twee. Over where other peoples could see how pwetty it is. That's what the other children's folks are going to do wif their twees, put 'em where other folks can see 'em."

"Of course," said Marjorie. "We want to give pleasure to others as well as ourselves."

There wasn't much more said about it then, but a kind of joyous expectancy began to pervade the house as it came to be a fixed possibility that there would be a Christmas.

Ever since she had arrived Marjorie had been planning what she would do, but there hadn't as yet been time to carry out her plans.

"Monday, you and I ought to go out and do some Christmas shopping," said Marjorie to Betty as they were putting everything in shining order Saturday evening after supper.

"Christmas shopping, my eye! A lot of Christmas shopping I could do. I haven't got ten cents of my own," said Betty ruefully.

"Oh, yes, you have," laughed Marjorie. "Look in your purse. I put some in there this afternoon while you were down at the store and it's for Christmas shopping and nothing else."

"Do you think I would go Christmas shopping with your money?" asked Betty scornfully.

"It's not my money," laughed Marjorie, "it's yours. I gave it to you so we could have some fun. You don't think it's any fun, do you, to do all the shopping myself, and not have anybody else be getting up secrets too? Now don't act that way. Let's have a real Christmas, gay and happy. Let's not think who the money belongs to. Let's just get the things for each other we know each likes or wants, and make up for all the other Christmases that I've lost in the family." She beamed lovingly upon Betty, and Betty softened.

"And I used to think you were selfish!" said Betty sorrowfully.

It was Sunday morning while they were getting breakfast together that Marjorie asked quite casually:

"Where do you go to church? Is it far from here?"

Betty stopped stirring the pancake batter she was preparing and stared at her.

"Go to church?" she laughed. "We don't go. We haven't since we left Brentwood. For one thing we didn't have the clothes to go there or anywhere else. And for another thing I guess we were all too discouraged and disheartened to bother about church. People don't feel much interested in going to church when they are having such a time as we've had. It isn't easy to believe in a God who lets people like Father and Mother suffer as they have done. I don't believe in a God myself. At least if there is one He doesn't know anything about us individually. He certainly can't care anything about us or He would make things different for us, that is, if He could."

Marjorie looked at her aghast.

"Oh, Betty! That's awful! You mustn't talk that way."

"Why not, I'd like to know? Do you believe in a God?"

"Certainly."

"Why do you?"

Marjorie looked at her thoughtfully.

"I never stopped to think about why," she said slowly, "but I do. I certainly do!"

"You do just because you were taught that way probably," said Betty bitterly. "But people aren't doing that any more, believing just because somebody else does."

"Betty dear! Don't talk that way," said Marjorie deeply troubled. "That isn't right."

"Right! Ha! What's that anyway? Who said I had to do right? Well, I didn't mean to worry you, only you asked about going to church, and I suppose you'll be disappointed in us if that's what you expect of us. Not one of us goes to church except Ted. He's the religious one of the flock."

"Ted?" said Marjorie lifting astonished eyes.

"Yes, Ted. He's as faithful as the clock. He walks away back to Brentwood every Sunday. He's got a crush on a young preacher back there, and we can't keep him away. He'll probably want to walk you way out there with him if you suggest church to him."

"Why, I'd love to go," said Marjorie. "Why don't we both go? It's a gorgeous morning."

"Thanks, no," said Betty coldly. "I don't feel religiously inclined, and anyway, I haven't any coat. You couldn't just divide your coat with me, though I presume you would if it were possible. Besides, it's you that wants to go to church, not me. Here, Ted," as the boy came in from the street, "here's a candidate to go to church with you."

Ted looked at Marjorie with a sudden sparkle in his eyes.

"Sure, I'll take her," he said diffidently. "But you haveta walk. There's no carline except a long roundabout way."

"I'll love to walk!" said Marjorie.

"In this snow?" asked Betty scornfully.

"Yes, the snow makes it all the nicer. But I can't go and leave you to get dinner all alone."

"I don't mind getting dinner. I enjoy it with all these nice things you've bought us. If you only knew how many dinners I've got with only a can of beans and some stale bread!"

"You poor dear! But that's all the more reason why you should have a vacation from it. You go to church and I'll get dinner!"

"Not on your life!" said Betty, using her brother's

phrase. "If I had any time for church I'd use it trying to fix up a little. My hair needs washing."

"We'll go to a beauty parlor tomorrow."

"No, we won't do that either," said Betty. "If I had any money for beauty parlors I wouldn't use it that way. Not with all the things I need."

Just then came a call from upstairs.

"Betty, your mother thinks she would like to have a little talk with your sister now, if you can spare her," called the father.

"All right, Father, I'm coming," called Marjorie. Then she turned to Ted.

"If Mother wants me perhaps I ought not to go with you this morning. But how about tonight? Do you go at night too?"

"Sure I do!" said Ted snapping his jaw together as if he had often had to contend for his right to do so.

"Oh, yes, he goes. You can't keep him home!" snapped Betty. "You'd think it was a saloon with a pool table they have there the way he's devoted to it. You can't pry him loose. Even the long walk doesn't stop him!"

There was a sneer in the end of Betty's voice, and Marjorie thought she saw resentment quiver over Ted's sensitive face, as if Betty's words were like whiplashes on his bare flesh, but he lifted his head proudly with a kind of defiance in his eyes. If she was going to laugh at him he was ready for her.

But Marjorie smiled warmly, with sympathy in her voice as she said:

"That's a pretty good recommendation for the church, I should say. All right, I'll go tonight if I find I can't go this morning. How soon do you start?"

"Ought to get going in a half hour," said the boy glancing at the clock.

"All right. If I don't get downstairs in time you just start without me."

Then she went upstairs to her mother.

"Your mother did not sleep at all last night," said the father, standing at the foot of the bed looking anxiously toward her. "She has been worrying a lot about you, and I told her it was best to send for you and just talk it out and get it off her mind. This morning she has just a shade of fever again, and I thought if we could only get to the bottom of the trouble and talk it through and have a thorough understanding Mother could rest and not worry, and maybe get a bit of sleep before the doctor comes."

"Of course!" said Marjorie eagerly. "But why should there be anything to worry about? I do hope I haven't made you worse, Mother dear, by coming now when you were sick! I didn't know, of course, but I guess I should have written first and asked if you were willing I should come."

"No, no, dear child!" said her father protestingly, "I'm glad you didn't. We probably would have felt it wasn't fit here for you to come now when we are in such straits. We would have been too proud to let you see to what we had fallen. And your poor little mother would have gone on grieving. No, it isn't about your coming at all that your mother is worried. Although of course she as well as all of us are ashamed that you had to find us in great poverty. Your mother has been worrying lest you may have thought that when she came to see you some two years ago you might think she came to try and get money out of your foster mother. The thought has fairly obsessed her until I can do nothing to take it out of her mind. She seems to think it will always be there in your mind when you think of us."

"Oh, my dear little Mother!" said Marjorie flinging herself down on her knees beside the bed and gathering her mother into her arms, brushing the tears away from the thin cheeks and kissing the trembling lips. "Of course not. How could I? In the first place I didn't know a thing about you until I found that letter that had been written before Mrs. Wetherill died. I only knew that you had given me up, and I did feel bad about that. I felt as if I had not been wanted, and I suppose that feeling made me love the Wetherills all the more fiercely. They were lovely to me, Mother, of course, and they did love me. But sometimes my heart would ache thinking how my own mother didn't want me, and wishing I could see you just once to know what you were like. But as for money, I never once thought about it. They told me when I was quite young that you were not in circumstances to bring me up the way you wanted me brought up, and so you gave me to them. I think that was all Mrs. Wetherill knew about it until a short time before Mr. Wetherill died. Then he told, but I do not know just what he told her. I do not think he told her much, because from her letter written just before she died she seemed to be very much disturbed at what she had found out from you, and terribly upset that you had returned in full all the money they paid for the privilege of adopting me. No, Mother dear, there wasn't ever a thing said to make me feel you were after money when you came to see me. I think that was what had made Mrs. Wetherill feel that she must tell me about you before she died. I think she was conscience-stricken when she found you still cared about me, and she felt she ought not to have kept you from seeing me. She rather put it upon me that I ought to come and find you, and she suggested that I would have plenty of money and was free to do what I would with it. I think she knew that she ought in some way to make up to you for her selfishness in keeping your child when you wanted her back. I think she understood herself that you were not the kind of people to whom money could make up for what they loved."

"Oh, I'm so glad!" sighed the sick woman with relief. "Then you didn't come here just out of pity for us?"

"My dear, I hadn't the slightest idea of pitying you. I felt that I was the one to be pitied. I was all alone in the world, and I didn't even know if my own people were still living. You know it was some time since you had been heard from. You might have all died for all I knew, or moved to another country!"

"You poor little girl!" said her mother softly, gathering Marjorie's hand into her own frail one and squeezing it gently. "You poor little abandoned baby!"

"No, Mother, don't say that!" pleaded Marjorie. "I was not abandoned, I was sort of cheated away from you, wasn't I? The letter makes it very plain that you were sick, and under great strain of worry about Father and my twin sister, and you were too sick to realize what you were doing, and goaded into doing it. At least that was what I read between the lines."

"Yes," said her mother, "they came to me when I was too weak to understand it all. They told me your father would not live unless he had certain care and attention. A specialist to watch over him, and a year or two in a quiet outdoor place where he would be absolutely free from worry. They said your little sister could not live, or at least she would be a cripple if she didn't have a certain difficult operation."

"And wasn't it true, Mother?" Marjorie was wide-eyed with consternation.

"Partly," said the mother wearily as if it were something that she had gone over and over so many times that it hurt her to remember. "But,—there would have been some other way. Oh, there would have been *something* else we could have done."

"But who told you all this, Mother? Not the doctor, surely?"

"No, it was Mr. Wetherill. He came to see me several times, till I didn't know what to do. He kept telling me how his wife loved you and would care for you as her own, and how he would see that Betty had every care that science could give her, and that your father should have a beautiful place to recuperate in, and all he needed. And he was as good as his word, too. He did all that, lavished things upon us until we had to protest. He seemed to think that made up for the other. And then the worst of all was that he gave me the impression that your father wanted me to sign the papers when all the time he was too sick even to be told that you and Betty were born, though I didn't know that yet. Your father did not know anything about the transaction until it was too late to stop it honorably. He was so sick for months that I did not dare to tell him what I had done, and so it wore in upon me all the heavier. And then when your father got better and I told him, he was broken-hearted. It seemed to me that he would never smile again. He felt that it was a personal disgrace, even though he hadn't done it himself, nor known about it, and as soon as he was able to travel he went to see Mr. Wetherill and tried to get you back. But Mr. Wetherill was very determined. He had the papers all ironclad. We had nothing to go on. We had given you up. He even had the doctor's statement that your father was not in condition to give consent, and I had the sole authority. He had managed it with witnesses and clever questions he had asked in their presence, so that we could do nothing. Of course it might have been different if we had had money and influence."

The mother sighed deeply and the quiet tears flowed down.

"There, Mother dear," soothed Marjorie, "it doesn't matter now, does it? It's all over, and we are together at last and understand each other."

"But I feel it was all my fault," wailed the mother. "Sometimes I wake up from dreaming that I am doing it all over again, and then I scream out. I felt as if I had done something utterly inhuman!"

"There, now, Mother, you are getting all worked up again, and you promised me you wouldn't if I called her up here."

"I know," said the mother again, trying to bring out a trembling little sigh.

"Well, Mother," said Marjorie gently, "I'm terribly sorry you've had to suffer so many years. If I knew any way I would so gladly take it to wipe out the memory of all this from your mind, but since we can't, suppose we just make the rest of the years so bright they will dim the others out of sight? You see, I was spared all that suffering. I longed to know about you of course, but I was only a child, and I was happy. They were very good to me. I didn't suffer in any way. But it is awful to me to know that you did, and why can't we play it never was. Why can't we just go on from here?"

The mother looked up with a little trembling smile on her lips as if she dared not quite fling off her burden.

"And you don't blame me?"

"No, I don't blame you, dearest Mother. And you mustn't blame the other mother either, because I don't think she ever knew the whole thing, nor had even the slightest realization that you wanted me until you came to see her. I think Mr. Wetherill always protected her from everything He adored her, and got her anything she asked for. He couldn't bear to say no to her in anything. I suppose he didn't scruple to do anything to please her. It was selfish of her of course, to want me who belonged to another, when there were so many other little babies in the world who had nobody to care. But I don't believe *she* realized until just before she died that she was selfish. So, mother, let's forgive her and forget all about the pain, and let's have a beautiful time together. Will you?"

"You mean " said the mother anxiously, "that you are willing to come down to being our child? That you are not ashamed of us?"

"Oh. Mother! Of course not. Of course I'm your child."

"But you have a different name from ours, and a different position. A position that you would not have had as our child."

"I can change my name," said Marjorie eagerly, "there is no one to be hurt by my doing it."

"No, my dear, you could not legally do that," said her father gravely. "I think it might affect your inheritance, and that would not be right. That is a small matter, of course. Neither your mother nor I would worry about your name. What Mother wants is merely to know if you really love us and are willing to forgive us for having allowed you to be put out of our lives. I am not saying it was not an advantage to you, at least a worldly advantage, but that does not make our act any the less questionable."

"Oh, Father, I do forgive, if there is anything to forgive, and I do love and honor you, and want to be your child. And as for name and inheritance, why all I care for the inheritance is to use it for you all, to make it more easy and comfortable. And Mrs. Wetherill practically suggested that in her last word to me."

"But, my dear, we can't live on you."

"Why not, Father? If I had been your child in the home all these years wouldn't I have been living on you? And now that I have come back to you, I have no other way to make up for the lost years except through the money. Why can't we just be glad in it and call it *ours?*"

"My dear, a man must provide for his family."

"That's all right, Father, when you get well and are able to do it, but just now *I* am able, and I'm going to enjoy getting and doing things for you all more than anything I ever did in my life. Please, dear Father! And- -don't you think Mother is getting a little tired? She looks to me as if she needed to go to sleep right away. Suppose you tell her it's all right. It will be, you know, and we can settle all these details afterward. We're just all a family together. If Betty had a legacy left to her, you wouldn't hesitate to let her put the family on its feet would you? Or Ted? And wouldn't they want to right away? Well, then, why not take me clear into the family and treat me just the same as you would them? I'm doing the very thing I want to do with my money, and it's giving me more pleasure than if I were to buy an airplane and a yacht and three or four estates in different parts of the world, so why not enjoy it with me? Besides what I have spent so far wouldn't even make a nick in the estate that has been left me, so why worry? Come, Father, kiss Mother and tell her it's all right and she positively needn't worry another bit."

The father stooped over and kissed his wife.

"She is right," he said tenderly, "she's our child, and it's all forgotten, and it's all right, and you're not to worry again ever any more. Will you cast it all away?"

"Oh, yes, I will."

"And will you go to sleep?"

She nodded, dropped happily back on her pillow and closed her eyes.

So Marjorie slipped away with a vision of her father sitting by the bed holding her mother's hand, a long loving look and smile passing between them.

"Aren't they sweet?" she said as she came down misty-eyed to where Betty was putting a clean tablecloth on the table.

Betty looked up admiringly.

"I'm so glad you can see that!"

"Why, did you think I wouldn't?"

"Well, you weren't brought up with them," she said evasively.

Marjorie studied her a minute, and then she said:

"It doesn't take long to discover they are sweet. But I suppose Ted's gone, hasn't he?"

"No, he's outside getting that ice off the step. He's afraid somebody will fall. He's been waiting for you. I think he's keen on having you go with him. I shouldn't wonder if he wants to show you where we used to live."

"Oh, is the church where we used to live?" asked Marjorie, and knew not that she had said "we."

Betty gave her a quick look and then said with satisfaction, "Yes."

"Well, I'd like to go in the daytime so I can see it. But are you sure you don't want me to stay and take care of the children?"

"Mercy no. They're used to taking care of themselves, and now that Bonnie's up again Sunny is no trouble at all. She invents things to keep him happy. Go on. Dinner won't be ready till after you get back, and you can help clear away if lack of work troubles your conscience."

So Marjorie and her brother started off to church.

Ted wasn't much dressed up. He hadn't anything to dress up in. But he had brushed his clothes spick and span, had combed his red curls to a shining polished mahogany, had shined his old shoes, and he was scrupulously clean.

Marjorie secretly admired his ease of manner and walk in spite of his clothes, though she could see he was conscious of his shabbiness, eyeing her handsome fur coat, and finally remarking:

"I guess you'll be ashamed of me, but they don't mind clothes where we're going."

"No," said Marjorie thoughtfully, "I'm not ashamed of you, I'm proud of you. Things like that are only comparative, anyway, aren't they? They shouldn't have any part in going to church."

Ted eyed her speculatively, and finally ventured another question:

"I guess you're saved, aren't you?"

"Saved?" said Marjorie altogether startled. The phrase was not common among the young people she knew.

"I am a church-member. Is that what you mean?"

Ted was visibly embarrassed.

"No," he said, "that doesn't getcha anywhere in being saved. That's what comes afterward. It's the sorta sign for others to see, but everybody who joins the church isn't saved by a long shot."

She gave him another keen look. What kind of a place was this church to which he was taking her? Obviously not an ordinary church. People didn't talk that way in the church to which the Wetherills belonged. They attended church and were very faithful in contributing to its support, but they didn't ask each other if they were saved.

"You haveta be born again, you know."

She gave him another keen look and as if he were answering the question in her eyes he said:

"You believe, you know, that's how you get to be born again. That's how you get saved. You just believe."

"Believe?" said Marjorie inquiringly. She didn't say "believe what?" But her tone said it. So he answered.

"Believe that Jesus is the Son of God and died to take our sins upon Himself and suffer their penalty." He explained it gravely, as if he had done it before, and understood thoroughly what it meant.

"Why, I guess I believe that," said Marjorie, "I've never really thought much about it, but I believe it of course. It's all in the Bible, isn't it? I believe the Bible. I was taught to believe that when I was very young, though I'm not sure I know much about it."

"Gee, it's great when you get ta studying it!" said Ted irrelevantly.

Marjorie looked at him in surprise.

"Have you studied it?"

"Sure! We had Bible classes twice a week at the Brentwood chapel. Gosh, I was sorry to move away! It's a whole lot harder to live the Christian life when you can't go where there are a lot of believers. Now I can't go any time except Sunday, and I certainly do miss those classes."

"You must have had a good teacher," said Marjorie wonderingly.

"I'll say he was! He was *swell!* He seemed ta know just what you'd been going through that day, and how to show you where you'd got off the track, see? Of course we have him Sundays too, but I certainly do miss the regular weekday classes. I tried for a while to keep up, but when you get up at four o'clock and serve papers, and then work all day, you don't seem to have much brains for study at night. But I certainly do miss it."

"Who is this teacher?"

"Gideon Reaver's his name. He's just a young fella, only been out of Seminary a little over a year, but he certainly knows his Bible. He can preach all around any preacher I ever heard before, even most of the big guns that come to the chapel now and then because they know him. He doesn't preach anyway, he just talks, and tells us what the Bible means. He's a great big fellow, six feet. And a pair of shoulders! Oh, boy! He's got a nice face, too. The girls all go crazy over him, but he doesn't seem to know it. He just looks right over them and smiles and goes on talking, and by and by they settle down and listen and get sensible. The fellows like him too. Oh, boy, do they like him! And how! But you'll hear him. You'll see what he's like."

"Well, I hope I shall be able to keep from going crazy over him," Marjorie smiled.

Ted turned red.

"Oh, you're not like that. You're sensible! But he's a prince, you know. I'm not blaming 'em for going crazy over him. If I was a girl I might do it myself."

"Did Betty used to go to church with you when you lived in Brentwood?" asked Marjorie.

Ted's face darkened.

"No!" he said shortly. "She wouldn't go. She said she had no time for church. She was all taken up with a poor fish in the office where she worked. He useta come out in a secondhand roadster and take her places. He made me sick. Had one of those little misplaced eyebrows on his upper lip, thought he was smart, could smoke more cigarettes in an hour than anybody I ever heard of, and wore his hat way off on the back of his head like he was bored with the world and thought he was too good to associate with common people. He useta call me, 'M'lad!' just like that, as though he thought he was some prince and I was to wait on him. I didn't stick around much when he came here. But he put Betts off the notion of going to church entirely. I couldn't get her near it. And then, even if she'd wanted to go she wouldn't attend a plain little chapel. She wanted some swell church where they had high-hats and swell music."

"Then she doesn't know Gideon Reaver."

"No, she wouldn't be introduced one day when I brought him home. She said she didn't care to know preachers, they would bore her, and it might be embarrassing to have him hanging around. Oh, she makes me sick, sometimes."

"I guess she's had rather a hard time," suggested Marjorie gently.

"Sure she has! We've all had a hard time. And she's been a good scout, worked like everything to take care of Mother and Father, and all that, but still—sometimes she makes me sick."

"Is she what you call saved?" Marjorie asked hesitantly.

"Not she!" said her brother sorrowfully. "She won't let me talk to her, and she won't go anywhere where she can hear the truth. She says she doesn't believe in a God who would let us suffer the way we have! I try to tell her about what the Bible says but she won't listen. There!" He suddenly broke off and his voice grew jubilant. "There's Brentwood now! See it up there on the hill? And that's our house, that long low stone house with the white pillars to the porch? Isn't that some swell location? And there! Upon my word if there doesn't come Gideon Reaver now! He must have been up on the hill visiting some sick person. Gosh, that's great! Now I can introduce you to him before the service!"

Then Marjorie looked up to see a tall finely built young man coming toward her with astonishingly wonderful eyes that seemed to have seen further into life than most men see, yet they had a deep sweet settled peace in them. She wondered if it could be real. She had never seen a young man who had that look.

X

MEANTIME back in Aster Street Betty was having a time of her own.

Bud had found a forlorn little alley cat shivering with the cold, rescued her from a ring of small dogs who were threatening her worthless life, and brought her into the house Her fur was caked with mud and ice, with a tinting of blood from her recent fight, and altogether she was a pitiful object. He hoped, faintly, to persuade Betty to take an interest in her, though he was pretty sure she wouldn't. Anyway he meant to sneak some food out for her.

But when he found that Betty had gone upstairs to make the beds it seemed to him an excellent chance to carry out his purposes, so with one free arm he filled the dishpan with nice warm water, took the dish soap, and plunged the poor astonished kitten into a lovely warm bath.

"There, kitty, there, poor pussy!" he said tenderly, holding the struggling frantic creature firmly, and dousing her under water in his efforts. "There, nice little cat! Can't you see you gotta be clean? Stop your scratching, you poor fish you! Didn't I rescue you from the dogs? You aren't a bit grateful. But you gotta be clean. Don't you understand? After I get you clean I'll give you some nice dinner. Nice warm milk. Won't that be nice, kitty?"

Appeared on the scene Bonnie, wide-eyed and eager.

"Oh, Buddie, what you got? Where d'you get that cat?"

"Sh-h-h!" warned Bud in the midst of his struggles, mingling his own life's blood with that of the dirty little cat. "Ain't you got any sense at all, Bonnie Gay? Dontcha know ya mustn't make a noise an' wake Mother? Dontcha know I gotta get this cat clean before Betty gets down here?"

Sunny came running. Yelling.

"Tat, where's a tat? I wantta see ze tat! Oh! Kitty! Kitty! See ze funny 'ittle kitty!"

"Can't ya shut up, Sunny Gay? Can't ya get outta my way?"

The children were plastered eagerly up to the sink, one on either side, Sunny with his chin on the edge of the sink, Bonnie holding on and watching, and suddenly the dishpan, which was a trifle too large for the inadequate sink, and much too full of dirty soapy water, tilted crazily, and Bud in his efforts to right it released one hand from the cat. That cat had learned to take any advantage no matter how small that came to her miserable life and she clutched and clawed at the edge of the pan, floundered away from Bud, and made a dive, anywhere out of that awful bath. One instant she wetly clutched Bud's neck, digging her nails in deep, the next she trailed sloppily across his front and slid from his grasp, thumping down on the floor with a flop and then scuttling dazedly like a little drowned imp through dining room and hall, finding refuge at last in the best upholstered chair the Gay family owned, and began licking away furiously at her outraged fur.

But the pan she had left behind her had attempted to follow her descent, and poured wildly over poor frightened Bud, with branches in every direction, one going right down Sunny's handy little neck and into his shoes, and another splashing into Bonnie's face and deluging her neck and arms and the front of her dress.

A united howl arose, Sunny dancing up and down with his eyes shut and screaming, and Bonnie setting up a wail like none she had ever given before.

"Aw, shut up, ya little pests ya! Now see whatchuve done!"

Betty came flying downstairs hushing them up, her eyes flashing fire! She beheld the dripping crowd in horror.

"Buddie Gay! What are you doing? You naughty, *naughty* boy!"

Betty seized Bud's arm and jerked him back from the sink, but some subconscious reaction compelled him to keep his hold on the dishpan which he had been trying to right, and when Betty removed him from the sink the dishpan with its remaining dirty water came along, and deluged Betty who had just changed her kitchen dress for the pretty little house dress Marjorie had given her that morning. She had been upstairs getting into array to meet the doctor when she heard the tumult downstairs.

Betty looked down at herself in horror and gasped, the more so as the nature of the element that was doused over her was gradually revealed by the dregs of dirt in the dishpan.

It was just at that opportune second that the doctor arrived and rang the bell. Only Bonnie heard it, and stopping her wail midway she went to open the door, then went on with her wail.

"Why, what's the matter, little girl?" he asked looking at her distressed face in astonishment.

"Buddie was w-w-washing—the—kitty!" she sobbed, "and the kitty—flew, an' it's all over us!" she explained and then opened her mouth in another howl and led the way to the kitchen where the two boys and Betty were carrying on.

"You wicked boy!" said Betty in a cold hard tone, never the tone she would have had the nice young doctor hear. "You wicked. *wicked* little boy! What on earth were you doing to make all this trouble?"

"I was—washing—a cat!" howled Bud, forgetting his years and reverting to babyhood. "She—was—all bluggy! The dogs were—f-f-fighting her!"

"Do you mean to tell me that you dared to bring a cat in here from the street and wash it in my *dishpan?* A dirty little alley cat? In my clean dishpan! And my dish soap, too!" as she sighted the sloppy cake of soap winking at her from across the floor under the table! "Oh, you unspeakable child! As if I didn't have enough to do without all this mess. And you've ruined this pretty dress too! You knew it was naughty to bring a dirty cat in here and wash it, didn't you? Answer me, Buddie Gay, you knew it, didn't you?"

"She—w-was—all cold—and trembling—and—and—s-s-scared!" howled Buddie now in paroxysms of hysteria.

"I don't care if she was frozen stark to death!" said Betty in a hard cold tone of fury. "Where is she now? Answer me, Bud! Where is that cat now?"

"I d-d-don't k-k-know!" howled Bud. "She—she—she —clawed me, and then she f-f-flew! I might bleed ta death mebbe, but you wouldn't c-c-care!"

Then Sunny put in with a cheerful excitement.

"Her went in ze parlor, her did! Her is in muvver's big chair wif the wockers, sittin' up an' wipin' her fezzers wif her little wed tongue!"

Sunny was dripping from neck to toes, and there were both tears and drops of dirty water on his cheeks, but his face was eager with excitement.

Then suddenly Betty looked up and saw the doctor standing in the doorway with the most comical look of amusement and pity on his face that a man could wear, and all at once Betty knew that she too was crying! The utmost humiliation that life could bring had descended upon her. The handsome young doctor had seen her like this, wet and dirty and angry! He had *heard* her like this. It was something she could never undo. The echo of her angry voice was still ringing in her ears, like the sound of a gong echoing long after the ringer is gone. No amount of apology or excuse could ever make him forget her that way. She was undone before him, disgraced forever.

And all limp and dirty as she was she sank down into a kitchen chair and burst into real weeping.

If she could have seen the doctor's face at that moment she would have been surprised. The comical look of amusement vanished utterly and a look of utter tenderness and sympathy came into his eyes. In one motion he set down his medicine case on a chair in the hall behind him and strode over to Betty.

"Poor child!" he said. "You've been working too hard. We'll have you down in bed the next thing if you don't look out. Here!" he said seizing upon a towel that hung on the rack above the sink out of harm's way. It was a clean towel. Betty had taken pride in hanging it there a few minutes before, thinking how nice her kitchen looked, all fixed up for Sunday. She had been so glad there was that clean towel.

The doctor wet the end of the towel and came over to Betty, lifting her face very gently and wiping off the tears with the wet towel.

"There!" he said cheerfully. "You'll feel better now. Nothing like cool water to brace one up. Hand over your hands too. There, now, don't you feel better? That dress will wash, won't it? No great harm done, is there? Anyway I don't wonder you felt you'd got to the limit. There! Go on crying if you want to. It will help you to react. It isn't everybody that can have the cat give a bath to the whole family at once on a Sunday morning."

Suddenly Betty looked up and laughed. Laughed with the tears streaming down her cheeks.

The doctor came over to her again, taking a clean handkerchief out of his pocket and lifting her chin with one hand gently wiped the tears away.

Betty stopped laughing and her face held something almost like awe.

"Oh," she said suddenly, "I'm such a mess! And you will get your nice clean handkerchief all soiled!"

She was coming back to herself now, with the hard usual edge in her voice, but somehow that little act of wiping her tears away had taken the shame and humiliation away from Betty's hurt heart.

"Well," she said after a minute, "you've certainly seen me at my worst! I'm sure I don't know what I said to those children."

"Do you often have as much cause?" asked the doctor with a companionable grin. "Now, let's see what can be done for these other drowned people."

Sunny and Bonnie were standing in the middle of the floor, still dripping, and staring at the two grownups, tears on their soiled cheeks Bud had returned to the window and was softly blubbering to himself.

"Ah—bbbbb--bah! Ah—-bbbubbubbub—bah!"

"I'll have to take them to the bathroom and scrub them," said Betty wearily. "And I'd just got them fixed up clean for Sunday!"

"Too bad!" said the doctor sympathetically.

Betty seized Bonnie's little dress and wrung the water out of it.

"There! Go upstairs and take off everything," she said. "I'll be up in just a minute. You can get into the tub and turn on the water."

She took off Sunny's outer robing, finding him less damaged than his sister, and sent him up to get his bathrobe

on. Then she turned her attention to Bud and her voice
had its hard edge now in full.

"Now, where is that cat?"

Bud turned a woebegone face toward her.

"I don't know."

"Well, find her!"

"Is this the lost article?" asked the doctor coming back
from a tour of investigation and holding up a dreary little
wisp of a meek stringy cat by the nape of her neck.

"Oh, mercy!" said Betty, and in spite of herself broke
into a laugh. "Here, I'll open the door and put her out!"

"You can't do that even to an alley cat," said the doctor. "She's too wet to put out in this cold. She'd freeze
solid in half a minute! The society for the prevention of
cruelty would be after you."

"Sh-sh-she's hongry!" announced Bud anxiously. "I p-
p-romised her something ta eat! An' you can't let her go
out there! There's about thirteen dogs chasing her out
there! She's scared!"

"Well, let's see," said the doctor still holding the cat,
"how about a box and some old rags? Couldn't you manage that, Bud? Isn't there a box in the cellar she would
like for a bed? And we could put it down by the furnace in
the cellar until she dries out, couldn't we?"

"Sure!" said Bud, brightening, and he stumped away to
get the box.

Betty shamedly brought a saucer of milk and set it
down on a newspaper in the corner, and the poor little rag
of a cat, crumpled and damp, addressed herself to the first
full meal she had had since she arrived in this vale of
tears.

They stood watching her for a minute, with an adoring
if damp Bud kneeling beside her, and then the doctor
said:

"How about that chair in there? Oughtn't it to be wiped
off before it dries in? Can I use this towel?"

"Oh, I'll do it," said Betty suddenly coming back to
reality. "You've already exceeded a doctor's duties several
times."

"Bud, as soon as that lady finishes her banquet put her
in her box and carry her down by the furnace, and then
come up and get off those wet clothes. Make it snappy,
too, hear, Bud? I don't want you for a patient, not yet
awhile anyway."

"Awwright!" answered Bud with an absorbed tone. He sounded enraptured over that poor little ratty kitten. It was a foregone conclusion that he would not leave her charmed presence nor think of changing his wet clothes until he heard someone coming after him again.

The doctor smiled indulgently as he hurried upstairs.

"And now where are my real patients?" he called as he came up. "If they've survived that tornado they must be getting well fast!" and he came with his cheery presence into the room where Mrs. Gay was just waking from her first refreshing sleep since she had taken to her bed.

Betty in the bathroom hastening Bonnie through her leisurely bath, smiled to herself and wondered if all doctors were so cheerful and comforting. It was probably just because he was a doctor that he had been so nice to her when she had been down there in the kitchen hysterical over the mess the children had made. But it thrilled her to think of his wiping her tears, of the touch of his smooth fingers lifting her chin so gently. It was that sense of being cared for that touched her, brought the tears to her eyes.

"Fool!" she told herself, "as if he cared anything about me. He's just a doctor and it's his business to heal anything, even a cat! He can't bear to see things suffer even with mortification, I suppose. That's probably why he chose to be a doctor!"

But she hurried Bonnie into her ragged little undergarments and got herself freshened up in the pretty knitted dress that Marjorie had given her. She would take it off as soon as he was gone of course, but she must appear decently if only for a minute, after he had seen her looking so disreputable.

So she came shining into the sickroom in an incredibly short space of time and gleaned an admiring glance from his nice eyes that made her feel warm all over.

"Fool!" she told herself again bitterly. "It didn't mean a thing! He was just kindly and impersonal! He's probably in love with some charming nurse, or maybe married to an heiress. Any good man might have done just what he did and think nothing of it. He was just being kind and helping me out of a mess. It's what any true gentleman ought always to do, put a girl at her ease. Of course there aren't many like that any more, but it's nice to know there is one left in the world who cares to be kind." She stared after him wistfully as he went out to his car and drove away,

and then she hurried upstairs to take off the pretty dress
and throw on her very oldest. She had to scrub the kitchen
now and she hated it, dirty cat-bath all over it! And the
children's clothes too! And she must find something to put
on Sunny while she did up his only decent suit.

Then it was time to put the vegetables on, and look at
the roast. Such a nice dinner! But she was too tired to
enjoy it. There were bright red spots on her thin cheeks,
and her tongue was sharp when she spoke to the children.
She gave Bud the worst tongue-lashing he had ever had,
and coming as a surprise after the doctor's merry chal-
lenge it hurt deeply. He dragged himself upstairs and
stayed a long time reflecting how hard grown-up people
were to get along with. He took off his wet garments and
put on the worst things he could find, out at the elbow and
out at the knee. He didn't care. He had the cat anyway.
Then he stole down cellar and sat on the rough dirt floor
beside the cat's box watching her sleep, all curled up in a
bunch. She had licked her fur fairly clean, and she was
drying out nicely. She looked like the fluff that came
under the bed when the room needed sweeping. He wondered why grown-up people hated cats so much. He
thought she was lovely.

If Marjorie sitting in the pretty little old stone church of
a hundred years ago, that was now called "the chapel," and
listening to the young preacher making salvation plainer
than she had ever heard it before, could have known what
had been going on back at the little house on Aster Street,
she would not have sat so comfortably absorbed in the sermon. But fortunately she did not know, and so it seemed
to her that she was happier than she had ever been in
church before. Always on Sunday she had gone to church
with a vague longing for something, she hardly knew
what, something that would satisfy the wistfulness of her
soul. And it had never been there. Sometimes her imagination would soar heavenward and she would try to feel as
she thought a good saintly soul should feel, but always
such forced emotions left her as she went from the
church, and the days passed on with that uneasy little rest-
lessness of soul back in her being somewhere, that would
not be entirely satisfied even when things were going just
as she had planned.

But here in this sweet old chapel with its lovely arched

ceiling of polished wood, and its fine windows of old-fashioned design, there seemed a different atmosphere from the churches she had known all her life. It was as if a strong sea breeze were blowing through the little audience room, waking up and freshening every mind to keener intelligence. As if a holy kind of glory pervaded the place. She heard one woman explaining to another: "Why, The Holy Spirit is here!" She wondered if that were what she meant. It seemed a place where God dwelt intimately, companioning with those who came to Him here in a way He did not reach the people who attended most church edifices. Maybe it was only a queer idea of hers. Her foster-mother used to tell her that she was queer sometimes, had quaint old-fashioned ideas. She often used to wonder if Mrs. Wetherill, much as she loved her, fully understood her when she tried to explain the strivings of her unsatisfied soul.

Then, too, the singing here seemed to have a different sound from that in ordinary churches. The people sang the words as if they meant them, and the music rose like incense from an altar and seemed to mingle with the heavenly choirs above. Of course that must be just fancy too, for the people around her were just ordinary people, some of them looked quite uncultured. It couldn't be the quality of their voices, or their training either. It seemed to be that they were singing because they loved to sing, and because they felt what they were singing. "Making a joyful noise unto the Lord." Wasn't that phrase somewhere in the Bible? Or was it in the ritual of the church? She wasn't very familiar with Scripture. She didn't know. Bible study had not been a part of her early training. She owned a beautifully bound Bible and it had its place on her bedside table, but she had seldom read it. She had no idea where 'to begin to read a Bible. The beginning seemed so unreal. So she had seldom read it, except in snatches here and there occasionally, as one might pick up a book of poetry recognized as lovely but not suited to practical life.

But now suddenly it seemed that the Bible was the guide book for the Christian's way, the indispensable source of all knowledge, the deep hidden treasury of a Christian's wealth. It had never occurred to her that the Bible could be all that; that it could be a thing upon which one lived and depended. She had looked upon it more as a clergyman's handbook, too mystical for ordinary mortals to comprehend.

So she sat and listened wide-eyed to the eager young preacher with the wonderful holy eyes who seemed as he talked to be looking into another world, listening to a higher authority than himself and merely passing on to his hearers the Word he received from Heaven. He seemed as he talked to be keeping his eyes above them, looking into the face of God Himself, using not his own thoughts nor even his own words, but merely repeating what his soul had caught from the lips of his Master.

When the sermon was over she felt breathless as if she had been privileged a glimpse into Heaven itself, as if God had been there speaking to her soul through the lips of this young man. She was filled with awe. Her heart throbbed a response as though she wanted to answer a high sweet call she had heard for the first time.

"You have shown me so many things," she said to him afterward as they stood together at the door a moment, waiting for Ted to gather up the hymn books and straighten the extra chairs for the night service. "Things I never knew could be! I never knew the Bible was a book like that!"

He gave her a startled look.

"Oh, didn't you? I'm glad I helped," he smiled. "I hope you'll come again."

"Oh, I will!" she said fervently. "What you have said seems to be something I've been searching for a long time."

His face lit up with a kind of glory light.

"Oh, I *am* glad!" he said quietly.

Then came Ted with his shy smile of adoration.

"Great service!" he said quietly, and it suddenly seemed to Marjorie that those two had some secret bond of fellowship that swept aside all inequalities of age or position or station and made them one. She looked at her new brother with wondering eyes, seeing him in another light, and remembering what he had said to her on the way over about being saved. It became at once apparent to her that this was the real Ted, this was his main interest in life. Whatever other relationships he might have in life were subservient in his eyes to this, whatever it was, that this

plain little old-fashioned chapel, and this strangely interesting young man, represented. She felt a pang of envy
going through her heart. Would that she might know
something of this mystic order that seemed to dignify all
other things of life, and make them more worth while for
its sake!

"I wish I could run you home in my car, Ted," said the
young preacher wistfully, "but I have a funeral in half an
hour, and just barely time to get to it. Queer time for a
funeral, isn't it, Sunday just after church? But some of the
family have come a long distance and have to be back
again to work tomorrow morning, so they are driving right
back as soon as it is over. Sorry, I'd enjoy taking you."

He included Marjorie in his smile.

"Oh, that's all right, Mr. Reaver," said Ted shiningly.
"I'm going to take my sister over to see our old place.
She's never seen it, you know."

And then as the minister looked at her inquiringly, Ted
explained:

"You know she's been away a long time. She's never
seen it."

"Oh," said the minister looking at Marjorie quickly
again, "then you're not the sister I saw before? I thought
there was something different about you. You're not twins,
are you?"

"Yes," smiled Marjorie, "and I guess we're quite alike
in looks, at least."

"Well, isn't that interesting. I'll have to take time off
some day and come and call and get acquainted with you
both. But you know, I really thought you were—different
—somehow—when I didn't know you weren't!"

They all laughed and then the minister looked at his
watch and said:

"Well, I'll have to be off. Hope you come again, Miss
Gay."

"Oh, I will!" said Marjorie, a bit breathless from hearing herself called a new name.

Then the brother and sister walked on in silence. Ted
was burning to ask her how she liked the minister, but his
boy-code forbade his opening his lips on the subject. Finally, as they turned the corner and the minister went driving by in his car, bowing to them and smiling as he
passed, Marjorie followed him with her eyes until he

turned another corner and was out of sight and then she said slowly, gravely:

"He's rather wonderful, isn't he?"

"You're telling me?" said Ted in a reverential tone.

XI

THE Brentwood house made a great impression on Marjorie. As they approached it Ted watched her with jealous eyes. She had liked his minister, now would she like the house he loved? These were the two tests he had set for this new sister, although perhaps he did not realize that he was testing her at all. But he did not miss a single expression on her face as she looked. and every question she asked proved to him that she was really interested in what he said. not just making talk to kill time, not merely to be pleasant.

"Why, isn't it occupied?" she asked as they came in sight of the "For Sale" sign.

"No," said Ted with a heavy sigh. "I've been expecting every time I come this way to find that sign gone. but it stays. I don't know what's the reason. Perhaps they are asking too much for these hard times. And then, of course. it isn't in the new part of town. The high-hatters are all moving to Rose Hill. That's half a mile farther over, and has a big fashionable church and a club house and golf course But I like Brentwood all the better for that. It's quiet here, and it's near the chapel. and besides we had enough land to do as we pleased. We were far enough from neighbors not to be bothered by what they did, nor have them watching us all the time."

"It's lovely!" said Marjorie. taking in the tall elm trees that were placed just right to make a picture of the house.

The long slope of snowy lawn, the shrubbery and hemlock trees heavy with their burden of snow making a delightful screen from the street, all added to the picture.

"Could we go up closer to the house?" Marjorie paused before the gate of iron grille work and looked up the long path.

"Sure we could," said Ted, lifting the latch and opening the gate.

As they went up the long path Marjorie was imagining a firelight's glow through those windows, the house filled with laughter and song, the children playing on the lawn, riding downhill on their sleds. It was indeed a lovely place. And in summer it would be wonderful.

Marjorie, used as she was to the great beautiful Wetherill house on the North Shore in a suburb of Chicago, with its delightful surroundings and perfection of detail, could yet see something most alluring in this lovely old stone house on its hill. The very ramblingness of its architecture, that was stamped with thoughts of generations past, spoke of lives unhampered by conventionalities, of freedom and love and a real home. The Chicago house was grand and she loved it, but there was something gay and inviting about this one that just seemed to fit her dear family. And suddenly Marjorie knew that she loved them all deeply. She didn't know them very well, but she loved them anyway. And she liked this house and loved to think of them as living here.

Ted led her around to the back and opened a loose shutter to let her look into the long low living room with its great fireplace, flanked on either side by bookcases reaching to the ceiling, and her enthusiasm for the house mounted till it equaled the boy's own.

She stood a moment on the front piazza afterwards and looked down toward the street, and the village, picking out the slender tower of the quaint little stone chapel, and her eyes grew quiet and thoughtful as she gazed.

As they turned away from the gate at last Marjorie took note of the sign board and made a mental memorandum of the name of the real estate agent.

"Now," she said as they walked on toward home, "tell me about it, Ted. How did Father come to lose it?"

"Oh, it was just one thing after another," said Ted sorrowfully. "First the head of the firm died where Dad was expert accountant, then the business went up, and after

Dad got their affairs straightened out for them he got very sick. And about that time the bank where Dad kept his savings closed its doors, and hasn't opened them yet. That's the story. We couldn't pay the interest on the mortgage, and we couldn't pay the taxes; three times it lapsed and Dad was getting into debt and nearly crazy, and finally the Building and Loan that held the mortgage went up too, and then the committee that had its affairs in charge got ugly and demanded the full amount of the personal bond right off the bat, and of course Dad couldn't pay it, and there wasn't anywhere he could borrow it. Anyway he was too sick to do anything about it, and of course I wasn't old enough to do anything. So they took the house away. It was awfully hard on Dad when he got better, because the way they did it they fixed Dad so he can't own any property any more. I don't know all the details but that's how it is."

"Are those people whose names are on the sign the ones who did that?" asked Marjorie.

"No, I guess not. They're only the real estate firm that's trying to sell it. They're a sort of trust company or something. Maybe they took it over. I don't know. But anyway it's gone and that's that!"

Ted rambled on about the school he used to attend in Brentwood and the way he came to get interested in the chapel, and Marjorie let him talk, getting sidelights on her brother's character that were interesting. But all the time she was carrying on a separate line of thought.

For it had come to her in the watches of the night, while she was lying beside her sister on the hard lumpy bed in Betty's room which they now occupied, with Bonnie's crib across the foot filling up most of the space between the bed and the door, that if she was to see much of her family in the future something had to be done about the place where they were living. She couldn't help realizing that she was in the way, as things were now. The very bed she occupied took from Betty's rightful rest, being only a three-quarter bed, and it was uncomfortable enough even without two people in it. And there wouldn't be room for twin beds if they had them.

Was she going to make her permanent home with them? She hadn't had time to think about it at all, she had been so engaged in helping them to meet the present crisis. Did they want her to stay? That was another question. Well, things would have to work out. She mustn't hasten decisions.

But even if she only meant to visit them occasionally, it meant discomfort for them all to crowd so to get her in. Of course they were lovely about it. Not even the belligerent Betty had made a sign that she was in the way. Of course she realized that she had been saving them from starvation and freezing and probably that had something to do with Betty's willingness to be inconvenienced. But there again was something that she must wait for. She must see whether they were going to grow together in real family love, or were going to irritate each other. She couldn't make any plans for herself until she was sure.

But meantime, even if she herself went back to Chicago to live her own life apart from them, they were cramped and uncomfortable in that little six-roomed house. There were too many of them. She could never be happy back in her home of luxury knowing they were living in poverty and discomfort.

But then there was that matter of their pride! What could she do to better their situation that would not hurt them terribly, humble them utterly? Her father could not hope to recover his fortune and be able to support them as he had done in the past, even if he got some little job right away. It would barely supply food and clothing for them all, even if it did that. Poor Father! What could she do to help him on his feet again? He wasn't an old man, but he looked older than his years because of the heavy burdens he was carrying. Was there something she could do about that? Something that wouldn't humiliate him too much?

But the Brentwood house. Could she possibly make some arrangement with the people who had taken it over whereby they would transfer it back to her father's name, *clear,* so that she could hand him the deed of it without any obligations for him to pay whatever? How she would love to give it to him for Christmas! Could a thing like that be done so quickly? There was still almost a week to Christmas!

So she carried on an undercurrent of thought while Ted rambled on, giving now and then a bit of information about the house that fitted right in with her thoughts.

"How many bedrooms are there in that house, Ted!" she asked suddenly.

"Seven!" he said promptly. "And then there was a servant's room over the kitchen, and two big rooms in the attic. Oh, it was great! I wanted them to keep it and rent the rooms or take boarders, but then Mother got sick and Betty got a job so that didn't work out."

Ted sighed. He was beginning to take a man's responsibility upon his young shoulders.

"I don't suppose Dad will ever get a job again," he said sadly, "there aren't many jobs now, and when a man has been out of things for a couple of years the way Dad has, people have forgotten how good he was. And then there are so many young ones coming on! I suppose it's going to be up to me to take care of the family, and I'm going to do my best. They're a swell family, I think, anyhow!" he finished with a half defiant look at the new sister.

"They certainly are!" said Marjorie turning a full frank gaze upon her brother. "And I'm with you, brother! You're sort of wonderful yourself, you know. At least I think so!"

Ted met her look of real sisterly affection for an instant and then his eyes dropped and the color swept up into his lean young face.

"You're pretty swell yourself!" he murmured embarrassedly.

"Well, but I mean that, Ted. It happens that I can do quite a little just now, and I am so glad I am able to, but the thing is, how can I do it best without hurting Father and Mother? I think you and I will have to work together in this. Betty is pretty proud too. I don't blame her. I like her the better for it of course, and all of you, but if I can just get them to realize that I'm one of the family as much as you or any of them are perhaps it won't be so hard for them. Shall we work together?"

"Sure thing," murmured Ted shyly. "It's great of you!"

"No, that's not the way to take it. You don't think it's great of you to want to do all you can to help your father, do you? Then why should you think it's great of me? Am I supposed to be any more selfish than the rest of you? Just because I happened to be brought up outside the family, which I couldn't help, does that make any difference? Just because I could get away with utter indifference, does that make me great, that I don't want to? And suppose, Ted, that tomorrow morning some great man should send for you and tell you that he had been watching you and he liked the way you were doing, and he had a fine position ready for you at, say, ten thousand or so a year, and he would give you some of it in advance if you wanted it. Would you think you were great if you decided to use that money for your home and parents instead of buying yourself a Rolls-Royce?"

Ted grinned.

"Fat chance!" he said.

"Of course," smiled Marjorie, "but if you had it I think I know you well enough already to know that you would just delight to turn in every penny you could to the family treasury and make them all comfortable before you thought a thing about any luxuries for yourself."

"Sure thing!" said Ted with shining eyes.

"And if some unheard-of relative off in Europe or somewhere should die and leave you a million dollars, I wonder what is the first thing you would buy? I wish you would tell me that, Ted. I'd like to know what it is."

Ted looked up and without hesitation replied:

"I'd buy the house back and give it to Dad!"

"Thanks!" said Marjorie with starry eyes. "That's the way I feel. Now, brother, do I belong to the family or not?"

"You belong!" said Ted solemnly.

"All right!" said Marjorie. "I appreciate that. And now, suppose we keep this to ourselves for awhile, shall we?"

"Okay!" said the boy solemnly, as they went up the steps of the home, and only a quick smile passed between them to ratify the contract, but both knew that something fine and sweet had happened.

XII

I've got to go into the city and do a little shopping," said Marjorie the next morning. "I wonder when would be the best time for me to go? What had you planned for this morning, Betty?"

"I? *Planned?*" shrugged Betty. "Nothing especially. But I couldn't go with you today, if that's what you mean. Mother isn't able to look after those kids. They were awful yesterday!"

"Of course not," said Marjorie. "I wasn't thinking of our trip together yet. But isn't there some special work to do today that I could help in? Isn't Monday your wash-day?"

"Oh, *that!*" said Betty with a sigh. "We haven't much to wash and that's the truth. I had to wash a lot of the children's things yesterday after the cat episode. No, there's nothing you need to help in. You go. I should think you'd be glad to get out of this crowded mess."

"No, I'm not glad to get away. I just must do a few things at once. I've got to make some telephone calls too. I came away in a great hurry and left a lot of things at loose ends. I really must attend to them. But I'll be back in the afternoon as early as I can. There's plenty of chicken broth for Mother, and I'll try and find something nice for dinner and bring it."

"Oh, you don't need to buy anything else. We've enough in the house for a week, I'm sure," protested Betty.

"Oh, you'll find it will go fast enough. Well, I'm sorry to leave you this way. I can see there is plenty to be done, but when I get back I'll make up for lost time," and with a gay smile she hurried away into the cold winter morning.

Marjorie went first to the real estate firm whose name had been on the signboard yesterday at Brentwood.

"I've come to ask about a house you have for sale in Brentwood," she said, and the man looked her over keenly, noted her handsome attire, and said "Yes?" in an eager tone.

He gave her a good sales talk.

"That's a bargain," he said, "it's just been thoroughly done over and modernized, and because the owner was caught in the depression we can sell it for a mere trifle."

Marjorie let him talk for a few minutes and then she said:

"Could I see the house?"

So she was soon in his car speeding toward Brentwood rapidly.

After she had gone over the house without comment, allowing the man to continue his sales parley without interruption, she said as they were about to leave:

"Well, now I may as well tell you, I am Mr. Gay's daughter. I was away for several years during the time my father lived here and I had never seen the house. I know all the circumstances of my father's having to give up the house of course, and I know how they hated to lose it. I have been wondering if there is any way in which my father can recover the house. Can you tell me the lowest terms on which he could recover it?"

The man's face fell.

"Oh, in that case you had better see Mr. Horgan. He has charge of all those cases. But I am quite sure that mortgage was foreclosed. We had to take over the house at a great loss, you know. I do not think that our firm could place any confidence in your father as one who could carry on and make his payments. He is not as young as he once was, you know, and even if he succeeded in getting a position now, it might not last."

"I was not speaking of putting a mortgage on the place. I was speaking of paying cash. As I understand it my father had only lapsed in his payments a short time. If he were ready now to pay up all obligations, and whatever other expenses you had been obliged to meet, isn't there some way that the matter could be settled and the property be taken off your hands?"

"Why, my dear young lady," said the man patronizingly, "what reason do you have to suppose that your father could pay his obligations now any better than six months ago when he finally surrendered the property?"

"When you finally took the property from him, you mean," said Marjorie coolly. "I understand you gave him no chance to refinance the mortgage and that you were very hard on him indeed. However, that has nothing to do with my question. I have some money myself and I would like to clear my father's home and put the deed in his hands for a Christmas gift if I find that your demands are within reason. I shall call up my Chicago lawyer, of course, and have the whole affair looked into before I pay the cash, but if I do this I shall want to do whatever I do quickly. Can you give me an idea what the demands were that my father could not fulfill, and would there be a likelihood, if they were paid now, with reasonable interest, of course, for the delay, that you could release the property?"

There was something about Marjorie's air of assurance, that impressed the real estate man, who had been having a hard time himself just now, and felt that in this property he was stuck with a house too large to realize its full value during the present depressed state of things. He looked at her a minute questioningly and then he said: "Well, we'll go and see Mr. Horgan. Perhaps he will know of some arrangement that can be made. It is very commendable of you, of course, to be willing to help your father, and I'm sure Mr. Horgan will want to help in any way he can. Of course you have been misinformed about the transaction. Your father was given every possible opportunity to recover himself."

He said it with a smug smile and Marjorie felt that she needed a very wary lawyer indeed to deal with this man. But she said nothing, and the quick drive back to the office was taken almost in silence on her part.

Mr. Horgan was an elderly man with gray hair parted meticulously in the exact middle and thin lips that seemed never to give an advantage to anyone. He had small steel-colored eyes that looked coldly through her, and tried to put her through a questionnaire about her family before he answered her question, but Marjorie held her head haughtily, and gathered her expensive furs about her and arose.

"Excuse me, Mr. Horgan," she said, "I have no time to answer questions. I want to know if there is any way in which my father can now meet the obligations. Perhaps I had better get my Chicago lawyer to attend to the matter, since you do not seem to be willing to name any sum that would satisfy the demands."

"Oh, not at all," said Mr. Horgan rising in protest, "I was merely interested to know just how sure a thing this would be. I can't, of course, enter into any more contracts that will eventually result in the same disaster and throw the property back on our hands again, with only more cost and delay."

"If I decide to do this thing," said Marjorie, drawing herself to her full height and trying to act as grown up as possible—though in reality she was very much scared—"I will see that you have a certified check for the full amount within the week."

Marjorie knew about certified checks. She knew their power.

Mr. Horgan became suave at once.

"Oh, well, in that case, of course everything would be different. You knew, of course, that the sum was quite large that your father was owing, did you not?" and he sailed into details of interest and principal and personal bond, while Marjorie stood her ground and tried to look cool and businesslike and not tremble.

"I would have to talk this matter over with my partner, of course, for usually you know we do not do things in just this way," went on Mr. Horgan. "The matter was formally settled up and the property handed over. But, since you are willing to pay cash we might find a way to get around the regular routine in such cases. It would be, however, you understand, at least—" and he named a sum so much smaller than Marjorie had dreamed that she was almost afraid she showed how surprised she was. However she had the good sense to keep still and merely bow her head gravely, and the man was left in doubt whether she was horrified at the amount or pleased.

"Of course, after we have looked over the figures of the actual cost to ourselves—" he went on smoothly with a smile which was meant to be patronizing, "we *might* be able to do a little better than that, if you found that was impossible, but I'm inclined to think *if* we find that we can make terms at all, it will be in the neighborhood of the sum I have named."

"Very well," said Marjorie taking a deep breath and hoping the man couldn't see how excited she was, "I will get my lawyer on the telephone and consult with him about this. He will know what I should do about it, and I shall either return sometime this afternoon for your answer, or send a representative of my Chicago lawyer to talk with you."

Marjorie, still holding her head high, sailed out of the office coolly, with only an icy little smile for the impressed agent. He bowed her out ostentatiously, almost afraid to have her go lest he was losing a prospect that perhaps never would return.

Marjorie, out on the pavement, summoning a taxi, found herself so excited that she could scarcely give a direction to the driver.

She had gotten from Betty a list of some of the best department stores, and she went straight to one and hunted up a telephone booth, calling the Wetherill lawyer on long distance.

"Well, I certainly am glad to hear your voice, young lady," said Mr. Melbourne, "I was beginning to think you had eloped or been kidnaped or something. A certain gentlemen in Chicago has besieged me night and day to discover your address so that he may send you Christmas greetings he says, and I have been deeply chagrined that I could not give it to him. Where in the world have you been and what are you up to? Nothing the matter, is there, that you take such an expensive way of communication?"

"No, nothing the matter," said Marjorie. "I'm quite all right, thank you. But I telephoned this morning instead of waiting to write because I want your help. I've found the house that used to belong to my own parents and I want to buy it. I want very much to get possession of it before Christmas if I can. I shall need several thousand dollars at once and I would like to have you put it into some bank in this city where I could draw on it within a couple of days. Would that be possible?"

"I suppose it would," said the lawyer. "I could wire it to them today. But are you quite sure this house is a wise buy? It's my business, you know, to advise you in such matters."

"I know," she said, "but I'm quite sure about this. And even if it were not a wise buy I should want it. But, Mr. Melbourne, of course I know I'm not very experienced in buying real estate, and I was wondering if there isn't some lawyer in this city to whom you could recommend me, who would take charge of this transaction for me? I think perhaps these people who have the house are a little tricky. It certainly seems crooked to me, the way they got possession of the property when my father was unable to pay the interest on the mortgage promptly."

"Yes?" said Mr. Melbourne. "Well, you certainly should have someone whom you can trust to look after the affair. Let me think. Yes, there's William Bryant. He's in the Federal Trust Company Building. I'll call him up right away and ask him to look after you. Could you go to his office at once? All right, I'll phone him about you. He's a very good friend of mine. In case he isn't in the office just ask for whoever is taking his place. I'll talk to whoever is there. You can trust Will Bryant or his representatives perfectly. But if I were you I'd have him go to see this house and look into the whole matter carefully before you make your final settlement."

"Oh, thank you, Mr. Melbourne!" said Marjorie in a relieved voice. "That was just what I wanted! I have wished so much that you could be here for a little while and fix this thing up for me."

"Well, I wish I could. I've an important case coming up today and tomorrow that I couldn't leave, or I'd fly over and see what you're up to. But I'm sure Bryant will look after you just as well as I could, and perhaps a little better seeing he is a local man. And by the way, Marjorie, I don't suppose you have any idea of selling your Chicago property, have you? Because I had a very good offer for it last week. Professor with a family coming to the University next fall. He's been scouting around looking for an ideal home and has pitched upon the Wetherill house. I told him I didn't think it was in the market, but I would inquire. He's keen to get it. Of course I hope you're not thinking of leaving Chicago, but I thought perhaps you might feel the house was rather large since you're alone. However, it's not a matter you need decide at once. Think it over and let me know if you should have any idea of selling."

"Oh!" said Marjorie a little breathless. "I hadn't got that far yet. I—don't—quite know what I am going to do."

"Of course," said the lawyer, thinking he knew pretty well that she would likely be married before long, and would have to consult a certain young man before she made any decisions, but he did not voice any such idea. "I just thought I'd mention it."

"Thank you, Mr. Melbourne. And—please, Mr. Melbourne, you won't let anybody, not *any*body I mean, know about this matter of my buying this house. I don't see that it's anyone's affair but my own."

"Certainly not, my child. You can trust me for that."

"Thank you. I knew I could. And now you'll need my address, of course. There isn't any telephone in the house where I am visiting, but I stopped at the nearby drugstore and made arrangements with them to send for me if anyone should call me."

"Fine!" said the old lawyer who had known Marjorie for years. "You have quite a business head, my child."

Marjorie laughed.

"I feel very young and inefficient," she said. "But I've tried to think things out beforehand. And, Mr. Melbourne, there's just one more thing. Would you have any connection in this city that would give you influence to get an opening for my father somewhere here? He's very much discouraged. He had a very fine position and lost it through the death of the head of the firm which resulted in the firm's dissolving, and he hasn't been able to get in anywhere since. He is a very quiet man, and not one who would push himself to the front, nor sound his own trumpet, but I have seen letters he has, and I know he was considered very fine in his line."

"What line?"

"He is an expert accountant!"

"Indeed? What was the name of the firm, do you know?"

"Hamilton, McIvor and Company," said Marjorie, glad that she had remembered to ask Ted that yesterday.

"You don't say!" said Mr. Melbourne. "They had a fine standing. I should say there ought to be something pretty good somewhere for a man whom they employed. I'll see what wires I can pull."

Five minutes later Marjorie turned from her expensive telephone call well satisfied. Mr. Melbourne had been just as kind and helpful as she had known he would be. And he hadn't asked for details nor tried to put obstacles in her way. She was a little surprised at that. She had thought he would demur at the proposition of her buying a house right out of the blue as it were, but he had evidently been somewhat prepared for her to do something of the sort. It must be that Mrs. Wetherill had given him a hint that there might be some such thing. Well, she felt a warm glow in her heart for the Mother who in her death had at least put her in the way of making restitution for the wrong she had unwittingly done during the years. How dear she had been always! The tears sprang to Marjorie's eyes and she had much ado to control them as she came out into the store.

But there was still much to be done before she could get to her shopping. She glanced at her watch. Half past eleven already! She must hurry. She must go to see Mr. Bryant at once and get the matter of the house well started. So she took another taxi to the Federal Trust Company Building and found to her joy that Mr. Bryant was in and had just been talking with the Chicago lawyer, so her way was smoothed for her at once.

Mr. Bryant had keen eyes and a kindly smile. He was not as old as Mr. Melbourne, but gave the impression of being able to comprehend a matter at a glance. He asked a lot of questions about the way the Gays had lost their property, some of which Marjorie could not answer, but she told him all she knew about it and confided that she wished to give the house back to her father for Christmas if it could be managed.

Marjorie was delighted with the kind interest he took in the matter and promised to return to his office at three o'clock to learn the result of his interview with the real estate company.

She went on her way with a lighter heart now, summoning her wits to remember all the things she wanted to buy.

First of all she had it in mind to get a warm lovely negligeé for her mother, and comfortable pretty slippers to go with it. The doctor had given them hope that she might be able to come downstairs to dinner on Christmas Day if she was reasonably careful beforehand. She needed something to wear down. Marjorie chose a charming one of wine red wool, exquisitely finished with soft, silk facings, a rich sash girdle, and frothy lace ruffling falling deeply from the wide sleeves and surplice neck. It was such a lovely thing that she couldn't resist it. She selected a rosy quilted dressing sack for wear now when Mother began to sit up in bed, and then a couple of very pretty simple dresses. She wasn't quite sure of the size and she must buy cautiously, for she did not want to hurt her dear new people. She merely wanted to get necessities now, and Christmas made a good excuse. But they all needed so many things, almost *every*thing, that she scarcely knew where to begin.

While she was eating a hurried lunch she wrote out a brief list of necessities. Some ready-hemmed tablecloths and napkins, mittens and stockings for the children, rubbers—? But how could she fit them? Oh, the list would be endless if she got all they needed. She must have Betty along to select things. The children's clothes were all too short and too tight and too ragged. But of course they didn't have to have everything before Christmas. Better just to get something for each and buy other needs after Christmas in a leisurely way.

So she hurried up to the credit department, opened a charge account, giving her Chicago references, and also Mr. Bryant, then went and found a squirrel coat for Betty that was almost an exact duplicate of her own. If Betty wanted to change it after Christmas she could, but she had admired Marjorie's so much that it seemed as if that might be her choice. Passing the millinery department she found a little soft gray felt hat with a bright dash of pheasant's feather cocked aslant in the crown. She was sure it would be becoming to Betty. She bought a couple of little brother and sister suits for Sunny and Bonnie. They were so cute she could not resist them; red jersey trimmed with braid for one set and navy blue sailor style with chevrons for the other. It didn't take long. Children's things were so pretty it required strength of character not to buy the store out.

It was getting near to three o'clock, when she was to meet Mr. Bryant. She hurried to the toy department and reveled in the bewilderment of delights for the children there displayed. She wished she could buy them all. A doll for Bonnie of course, blocks and some wind-up toys for Sunny, an electric train for Bud. Would there be room to set it up? Oh, but there would be plenty of room in the house at Brentwood. Her heart throbbed joyously as she remembered that.

After that it didn't take much time to select a warm house coat of brown for her father, a nice leather coat for Ted, and a thick, warm sweater for Bud with a bright Roman band of colors in the roll of the turtle collar. Then she was off breathless with anxiety to meet the lawyer.

She found a better report than she had hoped for. Mr. Bryant had looked up the records of the transactions at the time Mr. Gay had surrendered his property, and found more than one questionable trick that the perpetrators would not care to have brought to light by such a lawyer as William Bryant, so he had succeeded in bringing them to accept a reasonable sum for back payment with interest, and the transfer of the property was not going to cost quite as much as Marjorie had been told at first.

It is true that Marjorie had been in control of her property for so short a time that money as yet did not mean much to her, and she would have as readily bought the house at twice the sum she was paying for it, but it was nice to know that things were being adjusted in a way that would please both her lawyers, and would probably afford her father much satisfaction when he knew about it; so she went on her way homeward with a light of satisfaction in her eyes. She could hardly wait for her purchases to come home. They would probably wait for two or three days before sending them until they had looked up her references, but they had promised positively that the things would all be there before Christmas. Tomorrow or the next day she would have to go down to Mr. Bryant's office to sign the check and get the papers. Then she could get anything she had forgotten, and perhaps a few more Christmas things.

She stopped on the way out of the store to get a five pound box of candy and another of salted nuts. Those would be things she couldn't well purchase at the little grocery store near Aster Street.

She felt conscience stricken as she neared home to think she had left Betty so long, with her mother still in bed, and all the work to do. But she had got a lot done. That was good. And now she began to think of the things she should have bought and didn't. However, that didn't matter. They had got along without them so far and probably would keep on a few days more.

She realized as the taxi drove up to the door that the house had become home to her, so different from what it had seemed the day she arrived, only a few brief days before! Home because there were dear ones there, and already her interests were tied up with theirs.

The children met her at the door. Sunny holding up a smeary face to be kissed, and Bonnie clasping her arm and nestling against her. Betty came wearily from the kitchen peering out into the hall at her with a relieved look:

"Oh, I'm glad you've come! I thought something dreadful had happened to you in the strange city,—or else—!" She stopped suddenly.

"Or else what?" Marjorie looked at her with a sharp note in her voice as if her answer meant a great deal.

"Or else, maybe you had got tired of us and gone back to Chicago," she said with her eyes half-averted.

"Oh, and would you have cared?" asked Marjorie breathlessly. "Wouldn't you have been rather glad to get rid of me?"

"Well, I should say not!" said Betty with a catch in the last word like a sob.

"I should say *not!*" echoed Sunny with a stamp of his foot, and a funny little shake of his head, ending with a joyous peal of laughter.

And Marjorie caught him in her arms and hugged and kissed him, while her heart gave a great throb of joy, and her bundles flew this way and that. Bud had to rush from the dining room and pick them up, touching them with awe. New bundles! So many of them!

Suddenly a flood of happiness rolled into Marjorie's heart. This was her Home, where she belonged! They loved her!

XIII

It was such a pleasant homecoming, everybody had
something to tell her, how Sunny had slipped on the ice on
the front step and bumped his head against the railing and
a great blue lump had come on his forehead and Betty
had to put arnica on it; how Bonnie had mended a hole in
her apron all by herself so Mother wouldn't have to do it,
and the mended hole with its crooked stitches was proudly
exhibited; how Bud's cat had stood out against the neigh-
bor's dog, arched her back and spit at him bravely, with
all her feathers on end, and then had scuttled into the
house, jumped on the kitchen table and eaten every drop
of the cream off the tray Betty had ready for Mother; how
Ted had a job evenings the rest of the week selling in the
ten-cent store and Betty was mending a shirt for him to
wear tonight; how Mother ate all her egg for lunch and
took a nice long nap afterwards; how Father had been
helping a man with his books all day and maybe it would
last another two days; how Betty had been to the window
every half-hour all the afternoon looking for her to come!

And then came Ted with a happy face.

"Great! You've got back!" he said with relief. "I was
thinking maybe I'd have to go out and hunt you and be
late to my new job if you didn't come pretty soon!"

So! They were all glad to see her!

And then Mother rang the little call bell, and when

Bonnie ran up to see what she wanted it was Marjorie she asked for.

So she went to her mother and had a sweet little talk with her about how much better she was, and how she was going to sit up in bed tomorrow, and maybe in a chair the next day if she was good and very careful, and then perhaps the next, or the next, she might walk around her room. And the doctor had promised that if all went well she might come downstairs for dinner on Christmas.

Marjorie unwrapped the little quilted pink dressing sack and put it about her mother's shoulders, and they all trooped up joyously to see how pretty she looked in it.

Then Marjorie went down to help Betty with the dinner. Not that she knew much about the actual dinner, but she could order the dishes onto the table and make everything dainty and ready for the food, and not forget a thing, even to water in the glasses, and napkins at every place, though they were only paper ones. Tomorrow or the next day the new ones would come. she was glad of that.

They gave Ted his dinner early and saw him off, excited and happy, so glad to be earning the pitiful sum the store would pay him for his work. Yet Marjorie reflected that she was proud of him that he did not want to lie back and let her take care of everybody. He was a manly fellow, a brother in whom she could rejoice. She had wanted to tell him about the house, but there hadn't been any chance, and perhaps there wouldn't be now until it came as a Christmas surprise.

Mr. Gay came in a little after six, looking weary but with a strange new content upon him, a new self-respect. Marjorie, looking at the light in his eyes, realized what a hard thing it must be for him that he could earn nothing to support his family, and wished with all her heart that something might come of her request to the lawyer about a position for him.

That night after they had gone to their room the sisters talked for a long time. Marjorie got little side lights on various matters that Betty didn't realize she was revealing.

"Betty," she said, "isn't there going to be some way you and I can get out together shopping for a little while? If Father were going to be home tomorrow or the next day, or if Ted didn't have to work all day couldn't he take care of the children, now that Mother is so much better? I'd

like to have you with me. I really don't know how to pick
out Christmas gifts for them all. You know what they
want and need."

"Christmas gifts!" said Betty excitedly. "You've already
given us a fortune! What more do you want?"

"Oh, little pretty things and surprises," laughed Marjorie. "You and I could have a lot of fun shopping together!"

Betty was still a minute and then she said decidedly:

"I couldn't! I haven't anything fit to wear to go with
you. After a while when things get straightened around so
I have time to get my clothes in shape it will be different.
I've got to get my coat cleaned and pressed and mended.
You don't realize. And besides. Father said he would be
two days more on those books. I can see he's very proud
and happy about them, too. He wants to get Mother something for Christmas, I guess. He's always made a lot of
Christmas for us all when he had any money. And Ted
will be out hunting jobs too. No, I couldn't leave now."

"Well, why couldn't I stay with the family and let you
go out alone then. Betty? I want you to have some more
money and go get things you want them all to have. You
can wear my hat and coat if you like. I'm sure my things
fit you, and we needn't worry about clothes for you. I
have plenty."

Betty's hand stole over and gave hers a quick clasp and
slipped back again.

"You're good!" she said. "You're wonderful! It would
be swell, but I couldn't do it. I just couldn't. Besides,
there's a lot to be done here. I'd better stay. Don't bother
about Christmas. It's enough this year just to have you
and plenty to eat, and a warm house and Mother getting
well."

"Well," said Marjorie thoughtfully, "I don't want you to
feel uncomfortable, of course. but we're going to have a
Christmas if I have to get it myself. You see I had to call
up my lawyer in Chicago today and talk to him about
some business that I hadn't settled before I came away,
tell him where I was, and all that. and he's sending on
some papers for me to sign. They'll be at another lawyer's
office. I'll have to go there day after tomorrow likely. I
thought that after I got that done I'd get some trimmings
for the tree. Would Ted know where to get a tree? I'd like

a nice big one, wouldn't you, to celebrate our having found each other? And I'll buy ornaments and balls and things."

"Oh!" said Betty. "We haven't had a tree like that since I was Bonnie's age. Things were pretty hard up while Father was saving money, and trying to buy the house at Brentwood. We used to have a tiny little tree that we got late Christmas Eve when they were cheap, and we trimmed it with bits of tin foil, and strings of cranberries, and popcorn, and little paper things we cut from advertisements."

"I can imagine that would be fun," said Marjorie. "Perhaps the children would like that best. Do you think they would?"

"Oh, no! They don't really know much about a Christmas tree, not the kind you mean. Mother has always had something for them, but we've always had to work hard to make everything. Christmas would be nice if one didn't have to worry about it all the time."

"Yes, I can see how worry would spoil Christmas! Well, we'll have one without worry this time I hope, and whatever you say about a tree goes."

They lay and talked a long time and Marjorie succeeded in getting Betty to say that she liked a tree all in silver with just colored lights. She had always wanted such a tree.

"But I don't want you to spend a lot more money on unnecessary things," she finished.

"Well," said Marjorie thoughtfully, "I don't want to flaunt my money in your faces. It isn't my fault that I have a lot of money. I didn't ask for it. I didn't do a thing to get it. And it isn't any pleasure to me unless I can share it. If we could only have a nice time together and not think whose money it is, that would be a real Christmas for me. I've always had everything done for me before this, but it would be wonderful to be allowed to do things for other people, if I was sure I knew what they wanted."

"Well then, have your own way!" cried Betty and suddenly reached over and put a quick shy kiss on her sister's forehead. "I'll enjoy every scrap of whatever you do. I'd like to be able to give you the earth on a gold platter, but I can't, so I'll just let you do the giving and be happy over what you do."

They fell asleep at last, hand clasping hand, a real sisterly love growing in their hearts.

It was not until the second day later that Mr. Bryant sent Marjorie word that he had the papers ready for her. So Marjorie, amid a howl from the children, started off early in the morning again, having first set them to cutting out chains from silver paper for the Christmas tree. She had told them about the tree until their imaginations were on the qui vivé with joyous anticipation. She had bought silver and red paper, and two little pairs of pointless scissors and a bottle of paste at the drugstore, and given careful lessons on how to make chains, and the two youngest were established at the dining table with their tools before them with an order for many chains to be finished before she returned. Bud was acting as overseer and chief adviser.

To Marjorie the day was full of excitement. It was so good to know that the matter of the house was going through all right and that she would carry home with her that afternoon the deed which she might do up in grandest Christmas wrappings for her father and mother.

Mr. Bryant told her that Mr. Melbourne had told him about her father, and he had been looking up several good openings that might materialize after Christmas. He didn't tell her that he had been commissioned to look up Mr. Gay's record and had found it absolutely unimpeachable, both as to ability and character, but she sensed that he spoke of her father with respect and it cheered her heart. For more and more as the days went by she yearned to lift that burden of worry and care from his shoulders, and see his face calm and at peace.

"Do you suppose it would be possible, if there were an opening, that it could come as an offer from somewhere, and not have him know that I asked about it?" she asked the lawyer shyly. "I think he would feel better about it that way."

And he seemed to understand for he smiled and said:

"I should think that might be arranged."

So she went on her way to complete her shopping in a very happy frame of mind.

And then, right in the midst of the last few purchases whom should she come square upon but the young minister from Brentwood, Gideon Reaver!

"Oh!" she said, a quick color flying into her cheeks, "I didn't expect to recognize anybody in this big strange city."

He seemed as pleased as she was. He paused and talked

to her a minute, told her how much he thought of Ted, and what a fine fellow he was going to be, and then he hesitated and looked down at her wistfully.

"I was just going into the tea room to get a bite of lunch," he said, "I wonder if you wouldn't join me? It's lonely eating all by myself, especially in the midst of these gay Christmas crowds. It seems to emphasize one's loneliness."

"Why, I'd love to!" said Marjorie, with a sudden unreasoning feeling of having been crowned. She followed him through the Christmas throngs to a table in a corner where there was comparative quiet.

Marjorie, of course, had often been out to lunch with her young men friends, but somehow this seemed the rare experience of a lifetime. How silly she was! This man was an utter stranger. All she knew about him was that he could preach an interesting sermon, and her brother adored him. Well, he was perfectly respectable, and nice and pleasant. Also, there would perhaps be opportunity to ask him a few questions that had been going over in her mind ever since Sunday. Meantime, she was tired, and it was nice to have found a friend in this strange city.

So she relaxed and enjoyed her lunch and the pleasant talk that went on with it.

"I have been wanting to ask you something," she said at last as the dessert was placed before them and the waitress hurried away again. "Perhaps this isn't the place to talk about such things, but I would so like to know something."

"I'll certainly be glad to help in any way I can," he said.

"Well, then would you tell me please, how can you tell whether you're saved or not? My brother Ted asked me if I was saved and I didn't know what to tell him. I never was asked a question like that before. I didn't suppose it was a thing you could be sure about. I'm a church member of course. But is there a way to be *sure* one is saved?"

"There surely is!" said Gideon, his eyes lighting eagerly.

She met his gaze earnestly.

"Sunday in your sermon you talked a lot about the new birth, and I don't understand it at all. I've always been taught that if I was good I would go to Heaven when I die."

"So was I," said Gideon smiling, "but that is not true."

Marjorie gave him a startled look.

"No, because the law must be kept perfectly to be a means of salvation, and no one but Christ ever has or ever could be perfectly good, so it would be hopeless for us if that were the only way to Heaven. But thank God it isn't. We have His own word for it! Do you believe the Bible?"

"Oh, yes, of course. I don't know so very much about it I suppose, but, yes, I believe it."

"Do you believe its gospel: that Jesus was nailed to a cross for you, taking all the penalty of your sins by enduring God's righteous judgment upon them?"

"Yes, of course, I believe that."

"Well, do you believe that because He did that God raised Him from the dead and exalted Him in the highest heavens?"

"Yes, indeed, I believe that, although I never heard it stated in just that way before."

"You believe, then, that Jesus is the Christ, the Son of God?"

"Why, certainly."

"Well, then listen to what this says."

He took a small testament out of his pocket and opened to I John 5:1.

"Whosoever believeth that Jesus is the Christ is born of God."

The astonishment on her face changed slowly into illumination as she took in the wonderful truth:

"Then I am saved!" she exclaimed, her eyes softening with the wonder of it. "I am born again! Just because I believe, all that comes to me! I never knew it was as simple as that! I didn't know ordinary mortals who had not studied theology could ever quite comprehend it. Born of God! What a wonderful thing to happen to me! I am so glad you have made me understand it."

"Yes, it is as simple as that," said Gideon, his eyes drinking in her eagerness. "God said it and that makes it true. whatever your feelings are. And if you are born of God that makes you His child! If you are born of God, you have His life! If you are born of God, you are possessed of the divine nature. Just as you are born of your father Mr. Gay. That makes you have his life in you."

Marjorie looked up, her eyes filled with wonder.

"You don't understand how very apt that illustration is," she said gravely. "You see, I've only known my own earthly father a little over a week. I was adopted by some very lovely people who rather took advantage of my parents when they had been unfortunate, because they took a fancy to me when I was very young. I never knew anything about my own parents until after my foster parents died, leaving me a letter telling about it and so I came to find my family. But you know, while my foster father and mother were precious people and loved me dearly, there is something about being an own child that is wonderful! I've found that out already, although I only know my own father a very little yet."

"Ah! That is truly wonderful! The analogy is perfect. And you will find out more and more of what it is to be as own child every day if you continue to live with your parents, just as you will find out more and more of the love and beauty of your heavenly Father if you abide in Him and walk with Him and come into a deeper and deeper knowledge of His word. There has to be intimacy to understand the relationship between father and child. What you have told me is most interesting, the testimony of a child who has come to find and know its earthly father, and is thrilled by the precious bond of relationship between them. But suppose now you should go back to Chicago and live. You would grow away from your newly found father again, and perhaps become as indifferent as you were before. It must be a daily walk with God to make beautiful the relationship. Do you see?"

"Oh, I see! You have made it wonderfully clear! Why! I feel as I did when I first found out I had a family of my own! Thank you so much! I shall never forget what you have done for me."

Suddenly Gideon glanced at his watch, and looked startled.

"Excuse me," he said, "I have a wedding in half an hour and I've barely time to make it. I didn't realize how the time was going. May I talk with you again sometime about this?"

"Oh, I should love to have you," said Marjorie. "I know almost nothing about the Bible!"

"You'll have to begin to study it now." He smiled as he turned to the waitress to get the check. "I'd love to help if I may. I have a little book that may help at the start. I'll send it over to you. Good-bye, I wish I didn't have to rush away. You've given me a wonderfully pleasant hour."

"Oh, and you've shown me an inheritance I didn't dream before that I had!" said Marjorie with shining eyes.

As she took her way home an hour later she reflected how utterly changed was her life just in a short week's time. It almost seemed that she was a different girl from the one who had come up in the beautiful Wetherill mansion doing all the proper conventional things that a girl in her station should do, happy and care-free, a trifle wistful, and not quite satisfied. And now here she was in a new city, with a brand new family all her very own, a new home, new interests, and at least one new friend. Unless she might also count the lawyer Mr. Bryant a friend too, for he had been very kind. And not once had she felt a pang of regret for the things she had left behind her. Not once had she been sorry she had not accepted her other invitations for the holidays! Oh, of course, she sorrowed for the one who had stood to her for mother for so many years, but that grief had been so gradual and final when Mrs. Wetherill was gone, that it was a thing she had to put aside entirely from her life or else be in continual mourning. And she was glad she had such an absorbing interest to divert herself from the loneliness that would surely have settled down upon her if she had stayed in the home alone and tried to go on with her life as it had been.

The doctor was there when she reached the house. He was standing in the living room talking to Betty, telling her about a certain Christmas in his childhood when he had been alone among strangers, desolate and forlorn, his only Christmas present a maple sugar Santa Claus. He had stood by the window all the afternoon licking it and staring out on a strange little western town because he had nothing else to do. He never had liked maple sugar since.

Betty stood in the doorway listening sympathetically to the story, and Marjorie thought she saw a wistful look in the young doctor's eyes. She wondered if he had a home and family now to make Christmas merry for him, or was he lonely yet? If he was how nice it would be if they were only in Brentwood and could invite him to Christmas dinner. Nice to have Gideon Reaver too. But, of course, they couldn't do anything like that in this little house, especially with Mother sick, and nobody to help get the dinner. It was not to be thought of, but it was an idea for another year, supposing all went well. What nice times they could have in the lovely old house at Brentwood! Marjorie clutched the precious deed-papers happily in her hand and hurried upstairs to take off her hat and get ready to help with dinner.

That evening after supper they all gathered for a few minutes in her mother's room, all but Ted who had to go to his evening job.

Sunny came smiling in and pulled at Marjorie's dress.

" 'Nother Betty, story, please! 'Nother Betty! 'Nother Betty! Tell us a story, please!" he begged persistently.

"Oh, for pity's sake!" said Betty petulantly. "Stop calling her that silly name! Mother, what are we going to call my sister? We can't go around ignoring her, or calling her 'you' all the time. Nobody dares mention her, and I think it's time we had some understanding about it. I'm sure she doesn't want to go around as ' 'Nother Betty' all the time. I guess it's up to you, Mother, to tell us what to do. Are you well enough to think about it?"

The mother smiled.

"Oh, yes, I'm well enough, but I don't think it is exactly up to me. It seems to me that the sister herself should be consulted. Your father and I have talked it over, and he feels that she should keep the name with which she was christened. He says it is her legal name. It is so recorded on her birth certificate, and in the papers of adoption, and also it is courteous for her to keep the name given her by the people who were Father and Mother to her all these years."

"But they couldn't be hurt by it now," burst forth Betty.

"No, perhaps not, but there is a fineness of courtesy that goes beyond mere hurting people," suggested the father. "Besides, none of you realize that your sister has grown up with her name and it would be awkward and annoying for her to change it now. All her Chicago friends call her Marjorie, and if you will just think a minute you will find that we ourselves have spoken of her as Marjorie. Even you children have called that picture of your sister 'Marjorie.' You would probably have to work pretty hard to change to anything else."

They were silent, realizing that this was the truth.

"Well, I like Marjorie better than Dorothy, anyway," said Bud, as if that settled it.

"I'm not sure but I do too," said the mother. "How about you, dear child? What would you like to have us do?" She turned loving eyes toward Marjorie.

"Why, I've always liked Marjorie pretty well," she said, "but I wouldn't mind changing if you preferred the other. I would want you to call me what you liked best."

"Then she's Marjorie!" announced the father. "Don't you say so, Mother?"

"Yes."

"Say it, Sunny! Sister Marjorie!"

"Sitter Mar-dory!" said Sunny with great effort, and then laughed long and loud over his achievement.

The little conference was broken up, and the mother hustled off to bed soon after that, but Marjorie as she bade her mother good-night was taken in frail loving arms and tenderly kissed.

"My little Marjorie!" she whispered, and Marjorie felt that she belonged thoroughly, name and all. And it was a relief not to have to get used to a new name. Some people would call her Miss Gay of course, and her old friends would say Miss Wetherill, but what did it matter? It couldn't change herself. And now she had a family of her own what did she care about a name?

Downstairs, Bud, after a long silence during which he was supposed to be whittling a boat out of a stick of kindling, looked up and remarked thoughtfully:

"And when she gets married, she'll have to change her name anyway, won't she? That is, she'll change the end one. Isn't that so, Marjorie?"

Marjorie laughed.

"Yes, brother, when and if. But that will be something else again, so don't let's worry about it."

XIV

LAWYER MELBOURNE forgot to telephone Evan Brower until midmorning of the day before Christmas. He really wasn't to blame, for the case he was working on was a very important one and some new features developed suddenly which made it necessary for him to fly to the far west and be gone three days. Evan Brower never entered his mind again until his return home, when he chanced to come on a memorandum on his desk that Brower must be called.

So Evan Brower was in a state of mind when at last the message got to him late in the afternoon with Marjorie's address. He immediately went to work trying to get her on the telephone. Mr. Melbourne had not given the drugstore number. It hadn't occurred to him. So Evan Brower worked in vain.

At last he went out and sent a large box of wonderful orchids to her by telegraph with his Christmas greetings.

He made his plans to slip away from his mother's annual family Christmas gathering immediately after the old-fashioned midday dinner and take a plane to the city where Marjorie was staying. He would arrive in plenty of time to take her out for a late dinner and the evening somewhere. He did not let her know of his coming. It was better to take her by surprise.

The Gays, meanwhile, had been having a wonderful

157

time getting ready for Christmas. Marjorie, of course, had
done the ordering. There was a twenty pound turkey, a
wonderful bird, and all the trimmings. The girls waited
upon their mother joyfully, asking questions about the
stuffing and the roasting, and Marjorie had her first real
lesson in serious cooking.

Ted had brought the Christmas tree home two days before and stood it up at the back door to the envy of all the
backyard-gazers. Christmas Eve he brought it in and set it
up in the parlor where it glorified the shabby little room.
They strung holly wreaths and laurel about until the faded
wallpaper retired utterly from view and the ugly wooden
mantel became a thing of beauty.

The children were allowed to stay up and help trim the
tree, hanging their own silver chains, and pretty little
strings of silver balls and tiny ornaments on the lower
branches, while the older ones put on the lights and silver
rain and balls above. Then they hung up their stockings
under the mantel and went to bed with shining eyes and
rosy cheeks, almost bursting with excitement.

It was the next morning about ten o'clock while they
were just in the most interesting part of opening the presents that the doorbell rang and an enormous box arrived
from one of the big city florists.

"Miss Marjorie Wetherill," the driver announced. "Sign
on the top line!"

Ted who had gone to the door hesitated. "Miss Wetherill!" Then he remembered, and signed for it. He came
back into the room with a ghastly look on his face, the
Christmas joy all flattened out into a drab dignity as he
came over to Marjorie with the box. Chicago had reached
out its long arm and was claiming their Lady Santa Claus!
It seemed that the lovely illusions were about to be dis-
pelled.

Marjorie looked up and smiled.

"For me? How ridiculous! How in the world did anybody find out where I was? Oh, perhaps it's from Mr.
Melbourne, our old lawyer. Shall I open it now, or wait
till we are done with our own things?"

"Open it now and get it over with!" growled Ted in
such a bearish voice that his mother looked up.

"Why, Ted, dear! What a rude way to speak!"

Ted turned red. He tried to think of some apology but

the words didn't come. He couldn't express just what it was that had brought a cloud over his bright spirits.

"Oh, Mother! That's all right! I know how he feels!" said Marjorie laughing. "We both hate to have our own nice time interrupted just now. You know this is the first Christmas I've ever spent with my very own family and I don't like anybody else to intrude. Put the box on the stairs, brother. They're only flowers and they'll keep till afterwards."

"No, open them, open them!" pleaded Bonnie.

"Open!" echoed Sunny.

So Marjorie, laughing, opened the box and disclosed the wonderful orchids.

The card which lay on the top fell to the floor and Bud picked it up and read it aloud before anybody noticed to stop him.

" 'Christmas Greetings for Marjorie from Evan Brower.' "

"Who's Evan Brower, Marjorie?"

"Buddie!" said his mother severely, "that's very rude! You should never read other people's cards. Give it back to your sister at once. I'm ashamed of you!"

Bud hung his head and handed the card to Marjorie, but he repeated his question, "Who's Evan Brower?"

Somehow Marjorie felt the eyes of the family upon her in question, though they hadn't meant she should, and the color crept up into her fair cheeks. But she laughed.

"Oh, he's just an old friend of the Wetherill family," she said casually. "They're gorgeous, aren't they? But let's put them back in their box until we get through our fun. They'll keep better there. Then we can get them out and decorate with them."

"They're orchids, aren't they?" said Ted, almost accusingly, Marjorie thought. "They're about the most expensive flower there is, aren't they?"

"Why, I don't know about the expensive part. Yes, I guess they are considered rather rare. We'll give them to Mother, shall we? I'd like to have her have them. Now, let's forget them and go back to our stockings. Bonnie, wasn't it your turn next? See, there's a note in the top of your stocking that has a cord tied to it, and it reaches down to that box on the floor. Can you lift it up or do you want me to help?"

So the whole family were presently watching Bonnie with her lovely big doll and the orchids reposed in their box in the dining room, forgotten for the moment by all. How mortified Evan Brower would have been if he could have known. It was not until the girls went out in the kitchen to put the dinner on the table two hours later that Marjorie found Betty peeking into the box and touching a lovely bloom with the tips of her fingers.

It is safe to say that Marjorie had never had such a happy Christmas in her life. The thrill of giving had never been hers before. She had bought handsome presents for her friends and acquaintances out of the generous allowance she always had, but this giving to loved ones, especially what they needed, was a different thing, and she enjoyed every minute of that morning intensely. Such surprise and delight as there was over every little thing! The children went wild over their toys, and then got very still and sat and held them in a kind of wonder. Bud, of course, wanted the dining room cleared of everything so he could set up his electric train at once, but was persuaded to better things, and so the box with the electric train was relegated to the dining room with the orchids for a time, and Bud came back reluctantly to watch everybody and beam and enjoy.

The last present was a long envelope done up in a fascinating box with a great seal and long red ribbons hanging from the package.

"To Mr. George Gay with many wishes for a Happy Christmas that shall last all the year," read Ted as he handed it out with a flourish. Ted was as much in the dark about it as any of them, for Marjorie had decided not to tell anyone her secret, so they all stood about in awe and wonder and watched their father carefully open the box, while Mother leaned over his shoulder and looked with interest. Because it was so elaborately wrapped they both thought it must be some kind of joke, and cast amused glances of questioning about the silent young group.

But they had to wait some time, before the legal document finally came to light, and then there was a note within that had to be read. The astounded father studied the paper and then the note, and read them both slowly, as it dawned upon him little by little that the document he held was a deed to his beloved lost house in Brentwood.

But still he didn't quite understand. So he turned to the note and read it aloud:

"Dear Father,

This isn't exactly a Christmas gift. It's only an old possession come back to you, and this time entirely free from any obligation.

Hoping it may bring you joy and comfort for many Christmases to come,

Your loving 'Nother Betty!"

When it finally dawned upon them all that the dear lost home was theirs again, there was first an awful stillness, followed by the biggest tumult of shouting and hurrahing the Gay household had ever known. The children weren't quite aware yet what it all meant but they climbed upon their father and clapped their hands, and yelled at the top of their lungs, and then they climbed all over Marjorie, and then they started in on Betty and Ted, until suddenly Father noticed that Mother was crying softly. Smiling and crying like April rain in sunshine.

"Look here, this won't do, Mother! You're going to get all used up. You ought to lie right down and rest and have everybody keep still!" he said anxiously.

"Oh, no," said Mother smiling through her tears. "Don't you know that joy never kills? I heard the doctor say that the other day myself, down in the hall to Betty! I think he was talking about me, and I couldn't imagine what joy I could possibly be going to have that wouldn't kill. But now I know. Two wonderful things! To think they should both come together! My dear other girl, and my dear home, both back again! It seems too good to be true!"

"It does!" said the father, turning suddenly to Marjorie. "But I don't understand how you did it. I can't believe it yet. You don't know, daughter, but those men who took the house from me are tricky."

"Oh, yes, I do," laughed Marjorie. "I found that out. But I had a trickier one. I had a great lawyer that my Chicago lawyer recommended, and he made them see the error of their ways. They didn't exactly want Mr. Bryant to take it to court and make the whole thing public. I gathered that he had something else on them already and they were afraid of him, for they came right down to terms as soon as he went to them."

Mr. Gay looked down at the paper in his hand thoughtfully, gravely, smoothed it gently with his fingers.

"I ought to tell you, dear, I am not any better prepared to keep this now than I was when I lost it," he said with a deep sigh. "Not as well, in fact, for then I thought I would have a good job soon and everything would be all right. But now I have learned that there are no jobs any more for such as I. I hate to disappoint you, little girl, after you have been so thoughtful and taken so much trouble, but I'm afraid I should not accept this after all. You see, I understand business, and I know now that I never could possibly pay off this mortgage, nor even the interest on it. If I am able to supply food and a modest shelter and clothing for my family, it will be all I can possibly hope for. And I am exceedingly dubious about ever being able to do even that."

But Marjorie was beside him at once, her hand resting on his shoulder.

"You don't understand, Father," she said, her face full of eagerness, "the mortgage is all paid off. There isn't a cent for you to pay. Read your note. Didn't you see it said it was all clear? There'll be nothing any more on it but taxes and any repairs that have to be made, and I am going to look after those, at least until you get to be a millionaire."

"Oh, my dear!" said Mr. Gay, suddenly putting his head down on his hand. "This is too much! Too much! I never dreamed of such a wonderful miracle!"

It was a long time before the Gay family simmered down to real life again. Such wonderful things had happened that it didn't seem worth while to consider common matters any more. Until suddenly the turkey set up an outcry from the oven and sent Betty and Marjorie scuttling to the kitchen.

They were all too excited to talk connectedly. They went from one gift to another, rejoicing over first this and then that. The girls in the kitchen were getting the vegetables cooking, basting the turkey, putting celery and cranberries and olives on the table, and talking.

"Oh, I can't believe I've really got a fur coat!" cried Betty. "You ought not to have done it, Marjorie. It's much too grand for me, and I know it cost an awful lot. I could have got along with a cloth coat with just a collar of cheap fur. But oh, I *love* it! I never dreamed of anything half so grand!"

"You can change it for any other kind," smiled Marjorie. "I saw a beautiful beaver one, and a mink. Would you rather have mink or seal? I think fur is something each person has a special taste in."

"But mine has always been squirrel!" declared Betty. "I've just envied girls with squirrel coats. I used to think I'd do almost anything to get one. And now I have one without doing a thing! And that darling gray hat! Oh, Marjorie, I'm so ashamed of the way I used to think about you! I don't deserve a thing!"

"Nonsense!" laughed Marjorie. "Forget it! You and I are going in town the first day Mother is well enough to be left alone and get you some pretty dresses. You're not going to have to be wearing my cast-offs any more. You're going to have what you want, what you pick out yourself!"

"What I *want!* How could I possibly want anything better than the lovely things you've given me. No, you mustn't buy me anything more. I'll get my head turned. I'm going to get a job just as soon as Mother is able to be left and I'll buy the rest of the things I need."

Marjorie put a loving arm around her.

"I'm going to get you some pretty things right away," she said. "We're not going to wait for jobs and things. You need them now and you're going to have them. Come, let's go back in the other room a few minutes. There's nothing more to do till those potatoes are ready to mash, is there?"

Back in the parlor they found their mother lying down on the couch in her new negligee, looking as pretty as her girls, and the children still rejoicing over their presents.

Suddenly Sunny broke forth.

"Evwybuddy's got a lotta pwetty sings but 'Nother Betty!" he exclaimed. "Her only got hankies an' ittle sings!"

"She's got those stuck-up orchid flowers from Chicago!" growled Bud savagely.

Marjorie suddenly cast a quick glance around at all their faces, and her heart tightened with a glad hope. Were her family just the least bit jealous of her Chicago friends?

"But the flowers can't help being stuck-up, Bud," she said brightly. "You know they're parasites and they find

themselves stuck up on a high tree somewhere when
they're born, so it isn't their fault."

Bud stared.

"What's parasikes?"

Marjorie explained.

"A parasite is a plant that lives on other plants. Their
seeds float around and lodge in the crotch of a tree in
warm climates, and begin to grow there, sucking their life
from the juices of the tree. Parasites don't work for themselves. They lodge on some other plant and live from it."

Bud looked thoughtful.

"They're like tramps, aren't they? Won't work.
Suckers!" said the boy.

"Look out there, Bud! You're getting pretty near
home," grinned Ted. "If this family isn't living on somebody else just now I'll miss my guess. You're sure right
that some people are parasites."

Bud turned solemn eyes on Marjorie.

"Is the man that sent these orchids a parasite?" he
asked.

Marjorie laughed. What would Evan Brower think of
that?

"Oh, no," she said with heightened color. "He works.
He's a lawyer, and I guess he'll have to work hard before
he gets to be a noted one like his father!"

Bud lost interest then and went to examine the signal
lights of his new electric train, but the rest of the family
were quiet, thoughtful, as they looked now and then at the
gorgeous orchids flaming at them from the big china
pitcher on the bookcase where Marjorie had put them.
Somehow those orchids represented to them all another
world, an alien world from which had come this fairy sister. Would it sometime take her away from them again?
A hint of sadness hovered in the Christmas air and threatened the Christmas spirit. They were going to have Brentwood back, but would it be without Marjorie? Would
Chicago claim her?

Betty was just taking the turkey out of the oven and
Marjorie was filling the water glasses when there came a
ring at the door again. Ted went to open it and there
stood Gideon Reaver with a small white package in his
hand. It wasn't tied up in ribbons or seals like a Christmas
present, though it looked as though it would like to have
been. It just had a rubber band around it.

Ted welcomed the young man joyously.

"Come in!" he cried as though Santa Claus himself had appeared at the door.

"Oh, I mustn't," said Gideon smiling. "I just stopped in to leave this little book for your sister. I told her I'd send it over and this is the first chance I've had. Also I wanted to ask if you folks wouldn't come over to our Christmas service tonight at nine o'clock."

"Oh, come on in," said Ted, "I want you to meet Dad and Mother. You aren't in such a hurry you can't stop a minute, are you?"

"No, I'm not in a hurry at all!" said Gideon smiling, "but I don't believe in intruding on Christmas Day."

"Intruding?" said Ted, opening the door wide and pulling his adored pastor in. "Where do you get that word?"

Then he suddenly turned and caught the look on Betty's face as she came into the dining room exactly opposite the hall door, with the great brown steaming turkey on its platter.

Betty didn't like him to invite Gideon Reaver in! Betty would be sore! Now probably Christmas would all be spoiled! Poor Ted! He could hardly get through the introductions.

But Marjorie came shining into the room and welcomed the guest, and Ted felt better. Then his father and mother were both very cordial too, and Ted beamed, though conscious all the time of Betty and the turkey in the background.

Betty put down the platter and came and stood frowning in the hall door, but the frown suddenly died down. Betty was surprised to find how young and good-looking Ted's boasted minister was. She hesitated, wondering just what to do about the turkey, and as she hesitated Marjorie turned and introduced her.

"This is my twin sister, Mr. Reaver. This is the one you saw before."

And suddenly Betty was swept into the circle much against her will. But he was interesting-looking, and she roused out of her annoyance and greeted him pleasantly enough.

But Gideon Reaver had a lot of intuition, and he had seen that turkey.

"I'm just delighted to see you all," he said with a comprehensive glance which took them all in, "but I'm not going to stop now. I can tell by the delicious odors that are going around that dinner is on the table, so I'll just run away now and come back another time and call if I may. Far be it from me to delay a Christmas dinner!"

Suddenly the mother spoke up, almost eagerly it seemed.

"Why not stay and share it with us?" she asked. She had seen the eager look in her boy's eyes.

"Yes, do stay," said the father heartily. "I know everybody will be delighted."

"Oh, I couldn't think of intruding that way. Indeed I couldn't. I was just passing and thought I would leave the message."

"But you haven't had your dinner yet, have you?" challenged Ted wistfully.

"No, I'm just on my way back to my boarding house."

"That settles it," said Father. "Ted, go and see if there are enough chairs to go around, and Betty, put on another plate!"

But suddenly the front door which had the night latch off, opened again, and in walked the doctor.

"Well, now, upon my word, if I haven't walked in on a party!" he said. "I beg your pardon. I won't stay but a minute. I just wanted to make sure my patients were all right and fit for turkey."

"You're just in time!" said Mr. Gay happily. "Have you had your Christmas dinner yet?"

"Well, no, I haven't yet, but I'm used to waiting. You see I was called up on the hills to a serious case at five this morning and I'm just getting back. Haven't had my breakfast yet and it wouldn't do to eat dinner till I've had breakfast, you see. I'll just look at Mrs. Gay's pulse and then I'll be moving on."

"We'll call it brunch then," called out Betty suddenly from the doorway. "Come on, there's plenty to eat. You get the chairs, Ted, two from upstairs, you know. Hurry! The turkey is already on the table. The more the merrier."

They all turned and looked at Betty's gay face, so changed from a moment before. Ted breathed a sigh of relief, and the rest gave quick furtive glances at the doctor, and then Sunny broke into the silence with one of his funny little grown-up imitation laughs.

"Ha-ha! More th' merrier! More th' merrier!"

Of course they all laughed then and the stiffness was gone. Marjorie hurried off to get the extra plates.

Mr. Gay introduced the minister and the doctor and they studied each other a bit cautiously. But they were both staying, there was no question about that.

"Dinner is served!" said Betty, suddenly appearing in the doorway looking very pretty indeed in Marjorie's green knit dress with a bit of red ribbon knotted in her hair and a scrap of holly on one shoulder.

"It's going to be a tight squeeze, friends, but we thought it was better than waiting to put another leaf in the table and eating a cold dinner."

Betty's cheeks were rosy and her eyes were twinkling. She seemed like a new Betty to Marjorie. Ted drew another deep sigh of relief and beamed at Sunny as he lifted him into his high chair.

The doctor, without waiting on the order of his going, marched straight over to Betty and pulled out her chair, and then took the one next her. Mrs. Gay smiled and took her place where cushions had been arranged at her back and feet. The minister found himself seated between Marjorie and Ted. Then Mr. Gay's voice broke into the laughter of getting seated.

"Mr. Reaver, will you ask the blessing, please?"

Marjorie stifled a quick look of surprise. There had been no asking of blessings so far in the meals she had eaten in her new home, although she reflected they had been most informal, and her father had generally eaten upstairs with her mother. But her heart warmed to the words that were spoken and she thrilled at the sweet silence that had settled over them all. This minister certainly was a rare one. How great for Ted to have such a man for a friend!

"Lord, we thank Thee today for this sweet fellowship that has gathered us all around this board to receive of Thy bounties. We thank Thee for these Thy good gifts for the refreshment of our bodies, and we thank Thee most of all for this day to keep in memory the gift of Thy Son, our Savior Jesus Christ, who came to earth to take upon Himself our sins and their penalty of death, and who bore them all, with their shame and their punishment, that all we who believe on Thee might go free, and come Home to Thy House at last without spot or wrinkle or any such

thing. We crave Thy blessing today, and ask it in the
name of the Lord Jesus. Amen."

As the heads were lifted the doctor shot a quick keen
glance at the minister across from him, but it was the minister who spoke first.

"Do you mean to tell me, Doctor, that you can always
tell which of these twins is which?" he asked looking from
Betty to Marjorie at his side.

"Well," said the doctor, "I can always tell that this one
is Betty, but I'm not always so sure which one the other
one is!"

They all laughed heartily at that and Sunny gave his little laugh that always brought down the house, bending his
head down on the table until his curls were in his plate.

"Ha! Ha! Which one is 'nother!"

There wasn't much stiffness after that, and the bright
talk raced around the table gaily from one to the other, till
finally all the plates were filled and everybody hard at
work emptying them.

Ted was very silent, but his nice grin at all the jokes
showed he was enjoying everything immensely.

"You sure you're not overdoing, Mother?" asked the father at last as he finished carving and addressed himself to
his own plate.

"Oh, no!" said Mother quietly, and added brightly in
the lingo of her children: "I'm having the time of my life!"

The doctor cast a questioning eye toward her, and said:
"Perhaps it will do her good. She's been cooped up so
long. Anyhow I'm here to rescue her if she shows signs of
collapse. But what I want to know is, Mrs. Gay, with you
laid up, who cooked this turkey? I never ate one more delicious. It's the best turkey I ever tasted."

"Betty cooked it," called out shy Bonnie suddenly. "She
asked Mother how and she did it all herself!"

"Thank you, young lady, for the information," said the
doctor bowing. "I suspected as much but I didn't dare ask
so personal a question."

"Aw, she can cook other things, too," put in Bud loy-
ally. "She can make pancakes something swell!"

"Can she indeed! I'm coming around to breakfast some
morning if I may. And I'm certainly coming to Christmas
dinner again whether I'm asked or not, some time when I
get another Christmas afternoon off.

It was a delightful occasion, and everyone enjoyed it to

the full. They lingered at the table laughing and telling stories until Sunny, replete with turkey and his first mince pie laid down his golden head and went to sleep in his chair.

And then when they at last arose both the guests insisted upon helping with the dishes, and what a gay time they had at that.

It was after seven o'clock when the dishes were done and the young people came back to the tiny parlor.

Mother had had a nap on the couch and professed to be as fresh as a rose, which remark gave occasion for a lot of pleasant compliments from the two young men guests.

Strange to say neither doctor nor minister seemed to be in a hurry to leave. In fact both had confessed earlier in the afternoon that they had been alone and longing for company when they drifted toward Aster Street but hadn't in mind any such invasion as they had made.

By this time they were excellent friends, having discovered a number of tastes in common. The doctor had inquired where Gideon preached, and Gideon had suggested that he'd better come over his way and open an office. The doctor said he'd think about it, and Betty told him they were going to move back there and needed to have their doctor handy. He said he didn't know but he would look into it.

They all settled down, Marjorie on the floor beside her mother's couch with her mother's hand in hers. Betty and Bonnie together in a big chair at the foot, Gideon Reaver talking to Mr. Gay in the wide doorway into the hall, Bud watching Ted as he helped Sunny to make a complicated toy wind up and run the way it ought to, and the doctor standing behind Betty's chair looking down at her and talking.

Suddenly Gideon turned around to them all.

"Now, why don't we have a little sing?" he said. "Christmas isn't complete without carols. Suppose we make the kiddies begin. Bonnie, don't you and Sunny know a little Christmas song?"

Bonnie shyly nodded her head.

"Soor ve does," piped Sunny getting up from his knees and coming promptly to the front. "Ve knows 'Vay-in-a-manger!'"

So the little sister and brother stood up by the Christmas tree hand in hand and sang Luther's cradle hymn very sweetly. Then Gideon started "O Little Town of Bethlehem," and they all sang on. Ted slipped up and turned off the light, leaving only the lights of the Christmas tree, and it seemed a holy and beautiful time. Gideon's voice was rich and clear, and the doctor proved to be a good bass. Song after song was sung. Bonnie curled up beside Marjorie, and Sunny crept into the big chair with Betty, sleepy and content, replete with Christmas joys.

It was just as they were singing the last line of "Silent Night," that Evan Brower walked contemptuously up the narrow steps, and failing to identify the small insignificant doorbell in the darkness gave a thunderous knock on the door.

Coming as it did into the sweetness of that "Silent, holy night" of long ago, it was somewhat of a shock.

XV

TED snapped on the lights and opened the door, and there stood a tall haughty young man.

"Does this happen to be number 1465 Aster Street?" he asked.

Ted nodded gravely.

"Is Miss Wetherill here?"

"Wetherill?" Ted hesitated and was about to say no, then suddenly it dawned upon him again and he took a deep breath like one about to relinquish something precious and answered with dignity:

"She is." Then he added with what was almost haughtiness in his voice, "Won't you come in?"

Evan Brower stepped into the house leaving the taxi throbbing outside, and looked about the tiny hall, and the equally tiny parlor beyond, searchingly like a warhorse out for battle. And strangely that place which had before been large enough and sweet with quiet fellowship, seemed to shrink and reveal all its inadequacies. Betty gasped quietly and remembered that she had on one of her sister's dresses. Would it be recognized? She sighted a smouch of chocolate from ill-gotten candies against orders on Sunny's face. She realized how ugly the wall paper was, and that the only vacant chair left for the stranger to take was a shaky one that invariably squeaked when one sat upon it. These things had not been in evidence all the afternoon, even with their two young men guests present, but now they came out and mocked her as she gave one swift survey of the room.

But Marjorie, her color perhaps a trifle heightened, came forward at once.

"Why, Evan," she said pleasantly, "this certainly is a surprise! Let me introduce my brother, Theodore Gay, and my father, Mr. Gay. Father, this is Mr. Brower, a very dear friend of the Wetherill family. This is my sister Elizabeth, and these are our friends, Mr. Reaver and Dr. Sheridan—"

She presented them one by one as they were standing about in the doorway, and each bowed courteously, trying to veil their disappointment at the interlude in their pleasant evening. But Evan Brower merely acknowledged the introductions by a level stare at each and the slightest possible inclination of his head.

"And won't you come in and meet my mother?" went on Marjorie blithely, though she wasn't at all sure from the look in Evan Brower's eye whether he was going to follow her or not. "Mother has been very ill, and is only up today for the first time, or rather she isn't exactly up. She has to lie on the couch."

Marjorie led the way to the couch, and Evan Brower reluctantly stepped a few feet nearer and inclined his head again at Mrs. Gay, his face showing that all this was a matter of utter indifference to him and he wanted to get it over with as soon as possible.

"And these are the children," went on Marjorie. "This is Gresham, otherwise Bud for short, and this is Bonnie, and Sunny."

Sunny, nothing daunted, stepped forward and put out a sticky hand.

"Merwy Twismas!" he volunteered.

Evan Brower gave him but a casual glance, ignoring the friendly little hand entirely, and kept his eyes on Marjorie.

"I came," said he in a rudely lowered tone, "to take you out this evening. Can you get your wraps and go at once? Will you need to change?"

He glanced down at her pretty knitted dress with annoyance. This was a part of finding her in this little insignificant house in a common neighborhood, that she should not be dressed for the evening! Christmas night and in a daytime dress! Evan Brower was very punctilious about such things. He always dressed for dinner. Could it be possible that Marjorie could revert to type in such a few short days?

But Marjorie did not look embarrassed at his evident disapproval. She lifted calm eyes to his face, and speaking in an ordinary tone that she was not attempting to disguise, she said:

"No, I'm sorry, I couldn't go this evening. I already have an engagement for later in the evening, and this is our first Christmas together. I wouldn't break it up for anything. You know this is what I came on for, and we're having a grand time. Won't you stay and enjoy it with us? And then go on with us to the service later? Let me take your hat. Take off your overcoat. It's warm in here."

Betty gave a quick little frightened gasp almost like a smothered protest and arose precipitately, plucking a protesting Sunny from the midst and hurrying him upstairs to get his sticky hands washed. The grown-ups slid out into the hall and began to talk about the weather and politics in low serious tones, a pleasant masculine clique. Only Mother on the couch and little Bonnie, her arm about Marjorie, her head resting against her lovingly, were left to hear what went on.

"Really, Marjorie, I don't see that you are required to do duty all day and evening too!" Evan's tone was exceedingly annoyed. He spoke with an air of authority. "I should suppose when I have taken the trouble to come all this distance to surprise you that you might spare a few hours to me. I have something important to tell you."

Marjorie's face did not cloud over. She had made her decision the minute she saw Evan enter the door and she meant to stick to it. Not for anything would she desert her dear new family on Christmas night. Not for anybody would she miss the Christmas night service at Brentwood! There might be a time for Evan Brower later, she was by no means sure, but it was not tonight.

"Well, I'm just as sorry as I can be, Evan, to disappoint you, but it's quite impossible. If you had let me know that you thought of coming this way I would have told you not to count on Christmas at all as I had made other plans. I do appreciate your kind thought for me, I do indeed! And the orchids were lovely! So nice of you to send them! But you'll just have to excuse me tonight, unless you find it possible to join us?"

She looked sweetly up into his face with an unruffled brow, and suddenly she knew that she was hoping he wouldn't stay. He didn't seem to fit with the rest. He had a lovely rich cultured voice, but would he camp down with the the others and sing carols, and enter into the quiet spirit that had pervaded the room before he came? Would he know how? Would he understand it? And yet, Evan Brower was very active in the church at home. What did it all mean? Was something wrong in herself? She didn't know. She hadn't time to think it out now. She was here and this was Christmas, her first Christmas in her father's house, and she didn't want it spoiled.

Evan Brower's cold, haughty, hurt voice was replying:

"That would be quite impossible. I am hunting up some friends on the other side of the city!" Was there the least perceptible emphasis on the words "friends," and *"other side"?*

And then Evan turned and stalked haughtily from the room without anything but the merest nod in Mrs. Gay's direction.

The low conversation in the hall had suddenly ceased. The participants hadn't been able to think of anything to cover the haughty refusal of that strange voice. Ted cast dagger glances toward the intruder, and even quiet Mr. Gay lifted a grave disapproving look toward him.

It was just at that crucial instant, as Marjorie was following the offended caller to the door, that Sunny's voice rang down the stairs.

"Betty, vas that the man vat sent my new sister Margwy those or-or-orkid parasikes? Vas it, Betty? Is he a parasike hisself like you vas talking?"

"Shhhh!" came Betty's soft warning.

"Vy do I have to be shsh, Betty? Is he a twamp?"

"Shhhhhh!"

A sound of little feet jerked suddenly by force across the floor above, and a quick wail:

"I don't not like him anyvay. He vouldn't shake han's. He vouldn't say Merwy Twismus!" The last syllable was cut short by the sharp closing of a door upstairs, and Gideon Reaver turned quickly to hide the twinkle in his eye from Ted who was glaring defiantly at everybody.

But Marjorie, her color rising and her head a bit high, walked coolly to the door with her caller.

"Too bad, Evan, to have this ride for nothing, but it just couldn't be helped," she said sweetly, and smiled indulgently upon him.

At the door he turned savagely upon her and said in a low growl:

"When can I see you, *alone?* In the morning? Will you deign to lunch with me?"

"Why, yes, I think I could," said Marjorie, considering.

"Very well, I'll call you on the telephone. What is the number here?"

"Oh, we haven't a telephone," she answered brightly as though that were quite a usual thing in her circle of friends. "Suppose I just be ready when you say you will come. Half past twelve or one. Which will be most convenient for you?"

"Eleven!" said Evan crisply. "I'm flying back in the afternoon and I'm taking you with me! Better have your things packed and we can take them with us where we lunch."

"Oh, no!" laughed Marjorie firmly, "I'm not going back yet. I haven't finished my visit. But I'll be ready at eleven if you like. Thank you again for the orchids. So nice of you to think of me. Oh—" as he swung the door smartly open, "it's snowing again, isn't it? How lovely! Christmas always has twice the thrill when it snows sometime during the day! Well, good night! I'll be ready at eleven."

Then he was gone. They could hear the taxi chugging away down the little common street, and Marjorie came smiling and dropped down beside her mother's couch in her old place again.

"Come on! Let's get going!" said Ted. "I'd like to hear these two sing a duet together."

"Why not make it a trio or a quartette?"

The children slipped into their places again, a subdued Sunny with traces of recent tears damp on his gold lashes came creeping in close beside Marjorie and slid a clean little hand into hers. She squeezed it hard, and stooping, softly kissed his round cheek.

So they started in to sing again, discovering a lot of sweet old Christmas songs they all knew.

A little after eight Gideon rose.

"Friends, I've got to tear myself away," he said. "I have a service at nine. I came here originally to get recruits for it, but I haven't the heart to tear you apart on Christmas night. I'd appreciate it awfully of course if all of you could drive over with me and help with the singing, but I shan't blame you if you don't want to come. Though it would be great to have that last song repeated, and if the doctor would come too he and Ted and I could do the trio! As for the girls, well, we could have a mighty fine quartette if they two and you two men would be willing! There, now! I wasn't going to ask you to go!"

"He wasn't going to ask us! No, he hasn't the heart to tear us away! And yet he's fixed it all up for us to be on the program!" laughed the doctor. "But friend, you're going to have the surprise of your life. We're *going,* of *course,* aren't we, Betty?"

"Oh!" said Betty both eagerness and withdrawal fighting for the mastery in her eyes. "But I have got to put the children to bed—and Mother—"

"Yes, Mother's sat up long enough for the first time even if it is Christmas," said the doctor, "so Ted and I are carrying her up to her bed right now, and one of you girls can undress her and put her in, while the other one sees these two sleepyheads into their cribs. That oughtn't to take five minutes if you work fast, ought it?" He appealed to them both. "As for you, Father Gay, I shouldn't allow you out in the snow storm anyway, so you're elected to watch over your family while we go a-caroling! Come on, Ted, all set?"

"All set!" said Ted, and stooping gathered his mother into his arms, while the doctor made a very efficient second, and the procession started laughing gaily up the stairs.

Marjorie with Sunny and Bonnie in tow passed her brother as he was coming down the stairs, a kind of triumph in his tread.

"Is Betty going?" she whispered as she passed.

"I don't dare ask," he grinned back. "Leave it to Doc. Perhaps he can work the trick!"

But Betty was flying as fast as any of them to get ready. Here was a chance to go out with a good-looking young man and wear her new fur coat and her new gray hat, and Betty was not the one to turn that down, even if it was just a religious service in a little old despised common chapel! She came shining down in her glad finery as soon as any of them, and Ted looked at Marjorie and winked.

By common consent the doctor went with Betty. They did invite Bud to ride with them but he shrugged his shoulders and said he guessed he'd go with Ted. There was more room in the minister's car, so they drove off into the whitest loveliest Christmas snow that could be imagined.

Seated in the laurel-and-hemlock-decked chapel between Bud and Ted, Marjorie studied the pleasant keen face of the doctor sitting in front of them beside Betty. She wondered if he was a born-again-one too, or just a man of the world? She studied her sister's face too, and saw the alert keen interest in everything that went on.

It was a beautiful service. The singing was from the heart. Cultured and uncultured voices, mingling in one Christmas song of the redeemed.

There was much singing and prayer, wonderful, tender prayer from both minister and people. There was a heart-searching talk from Gideon Reaver pressing home the fact to each soul present that the Lord Jesus was born and suffered and died just for him. Marjorie had never realized it as a personal thing like that before. She was deeply stirred. Young Bud sat and listened wide-eyed. He had taken a great liking to the minister that afternoon. He appeared to be hearing the gospel story for himself for the first time in his life.

And then after another tender brief prayer Gideon called for his quartette, and Ted calmly arose and led the way to the front. Marjorie as she walked behind him marveled at his coolness, his reverent attitude, as if he were a young priest going to perform his duty at the altar. She found herself a little nervous about Betty, whether she would come up after all. Betty hadn't *said* she would sing at the service, though she had joined with them in the few minutes' practice they had just before the service.

But Betty came, and her alto was deep and sweet. Betty had a nice voice. Marjorie found herself thinking that Betty should have some lessons by and by when things got straightened out.

Then they sang:

"Oh, listen to our wondrous story,
    Counted once among the lost,

> Yet, One came down from heaven's glory,
> Saving us at awful cost!
> Who saved us from eternal loss?
> Who but God's Son upon the cross?
> What did He do?
> He died for you.
> Where is He now?
> Believe it thou,
> In heaven interceding."

It wasn't exactly a Christmas hymn, but it exactly fitted the Christmas message that Gideon had given. Marjorie found her heart swelling with the message, which a few short days before she would not have understood so well. And when they came to the last verse she found herself thinking of Betty and making the song a longing for her to know something of the wonder and joy that had just come to her own heart.

> "Will you surrender to this Savior?
> To His Sceptre humbly bow?
> You, too, shall come to know His favor,
> He will save you, save you now!"

Her whole soul was in the words as she sang them, and she found herself longing for the salvation of all those around her, who perhaps did not know the truth of what it meant to be saved, as she had but just discovered it.

Ted was singing earnestly. His voice was going to be good. It had a fresh sincerity that makes people listen. Astonishingly the doctor seemed to be enjoying the singing too. It must be that even if he wasn't a Christian he had a Christian background somewhere, for he had seemed familiar with that song, though it wasn't a common one. And he had certainly listened to the message.

"Something real about this place," she heard him say to Betty half an hour later as they stood at the door about to plunge into the snow and go to the car.

Betty didn't answer, but she gave a quick glance up at him as if she were trying to understand his point of view.

Then they went home with the memory of the little chapel in its gala greenery, and the sweet songs, the tender looks on faces, the Christian testimonies with which the meeting had closed, all a holy beautiful ending to a day that had been wonderful from start to finish.

Marjorie lay awake for a long time and thought it over, step by step, thrilling anew at the memory. There was just one part she forgot to review, and that was the interlude in which Evan Brower figured. But then, she was having to go home to Chicago pretty soon, and there would be plenty of time to deal with Evan Brower. That was what the back of her mind thought, while she brushed lightly over the episode of his coming to call, and held on to the things she had most enjoyed.

Of course she was having to go to lunch with him tomorrow, but there was time enough to consider that when tomorrow came. She wanted to hold on to each moment of this day and get the last drop of joy it had to give before it passed into oblivion.

And none the least among her memories was that of Gideon Reaver, what he had said, what he had done, the comical expression of his face now and again, the quick deep fervor of his voice as he spoke, the merriment of his laughter, the true look in his eyes, the simplicity of his prayers, the earnestness of his message. These all hovered in her memory making a picture that intrigued her. What a wonderful young man to be a minister! Would he grow dignity and conceit as he grew older? She couldn't believe it. He seemed as utterly unspoiled and humble as a little child. He seemed—was it irreverent to think so?—almost like his Master, the Lord Jesus Christ! But no, that could not be irreverent. Wasn't that what Christians were meant to be, like Christ? Only she had never seen a young man before who had impressed her with the thought as he did. She feel asleep thinking about it, thrilling at the memory of how he had led her in a few brief words, to understand that she was saved, and to long to walk with God.

She must ask him again some day about that walking with God. It was a wonderful thought, to walk with the eternal God!

Betty lay beside her, eyes staring wide ahead at the blank wall of the room in the darkness. Betty was thinking of the look on the doctor's face when he had said, "Something real about this place!" Wondering about the doctor, thinking of all the fun he had made for them during the afternoon and evening. Contrasting it with a few experiences in her meager past that she had called "good times." She was being searched as her bitter eager young soul had never been searched before. Real things! What were real things? She wished she could know Dr. Sheridan better, dare to call him by his first name, go out with him sometimes, but of course that was unthinkable. It wasn't in the least likely that he would ever think of her again. He was too busy to spend time on girls anyway, and if he did he wouldn't pick her out for a companion. This had just been an off day with him, all his friends busy elsewhere, and he hindered from being with them by that call to the country which had made him too late to get to house parties, and things that he would of course be invited to. It wasn't probable that a rising young doctor would choose to spend his Christmas Day in a poor plain little house on Aster Street if he had been home in time for more interesting places. Yet he had seemed to enjoy himself. Or was it only a rare quality he had for adjusting himself to circumstances? Well, she had had a good time anyway and she liked him. It was nice to have a memory of such a day even if it never happened again. Maybe he only stayed because he liked to look at her pretty new sister. Of course they all said she and Marjorie looked alike, but she knew herself that there was something more sophisticated about Marjorie, an air of being to the manner born that she, Betty did not have, and that no amount of make-up could simulate In fact, perhaps it only made the lack more apparent And then there had been the way the doctor had acted in that meeting, taking it all so seriously, actually interested in it! Well it was interesting She had to own that. She hadn't been able to disconnect her mind from what was going on the way she usually could in churches—though she hadn't been to any very often of late. She couldn't blame Ted for being so devoted. That young minister was very interesting, and very good-looking. Though she told herself she preferred the doctor's type. Gideon Reaver was a little too quiet for her. However, why quarrel with anything that had happened in that wonderful day? Here she was lying and thinking over differences in mere people that she likely wouldn't see much again, when she had a wonderful new fur coat and a hat that looked as if it was imported! She, Betty Gay, all rigged up like that sitting beside a handsome doctor and singing in a church! It was unbelievable!

But just as she dropped off to sleep there came the words of the chorus she had helped to sing:

"What did He do? He *died* for you—" it trailed off

vaguely and blended with her dreams. Was it possible that the dying One had really ever thought of Betty Gay, so long ago when He died on Calvary?

And down on his knees beside the sleeping Bud knelt Ted, thanking God for the wonderful Christmas Day, and praying for his family.

XVI

THE next morning Marjorie became aware of something strained in the atmosphere that hadn't been there the day before. She didn't quite know what it was. It was subtle. It evaded her in glances, even loving glances. It was a kind of shy embarrassment upon the whole family. It troubled her, though she tried to put it away and tell herself she was imagining things, but it kept returning.

"No, don't try to help wash the dishes this morning," protested Betty. "You're going out and you'll get your hands all red."

"The idea!" said Marjorie laughing. "Give me that dishcloth! What do you suppose I care about my hands?"

"Well, you ought to care," said Betty reprovingly, "with a particular man like that you might be criticized. He's critical. I could see that!"

"Well, I'm not afraid of him," said Marjorie, "and I'm going to wash these dishes! I'd better open another box of soap powder, hadn't I? This one is nearly gone."

"There's plenty there," said Betty frugally. "I wish you wouldn't feel you have to wash dishes and things like that all the time. I know you're not used to it."

"Why continually remind me of that? I suppose you judge because I do it so awkwardly," smiled Marjorie, "but I'll get over that in time, you know. What I would like to know is why you are so much more solicitous about

182

my washing dishes today than you were before? Have I done something wrong?"

"Oh, mercy, no!" said Betty sharply. "It's just seeing that high-and-mighty friend of yours, I suppose. Have you known him long?"

"You mean Evan Brower? Oh, yes, I've known him practically all my life. His mother was Mrs. Wetherill's most intimate friend. They lived not far from our house. But he never took much notice of me till I grew up. He's very pleasant."

"Yes, he acted that way last night!" said Betty sharply.

Marjorie gave her sister a quick look.

"He wasn't very nice, was he?" she agreed. "I was ashamed of him. But he's not like that usually, he's most punctiliously polite. I suppose he was a little annoyed at me for running away from his mother's Christmas party. I never dreamed that he would come all the way down here to see me. I suppose they feel a little responsibility about me on the Wetherills' account, now that they think I'm all alone in the world."

"Oh, *yes?*" said Betty with an upward accent. "Well, his royal highness certainly knows how to give orders. I admired the way you held your own, but you won't do that today, lady! He intends to give you his orders. I could see it in the corner of his eye and the droop of his lips. He means to take you home with him. Excuse me for listening, I was standing at the head of the stairs trying to get Sunny's face clean without stopping to turn on a light upstairs, and I heard him say he was taking you home today. You'll go, too. I can see that! And if you do it'll be good-bye sister, all right! Are you engaged?"

"Mercy no!" said Marjorie. "Where did you get that idea?"

"Out of his masterful manner. If you aren't, you probably will be by the time lunch is over. You ought to have told us about him before you let us all get to caring about you. It wasn't fair, after all these years without you."

"Betty!" Marjorie lifted her hands out of the dishwater and whirled about toward her sister.

"What in the name of peace is the matter with you, Betty?" Marjorie said, half ready to cry, "there wasn't anything to tell. He's just a friend of the family and there's nothing at all between us. I'm not engaged to *anybody*, and don't mean to be for sometime, if I *ever* am. I'm not interested in such things yet. I've got a family and that's enough for the present."

"Oh, *yes?*" said Betty again incredulously. "Well, wait till you come back—*if* you come back! Don't you mean to pack your things? Or will you trust me to send them to you if he carries you off willy-nilly?"

Suddenly Marjorie rushed at her sister, half laughing, half crying, and gave her a loving shaking.

"There!" she said breathlessly. "Stop this! I'm not going away with him. I wouldn't think of such a thing, and he hasn't a right in the world to make me, so please be good and let's have a nice time the way we usually do."

Thus appealed to Betty put aside her bitter little flings, but Marjorie could see there was something still in her mind that fenced them apart. She sighed as she went upstairs to dress. There really wasn't much time, for they had slept late that morning. She tried to get away from the things Betty had said but they annoyed her.

When she went in to say good-bye to her mother in her wine red velvet dress she felt the same thing again.

"I hope you'll have a very nice time, dear!" said her mother wistfully. "Is this young man a very special friend?"

"Why, no, I don't think so, Mother. He's been a friend of the family for years. I haven't any specials yet. I'll tell you when I do!" and she kissed her mother and ran down to open the door as the taxi drew up.

"Bye!" she whispered toward Betty in the doorway and blew a kiss from the tips of her fingers toward her. "Don't you do a thing toward getting dinner till I get back!"

Then she was gone.

Her father was watching her from the window.

"I'm afraid he is," he said as he turned away with a sigh. "Or at least he thinks he is. He has a very possessive manner."

"He would!" said Marjorie's mother. "He's that kind. George, don't you think we ought to have a talk with her about what we're going to do next, and what she's going to do? She asked me last night if we wanted her to live with us."

"I certainly do," said the father. "We oughtn't to stand in her way. It's going to be harder than ever of course,

now that she's been here, to let her go, but—it's her right!
That's her natural setting now, a sort of a birthright that we
wished on her! She has a position in Chicago, in social
life, I suppose, that she never could have here as our
daughter, no matter how successful I got to be." He
smiled ruefully. "And you know how likely that is."

"Yes," said the mother tearfully.

And then they sat down and talked the whole thing
over, and presently Betty could stand it no longer and
came up to listen. Then came Bonnie and Sunny in from
playing in the snow and caught a few words, and began to
cry.

"Where is 'Nother Betty?" demanded Sunny. "I vants
'Nother Betty!"

And Bonnie came close to her mother and asked sadly,
"Is our new sister going away?"

At noon Ted came in. He had a job for the evening
again, cleaning up after Christmas. He listened to the dole-
ful tale. Then he shook his head.

"Aw, you're crazy!" he told Betty. "She won't fall for
that poor sap! She's got too much sense! Come on, let's
have lunch!"

Down in the city, meantime, Marjorie was having troubles of her own. It was Evan Brower's idea of a good time
to make Marjorie suffer plenty for having gone off without
leaving him her address, and for having refused to go out
with him last evening, and then to show her how generous
and forgiving he could be afterward.

So Marjorie was seated at a sumptuously appointed table
in one of the most exclusive hotels in the city, with a stern
companion who lectured her as if she were a naughty little
girl.

At first she laughed it off, and pleased herself by remembering what a good time she'd had yesterday.

She was wearing the orchids he had given her, but before he was done disciplining her she wished courtesy
would permit her to take them off and fling them at him.

He was not blind however. He knew that she was looking very well indeed, and that others at neighboring tables
were aware that they were a noticeable couple. In his heart
he was swelling with pride over her beauty, and her air of
gentle breeding, though he prided himself that no small
part of her distinction came from his orchids which she

wore so graciously. But she really was going to make a very fitting wife for him, and she certainly was taking her punishment well.

At last she look up and smiled:

"Now, Evan, don't you think we'd better talk about *you* awhile?" she suggested. "What have you been doing the last week? Did you go to hear The Messiah? Was it good with the new soloists? And what did they do about the Christmas party for the crippled children? I promised to help at that, you know. Who took my place? And is your mother well? You haven't told me a thing. And how in the world did you get away from your family Christmas party? I'm afraid you hurt your mother's feelings terribly."

That was an unfortunate thought. She saw it at once. Evan stiffened immediately.

"I *came* away. I *had* to. I felt that you needed my protection and I had something to say to you."

"But I didn't need any protection, you know," smiled Marjorie, "and I told you I wasn't ready to talk to you."

"Marjorie, you did a most unwise thing when you came all alone to hunt up your family. You didn't know in the least what you were running into."

"We won't go into that!" said Marjorie coolly. "I ran into the happiest thing that has ever come into my life thus far, and I'm glad I came."

"Do you think that statement is kind or fair to your foster parents? Do you think you are being loyal to dear Mrs. Wetherill who so adored you?"

"Yes, Evan, I do. I do not love her less because I have found my own mother to love, and it was at her suggestion that I took up this matter at all. Now, will you please not talk any more about it? Some day you will learn, I hope, how wrong you are, but at present I would rather not discuss it. Let's have a nice time together until you have to go. Don't you think my orchids are lovely with their creamy leaves against this dark red velvet?"

"They certainly are," said the young man half grudgingly. "I had begun to think you didn't care for them."

"Care? Why, I love them! They are such wonderful specimens, and it was so nice of you to send them to me when I was away. I was proud to have them. We all enjoyed them a lot."

The young man was silent for a little, studying her. He didn't exactly care whether the rest of her family had enjoyed his flowers or not, and he was pondering whether to tell her so but he had been steadily working along such lines for a half-hour now and had got nowhere; perhaps he had better try a new tack.

"I've brought you something else," he said with a swift change of manner and a lighting of his eyes, "something that is just for yourself. I hope you'll like it."

"Oh but you shouldn't Evan." she protested. "The orchids were enough! They were wonderful. I love having them. especially to wear today, too."

"Well this is something very special." he said with an engaging smile She thought to herself that he was handsomer when he smiled than when he was trying to lecture her. He had a nice smile.

He put his hand in his pocket and pulled out a tiny velvet case of the color of violets. She looked at it and an anxiety entered her soul.

"Oh. Evan, not some great gift now, please. I don't somehow seem—ready—" she gave a half-frightened glance at the box. perhaps divining what it held.

But he handed it across to her. smiling.

"Open it!" he said, "I want to watch your face when you see it."

There seemed nothing to do but take it and open it. She held the little box gently in her hand as if it were a living thing that she might hurt. and hesitated. looking at him, and trying to think what to do. Then she touched the pearl spring and disclosed the wonderful blue diamond set in a delicate frostwork of platinum.

For an instant she caught her breath at its beauty, for it was a charming ring Then suddenly the trouble in her eyes grew definite and she shut the cover down sharply with a snap.

"Oh, Evan! Please! You ought not to have done this! Not now anyway! I told you I could not think of such things now. Please! I'm sorry. but I couldn't take that!" She handed it back across the table but he did not move to take it.

"Please!" she insisted. "I could not take a thing like this until I was sure!"

His face was haughty and frozen.

"And why aren't you sure?" he asked. "It's been nearly ten days since I asked you to marry me. You've had plenty of time to think it over."

"No," she said firmly, "I haven't. I've had other things to think about and settle. They had to come first before anything."

"Well, haven't you got them all settled?"

A gleam of something like joy flitted across her face, but she shook her head.

"Not all, yet."

"How long will it take?" There was a trace of anger in his voice.

"I'm not sure, but when I come home I can talk with you about it. I shall know then what I am going to do."

She laid the box down definitely on the table between them, and sat back with finality.

"Well!" he said after studying her face a minute, "it won't be long then, for you are going back with me on the plane that leaves the flying field at three. We can talk about it on the way."

"Oh, no!" said Marjorie. "I have no idea of going back today. And I have asked you, both today, and back in Chicago before I left, please not to talk about this now. I must settle several things in my own mind before I shall be able to talk with you."

"But I love you, Marjorie!"

She studied him rather hopelessly for a minute and then she said:

"If you truly love me won't you prove it to me by putting that ring back in your pocket and just sitting there and talking to me in a pleasant natural way as you always have done, without any perplexing questions or anything? Just let's talk!"

He looked at her keenly for a minute and then he said quietly, with an inscrutable mask on his face:

"Very well. What shall I talk about?" She knew by his tone that he was angry, but she could not help it.

"Oh anything! Suppose I ask you a question. It's something I've been wondering. Evan, you were brought up a good deal as I was, you're in the same church, and active in it. What do you believe about being saved? Did you ever know there was a way to tell definitely whether or not you were saved? Because I never did till a few days ago, and I've been wondering if it was my stupidity, or if it was a lack somewhere in the teaching? Have you ever thought about it?"

He looked at her as if she had suddenly gone crazy.

"Saved?" he said. "What in the world do you mean?"

"Why, saved from your sins. Fit to go to heaven, you know, when you die. I have always supposed that you had to be as good as you could to get to heaven, but you couldn't be sure you were going to get there even then, till after you died. Didn't you?"

His face softened and he spoke to her as if she were a sick person, or a very young child.

"My dear! I am afraid the long strain of nursing Mrs. Wetherill, and then seeing her die, has been too much for your nerves. I thought there was something the matter with you before you left home. I thought you did not look well, but I never suspected you were growing morbid. I'm sorry. I should have been more gentle and tender with you, and tried to cheer you up. Come home with me now, dearest, and let me try to make life bright and cheerful for you and help you to forget the fearful shock you have had."

"Oh, no," said Marjorie looking up brightly, "you don't understand me. I'm not in the least morbid. In a way I'm happier than I ever was in my life before, because I've found that I have a Savior from sin, and that there is a way to know without a doubt that I am saved and needn't go all my life with that worry even in the back of my mind! It's all plainly written in the Bible, only I never searched it to find out before. I was only wondering if you had known about it all the time, or if you didn't know it yet."

He studied her face with vexed unresponsive eyes a moment and then he said coldly:

"So, that's the line of your new family, is it? They are fanatics!"

She sprang up as if he had struck her, and her eyes grew suddenly alien.

"No, Evan, you are mistaken! My family are not fanatics. I do not know yet whether they even know this or not. Except my brother Ted. He is a Christian, but he is not a fanatic. But I heard this in a sermon, and then I read it in the Bible. It is there quite plainly if you will hunt for it."

She was speaking almost haughtily, as if he were a stranger. Then she glanced down at her watch. "And now if you will excuse me I will take a taxi back home. I have something else to do at once, and you will be going to the flying field soon. I will let you know when I get back to Chicago. Good-bye!"

She flashed a distant little smile at him and walked out of the dining room.

He followed her, of course, instantly, his face haughty and indignant, but he summoned a taxi and put her in.

"You are very headstrong!" he said as he gave her hand a cold hard grip. "I didn't dream you had it in you to be so hard. When are you planning to return?"

"I'm not hard, Evan, really. Only you've said some things that were rather difficult to bear. But we'll talk about that when I get home. I shall probably come a few days after New Year's."

He watched her gravely as the taxi took her away into the light falling snow, his own face stern, reproachful. Well, he had done his best. She would have to go her own gait and learn her lesson.

As the taxi rounded the corner and went away out of sight a wild idea of taking another and following her, compelling her to listen to him, to *make* her accept his love and let him have a right to protect her, came to him, but his natural restrained nature told him that would be very bad policy, if he ever hoped to train her to be a sweet submissive wife. It was only a week till she would return anyhow, and it would be far better to let her see how she had jeopardized such a love as he intended to give her. She would come to her senses. She wouldn't keep this up. She was young and out from under discipline and a little skittish. This religious line of course was bad for one like Marjorie, with an already uncomfortably keen conscience, but once she got home he would see to it that she had something to offset such nonsense. The best thing he could do now was to take a plane home and get some work done, laying his plans for a campaign against her return.

All the way home he was planning. It didn't take him long to lay aside worries when he once decided what line of action he should take. So he gave his whole energy to thinking out his future, his and Marjorie's.

It was very annoying that Marjorie had acted so about the diamond after he had taken so much trouble to select it, but he would make her regret that, and after all, perhaps she intrigued him all the more that she wasn't too eager. Although he didn't at all like this family complex she had suddenly acquired. He would have to be very firm indeed about them. He couldn't have a family hung around his neck, no matter how much she wanted it. That was why it was such a pity that she had not been willing to come with him at once. But perhaps. on the other hand, if she stayed a little longer in such close quarters with them she might get thoroughly over her infatuation and be but the more ready in future to ignore them perhaps even be willing to acknowledge her mistake in hunting them up at all. It was only to be hoped that she didn't get too generous while she was with them and endanger any of her fortune. That man, the father was probably capable of begging her to let him handle her property! Well if worst came to worst and she had done anything unwise he could get Melbourne to exercise a little well earned authority over her. Even if she was of age he could profess to have been put in charge in such a way that his advice must be asked before anything definite was done with regard to disposal of stocks or anything of that sort He would wait until she came home. and if she had been unwise—of course he would have to be most careful in trying to find out from her what she had done or she might fly up again—but if she had done more than give them reasonable presents at Christmas. he would have a very confidential talk with Melbourne He was sure he could easily make Melbourne see his duty in the matter, even if the will didn't give him an actual authority to control her Of course it would be best to urge her to marry him at once Then he would be able to stop any further leaks family-ward. Poor child! She knew nothing of finance of course. But just fancy her getting all up in the air that way at his remarks about her family. A family she had known only a few days! A family who lived in a little tucked-up house like that in such a neighborhood!

Well, he would certainly have some training to do when he married her and it had better begin as soon as possible before she went off on any more tangents.

But she was beautiful! Yes, she was very beautiful!

XVII

THERE was an alert strained something in the atmosphere when Marjorie got back to her father's house that melted at once under her smiles and her obvious gladness to be with them once more.

"Well?" said Betty coming out of the kitchen with the dishtowel in her hand, "did he go?"

"Yes, I suppose he did. I didn't stay to see."

"Do you mean you didn't go to see him off? Do you mean he didn't even bring you back? He let you come in a taxi all alone?"

"Oh, I wouldn't let him come back with me," said Marjorie, omitting the fact that he had not suggested it. "It was time for him to go to the flying field."

"But didn't he try to make you go back with him?"

"Why, yes, he suggested it. His mother is having a family Christmas affair and wanted me to come back and be with them. But I had no idea of going."

"H'm!" said Betty. "Well, I'm glad you're back, but I certainly didn't expect it."

The children came flying downstairs with eager eyes.

"Has she come back?" they chorused.

Bud appeared from his room.

"I wonder if you can make my 'lectric train go together? I got 'em all laid out on the floor in Ted's and my room, but they don't seem ta fit."

"Well, I'll look at it, Bud," said Marjorie smiling. "If I

can't Ted can, and he ought to be coming along home soon now."

"Marjorie, did you really mean you would make some more clothes for my dolly sometime?" This from Bonnie.

"Mar-jo-wey vill oo vind up my nauti-mobile?" demanded Sunny. "Betty's twoss. Her von't any more."

"Poor Betty, I expect she's tired," said Marjorie. "Yes, I'll wind it up. Wait till I take off my things, and look in on Mother."

"Okay wif me!" said Sunny.

Oh, it was good to get back where she was wanted and see them all glad to welcome her.

Her mother was asleep so she went down and patiently wound up the automobile a dozen times for Sunny while she talked with Betty. and helped straighten up the kitchen Betty was tired and she showed it. She had been worrying all the morning but she didn't let that be known.

"Didn't we have a good time yesterday?" Marjorie said to Betty thinking aloud.

"*We* all did, but I can't see where the good time came in for you," said Betty sourly. "You didn't have a single present that amounted to anything. Next year I'll have something to give to you if I have to sell the last rag I have."

"Oh, my dear!" said Marjorie twinkling. "Not that! But please dear I had the best time of my life seeing you all open your things And wasn't it funny the way we had company come right down upon us that way, and weren't they nice?"

"They certainly were," said Betty more mollified. "I wondered what you'd think of that. Your dinner and your everything and we asking outsiders to help eat it."

"Look here Betty! If you keep on talking that way about things being mine I'm going to run away and never come back. If that is what you want to have happen, all right go right on! But I mean it! You take every bit of delight out of life talking that way."

"Well I won't!" said Betty fiercely, winking hard to keep back the tears "Only I've been so afraid you wouldn't come back or if you did that you'd be running right away back to Chicago again. You know you only said you'd come to spend Christmas when you came, and I know if you go Mother is going right back to crying in the night again, and all of us are going to slump!"

"Well, I haven't any intention of leaving you unless you want to get rid of me!" declared Marjorie. "I'm only too happy to get a family! Of course I'll have to go back pretty soon and do something about my house and furniture and servants and so on, but I shan't stay long. Not if you want me!"

Betty's fears were quieted for the moment, but that evening after the children were put to bed they all gathered in the little parlor again, with the soft lights of the Christmas tree glowing, and talked.

"Marjorie," said her father, "your mother and I have been talking things over and we feel that there is grave danger, in our love for you, and our longing to have you always with us, that we shall be unfair to you. Since seeing the young man who called upon you last evening we realize more than ever that there are others whom you have known far longer than you have known us, who perhaps have a prior claim upon you. You have doubtless a lot of friends in Chicago whom you love and who love you, and who are in a social life that we have never had and never could have. We have always lived quietly. We shall probably continue to live quietly the rest of our lives. We have no great social standing and no wealth to bring about such standing for you. We have been talking it over and we do not feel that it would be right for us to allow you to make so serious a change in your life without careful consideration. You understand of course that this is not said because we *want* you to go, but because we feel that you should feel entirely *free* to go and live your own life as you wish."

"Oh, Father!" said Marjorie in dismay, "why should I care for social standing? I've had it all my life and I never enjoyed it at all. It means nothing to me!"

"But my dear, have you ever considered what it would mean to be without it? Your mother and I would far rather lose you than to urge you to stay with us at the expense of having you sorry afterward, when you are missing something that you have never had to think about before because you had it."

"I should never feel sorry about a thing like that!" said Marjorie.

"But you do not realize what it will be to be alienated from all your friends."

"Father, if a thing like that would alienate friends then they aren't friends, are they?"

"Well, that is a question, but in some cases it would undoubtedly alienate them."

"Father, I don't mind," said Marjorie. "There isn't a soul among my old friends that I would actually break my heart about if I didn't see them any more ever. Oh, there are some pleasant people whom I like, some of them I admire, but I've never had many intimate friends, just a few schoolmates. But most of those live in other places, and some are married. In any case, I shouldn't see much of them."

"Hasn't it occurred to you, my dear, that you might marry, yourself, and that if you came to live with us in our quiet circumstances it might make a difference? Some people might not care to marry a girl under such circumstances."

"Do you think anyone who felt that way would be worth marrying?"

"Well, there again opinions might differ. I might not think so, but it might be possible for some very good worthy person to have been so brought up as to have his point of view entirely different from mine. It certainly is not what I would choose for you. I would not call it an ideal marriage, but yet on the other hand a test like that might alienate someone who had grown very dear to you. Take that young man who called here yesterday. My dear, I do not think he would care for any of us. You know him better than I, and he may have some very good qualities, and be a most estimable person, but I would feel that if you meant to marry him, living with us might make trouble for you."

Marjorie was very still staring at the soft brightness of the Christmas tree, seeing the future perhaps in miniature in those bright balls, trying to work it out.

"Father," she said at last, "is that what you would rather I would do, go back to Chicago and make a brilliant marriage, instead of coming to live with my family? Remain alienated from you always?"

There was a choking in her voice and her father reached out his hand as she sat on a low footstool by her mother's side and laid it on her head tenderly.

"No, little girl, that is not what we *want*. But we want

you to be truly happy, and to have no regrets if you should decide to come and live with us. What we want is for you to go back to Chicago for a time and think the whole matter over, consider it from every possible angle, and then make your decision. Will you do that?"

Marjorie was still a long time and then she looked up sadly:

"Yes, I'll do it if you will do the same thing. If you will honestly talk it all over with the other children, and decide whether you want me or not."

"There is no question of that, daughter. We want you with all our hearts, every one of us, even the babies. But we are willing to sacrifice our own wishes for your sake, since we were the cause of putting you into another environment, we want it to work out in the best way for you."

"Well, Father, I feel the same way. It really is silly for me to go to Chicago just to consider that, for I knew almost the first day I landed here that this was where I wanted to be. But you must realize there are things for you to consider, too. I think you ought to go over them all and consider just as you want me to do, and agree to be honest about it, no matter how much you think it will hurt me."

Her father looked at her mother, and they smiled tenderly over her bowed head.

"All right!" said her father, "we'll agree if you will."

Marjorie's face brightened.

"Well, then I'd better get it over as quickly as possible. I've got to go back of course and see to things. I came away without closing up or packing or anything. I told the servants I'd be back after New Year's or maybe before, and I gave them a holiday. The chauffeur and his wife are living over the garage and looking after things But I can't leave it that way indefinitely I'll write them and set a date for coming, and I'll stay there a week to consider, no more. A week is plenty. If *you* need more all right, but I shall wait for your answer eagerly. But I did want to get the Brentwood house cleaned and you moved into it. I would hate to miss that."

The father's face softened and then grew reserved.

"Well, that's another thing, again, dear. We don't want to do anything about that, Mother and I, until this other matter is settled. You needn't think that you will be left out of things, but I've got to get into a position to be earning something before we go into a more elaborate style of living, that is, if it seems best for you to stay in Chicago."

"Father!" said Marjorie in a hurt tone. "You don't think I wanted that house just for my own comfort, do you?"

"No, dear, I know you didn't. I know your dear generous nature wanted to make your mother and us all happy and comfortable. And we do appreciate it with all our hearts. And of course we're deeply grateful, and shall keep the house and try to get into shape to live there, but we felt just now it was better to wait and settle this other matter first."

"Father, that house is going to be financed all right whether you let me come and live with you or not. That was a part of my Christmas gift. And if you or any of you, are going to keep talking about my money as if it were poison that you mustn't touch then I'm not coming back. I told Betty that this afternoon! The only reason I'm glad I have money is so I can do things for you all. There isn't anyone else who belongs to me."

"Don't you realize that wouldn't be fair to your husband if you should marry?"

"No, I don't! If someone wants to marry me for my money I don't want him. I'm not sure I shall ever marry anyway! Anyhow I don't care a thing about my husband now. He can take what he gets if he ever comes into the picture."

"All right, little girl! Have it your way. We'll put down our pride and let you fix the matter of the house the way you like, only we're not going to move in until we hear from you."

"But will they let you stay here?"

"Yes, I arranged to keep the house till the end of January. Ted went and paid the rent the day after you came, with some money he says you gave him. Besides, Mother isn't quite fit to look after moving just now anyway, and I've got to get out and hunt a job."

"All right!" said Marjorie with a sigh, "but there won't be any harm in getting some of the cleaning done and having the plumbing and heating plant gone over and things like that. Then when we are ready to move it won't take long."

Betty giggled.

"It wouldn't take long anyway," she said. "Have you considered how little we really have to move? One truck

load! You'd better think twice, Marjorie. It will be quite a
comedown to go into a big house and see our few sticks
rattling around in those big rooms, after the luxurious
home you've always had. When you get back to Chicago
you'll see the difference right away from this little old
dump."

Marjorie smiled.

"I'll see the difference all right. I wish I could take you
all with me, but I know you wouldn't like that, any of
you."

"Dear, you're going to mind giving up that lovely house
aren't you? But it doesn't just seem right for us to go
there, if we decide to be together. Mrs. Wetherill's friends
would criticize," said the mother.

"No, of course not!" said Marjorie briskly. "But anyway
I like Brentwood best."

They talked of other things before they went to bed,
and had a happy time together, although they were all
quiet, thoughtful. The shadow of the testing time that was
coming had already fallen upon them.

The next morning after the breakfast work was done
Marjorie wrote to the servants. She would be at home two
days after New Year's. Then she had a talk with Betty.

"You and I should go shopping," she said. "I want to
watch you buy some pretty things for yourself, and there
are things the children ought to have."

Betty, nothing loath, consented.

"We can go tomorrow," she said. "Father says his work
on those books will be finished then and he can stay home.
Anyway Mother feels so much better now that she will be
all right with the children. If it only weren't for Bud. He'll
drag in a goat or a rabbit or something from the street
and wash it in the dishpan again, I suppose. He does think
of the most impossible things to do."

"We'll talk to Bud and put him on his honor. I'll promise him a crossing light for his train if he cares for them
all beautifully."

"You mustn't begin by giving him everything he wants
or he'll be utterly spoiled," warned Betty.

"No, I won't, but this is a special time, holidays, and
Mother not well, you know."

"Mother won't be really well till this thing is settled,"
said Betty with pursed lips.

"No, I suppose not," said Marjorie with a sigh, "but I don't know what to do. They would have it this way."

"I know," said Betty with a sigh, "I guess it's right, too. You oughtn't to be tied down by us."

"You don't suppose I feel that way about it, do you?"

"Well, maybe you don't now, but you might sometime." Marjorie smiled.

"You'll see!"

So they went shopping.

They had a lovely time and bought a lot of fascinating things. Betty said it was Christmas all over again.

She looked very pretty as she waited for Marjorie who had gone to another part of the store to get Bud's signal light. She watched the throng of shoppers, well-dressed and happy, moving by. She was conscious of looking just as well as any of them. Fur coat and chic little hat, new gloves, and trim shoes. She had never been so handsomely dressed in her life. She glowed all over with comfort and satisfaction, and her cheeks had a pretty pink that was very becoming.

Just then a long, lank, sallow youth with a daredevil in his eye, and a loose handsome mouth, brought up standing before Betty and gave her a long admiring stare.

"Well, some baby-doll!" he exclaimed. "Am I seeing aright? Is this my onetime co-laborer in Old Jamison's musty office, or is it some millionaire's daughter?"

XVIII

It was Ellery Aiken, who had been in the office where Betty worked before her mother was taken sick. It was he to whom Ted had referred as a "poor sap."

He grasped her hand in a long lingering clasp that expressed as much as the languishing look in his bold eyes.

Betty was delighted. Here was a chance to show off her fur coat where it would be appreciated. Here was a chance to impress the young man who hadn't taken the trouble to come and see her after she moved. She had never been quite sure that Ted had not had something to do with that.

But now here he was and taking in her changed appearance!

She lifted her chin proudly and smiled, and he let his eyes linger on her pretty face with that intimate glance that all the girls usually fell for. A kind of triumph filled Betty's heart. She hadn't lost her power over him yet.

"Well, beautiful, you're lovelier than ever. Where did you get the glad rags? Struck oil or anything?" His eyes roved boldly over her garments as if he had a right.

"How about a date, Baby?" he asked. "Got anything doing tonight or tomorrow night? How'd you like to do the round with me? Little supper, dance, and go the rounds of the night clubs? Like to show you something real."

Betty flushed proudly and her eyes sparkled. Ellery had never asked her out before. She suspected that it was because her clothes were plain and worn. But now he wanted her, did he? Well, he would have to ask humbly. With a coat and hat like that she could afford to be the least bit haughty.

"Thanks, that's kind of you," she answered trying to feign an indifference she did not feel. It was going to her head to have attention. Two young men in one week, even if one had taken her to church!

Of the two dates she preferred the night clubs.

Of course the doctor was much higher class than Ellery, who was only a subordinate with a very small salary, but she had always secretly yearned to see a real night club, and she had heard Ellery boast of his intimate acquaintance with them. "I don't just know what free time I shall have the next few days," she said casually. "My twin sister is visiting us. I wouldn't feel like leaving her."

"Twin sister!" said the young man deeply impressed. "Lead me to her! Is she as pretty as you are, Baby?"

"People say we are alike," said Betty with a toss of her head.

"All right, bring her along," said the Lochinvar graciously. "Be delighted to entertain you both. Just phone me at the office and name the night and I'll be ready to go."

"Well, I'll talk to my sister," said Betty, flattered as she could be. Poor Betty had been bitter that she could not have nice things and go out like other girls.

Marjorie was longer being waited on than she had expected, and young Ellery's lunch hour was over-past, so he left a minute or two before Marjorie arrived, but Betty's cheeks were still blazing proudly and her eyes shining.

"You just missed meeting an old friend of mine," said Betty.

"Oh, I'm sorry. Who was it?"

"Oh, just a fellow that worked in the same office with me on my last job. Maybe you wouldn't have thought much of him, but he's awfully good-looking. He's asked us to go out with him some evening this week. I told him you were here and he's crazy to meet you. Would you like to go? His name's Ellery Aiken."

Marjorie had a sudden memory of Ted saying "he's a poor sap from the office where she used to work." Could this be the same one?

"Why, that's very kind of him," she faltered. What

should she do? Not antagonize Betty if she could help it, of course. Maybe she ought to go along and find out what kind of a person he was. Ted might be prejudiced, of course. Boys were, sometimes. "Where is he going to take us?"

"Why, he'll take us somewhere to supper and then the round of the night clubs," said Betty enthusiastically. "He knows them all. I've heard him talk about them at the office. He's awfully good-looking, and very popular—" Betty's knowledge of Ellery's popularity was mainly gleaned from his own words— "and he knows the ropes all around places. We'll really see things!"

"Night clubs!" said Marjorie in a dismay she could not keep out of her voice. "Oh, my dear! Do you go to night clubs?"

"I've never been, but I've always been crazy to see one. Why? Don't you like them?" She almost glared at Marjorie. Was Marjorie going to high-hat her now when she had been so pleased that she had a social advantage to offer her?

"I've never been to a night club of course, but I don't think I would care to go," she said gently.

"But if you've never been how do you know you don't like them?"

"Why, I shouldn't care to go among people who are drinking," said Marjorie with a troubled look at her pretty sister.

"Drinking! Why, for pity's sake, you wouldn't have to drink if you didn't want to, would you? And anyway, everybody drinks in society today. It isn't courteous not to drink, I've heard."

"*Every*body doesn't drink, Betty, not in the society I know, and we were well acquainted with some of the nicest people in Chicago. None of them drank. Of course Mrs. Wetherill was particular about the people she was intimate with. She just didn't go with that kind of people."

"For pity's sake! Why not? Was she very religious?"

"No, I wouldn't call her religious. She went to church of course, but she did not say much about religious things. I wish she had said more. I grew up without much idea of such things except that it was respectable to go to church. But the churches she picked out were rather cold and uninteresting. Lovely services and excellent music of course, and nice people there, but—no, I wouldn't say she was religious. She just didn't like to be with people who drank. She didn't think it was nice. She didn't like fast society. We were rather quiet people, you know!"

"For pity's sake, and I've been envying you all the chances you've had to see life."

"But I don't believe that's life, Betty," said Marjorie thoughtfully. "The people I've seen who go in for that sort of thing look to me more as if they'd been seeing death than life. It always fills me full of horror to see people under the influence of liquor."

"Oh, I don't mean really drunk," said Betty glibly, "people don't need to drink too much."

"Don't they? I wonder why so many of them do, then!"

"Oh, you don't see so many drunk! They're only a little gay. They say a little drink or two makes you bright and interesting."

"It makes people utterly silly," said Marjorie, "and entirely disgusting. I've seen girls coming home from parties, sometimes in the public railroad station, acting like fools. If they could once have a picture of how they looked and see it when they were sober, I shouldn't think they'd ever be able to hold up their heads again!"

"Then you won't go?" said Betty vexedly.

"No, Betty, I couldn't. I wouldn't feel at home in a night club."

"I didn't know you were strait-laced."

"Is that strait-laced? I thought it was only a kind of refinement. Just plain decency."

"Well, I'm sure most young people do those things today. All except fanatical people. Religious cranks, you know."

"I guess a good many do," said Marjorie, "but I don't like such things. I can't help it. I've never been religious or fanatical that I know of. But I just don't like a letting go of the fine things of life. It seems to me that people who do things like that are just letting go of everything worthwhile."

"Oh, heavens! You sound just for all the world like Ted!" said Betty almost angrily. "Here I thought I had something nice, to show you a good time, and you've spoiled it all."

"I'm sorry, Betty, but I couldn't help it. I couldn't go to

places like that. I just wouldn't belong. I wouldn't feel it was the right thing."

Betty sulked almost all the way home, with stormy eyes averted, looking out the other side of the taxi. At last as they were nearing home Marjorie said sadly:

"Well, now I suppose you won't want me to come back and live with you, since you've found out I don't agree with you on the way to have a good time."

"Oh, forget it!" said Betty unhappily. "I suppose I've been terribly disagreeable to you again, and you won't want to come back. But I can't help it, I've always wanted to have a good time, and I've always wanted to go to a night club."

Marjorie looked at her earnestly.

"I don't believe you'd really like such things, Betty. I think you'd be disappointed."

"How do you know if you've never been there?"

"I know the kind of people who go to such places. In fact I know personally a few, that is, they are not my *friends*, but they are acquaintances, and—well they are not like you, Betty. I think you really like fine lovely things, not wild hard-boiled places and people who are just out to do some new crazy thing and find a new thrill, no matter how dangerous. or unconventional it is. Oh, Betty, dear, I don't know how to talk about such things, but I just feel they are not the thing for you and me to do. They are not things that our mother and father would approve, at least it seems that way to me."

"They belong to another generation," pouted Betty.

"What difference does that make? The world is the same in any generation, and human life is the same. Good and bad are the same. Kicking over pleasant helpful rules and running wild doesn't change results."

Then they reached home. and Betty with a sigh went in and took off her beautiful finery. That night before they went to sleep she had the grace to apologize to Marjorie for being disagreeable after Marjorie had got her so many lovely things.

But Marjorie lay wakeful through several hours, and in her heart began to pray for her sister, the first prayer she had ever made for anybody else.

It troubled her, too, that they had found a point of disagreement. What if they came to live together and found more and more that their ways differed! Would it make life unhappy for them all? Was this one of the things that her father and mother wished her to consider before deciding whether or not to cast in her lot with her family?

But then other families must differ. What did they do? They didn't go off and live away from home because they differed, at least not many of them, not nice people. They learned to adjust their differences, and to help one another to find the right values, and make a happy home for all. Wasn't that what God had meant people should do? How she would like to talk it over with Gideon Reaver!

And then she suddenly realized that he was one very strong reason for her coming to live with her parents. She wanted to hear Gideon preach. She wanted to learn more of the way of Life. She wanted to be able to ask him a lot of questions. Not just once, but many times. She wanted to learn to study the Bible in the right way, the way Ted said was so interesting.

If it should come about that as her parents suggested, she should meet with hindrances and find her way hedged from coming back, would she ever meet one again who could tell her more about the things of God? Perhaps Gideon Reaver knew of someone in Chicago who talked and thought as he did. She would ask him.

But no, she would not admit even so much the possibility that she was not coming back. She must come back. Her heart cried out for her dear family. She must know them better. And she must somehow try to help this precious sister Betty, if indeed she was in danger as Ted seemed to imply. How she wished she could talk it over with the young minister! That was what a minister was for, to help people about things like that. He would keep her confidence she was sure. He had such a wonderful face, so full of peace and yet so strong. He seemed to walk with God so closely. How she wished she might walk with God and find out daily His will. She must learn more about it before she went away, for she could not bear to wait even a week, or a few weeks, without knowing. It seemed a long time to waste.

The little book that Gideon had brought her was a great comfort, though she had found very little time in which to even look it over. It had references to Bible passages to read and study. He probably did not dream she had no Bible with her. She must get hers out as soon as she got back to Chicago and begin reading it. That would be another thing she must ask him, how to study the Bible.

But in this little crowded house with so many daily tasks there was little time to read, and no place to read alone, nor to pray free from interruption. And Marjorie was shy about prayer, it was all so new to her. Oh, she was used to kneeling beside her bed and going through a routine petition, and that she had done the first night she slept with Betty, without a thought but that Betty would likely kneel also. It was the conventional thing she had been brought up to do, and it had meant nothing but a form until she had heard Gideon Reaver and Ted talk about being saved. But now prayer had taken on a different look. She wanted time and quiet to look into the face of the Lord and ask Him what to pray for. Perhaps the Holy Spirit was already beginning to teach her things that she had never dreamed of before, things that many an older Christian had not yet looked into.

It came to her to wonder if God might not Himself do something about Betty and this Ellery person who seemed to be going to appear on Betty's path again. She couldn't see anything else she could do immediately but ask God about it. It wouldn't do to tell even Ted, for he might talk to Betty and make her angry and do more harm than good. Brothers did that sometimes, though Ted seemed to be unusually wise for his years.

She fell asleep at last thinking of that happy Christmas day, and how well all of them seemed to fit together. What nice friends those two young men had been, what delightful company! And what a pity that Evan hadn't been able to see how fine and wonderful they all were! Evan had fine things about him too, but in another line. Would she ever be able to make him understand the great thing that had come to her life through the last few days? How utterly he had misunderstood her when she had tried to ask him about being saved. Was she ever going to feel toward Evan as she ought to feel if she were going to marry him? Well, she was still not ready to face that question. She must put it off till she got back home and then she would take time from everything and settle once and for all whether she could ever love Evan Brower. At present it seemed such a troublesome question. And yet Evan was fine and good and respectable, and her foster mother would have been altogether pleased with such a match. That her own father and mother would not approve him she somehow knew without asking. Oh, why did Evan have to act so disagreeable when he came here on Christmas Day? Why did he have to come then anyway, just when they were having such a wonderful time, and Heaven seemed so near? He had made a false note, a harsh jarring note in the harmony of the occasion!

Oh, if Evan could only be more like those other two! Like the young minister!

And then she fell asleep and dreamed that it was Gideon Reaver who had sat across from her at the hotel table and handed her the blue diamond and watched her while she opened the box. Even in her dream a thrill of joy went through her heart. And then in the dream they seemed to lose the blue diamond and could not find it, but it didn't matter. They were happy even without it.

When she awoke in the morning the first part of the dream was vivid, and the thrill in her heart was there whenever she thought of it, but it was Gideon Reaver's eyes who looked into hers above the blue diamond, and not Evan Brower's eyes, and that troubled her. She must not allow her thoughts to wander off to absurd things like that. As if Gideon Reaver had any special interest in her, a stranger to offer her diamonds, and touch her hands with that strange wonderful thrill. It was Evan Brower who had offered the diamond, and Evan Brower and his pleas whom she would have to face when she got back to Chicago.

But meantime, she could not and would not consider him. And she must put away all thoughts of that ridiculous dream or else she would never be able to face Gideon Reaver again and ask him the questions about things she so longed to understand. It seemed a profanation to approach him even in her thoughts, in any more intimate way. A man like that was set apart to holy things. His love would be a wonderful treasure to possess, but it was not to be sought after even in thought. The girl whom such a man would love would not dream of presuming to hope for his love. It was something he must bestow, it was not to be won by human arts.

So she put it by, and although she could not help the thoughts recurring, she decided she could help entertaining them, and she was determined to keep this friendship upon a sane, healthy footing. It was a privilege just to have met him, and to have learned at his feet.

So the morning came and Marjorie arose with a gladness in her heart that promised better things even through a perplexing way.

XIX

BUT Betty had slipped down to the store on some pretext a little after nine that morning and telephoned Ellery Aiken in the office She told him that her sister could not come and therefore she would not be able to. But she had finally let him persuade her that she could come for just a little while. He told her that he wanted to show her a good time, and had some friends he knew she would like to meet.

She came back to the house with a shamefaced look, and worked madly all day doing little extras for everybody, to make up for what she meant to do that evening.

After the dishes were done that night she hurried upstairs and came down in the pretty velvet dress that Marjorie had bought her. She had been careful to wait until Ted had gone out and her father was safely upstairs with her mother. who was still supposed to rest a good deal and go to bed very early.

Marjorie looked up surprised.

"How lovely you look. dear. Are you going out?"

"Why, yes," said Betty apologetically, "I have to, just a little while. I'm sorry to go when you have so few nights left, but I really couldn't get out of it very well. But I'll be home early. However. don't sit up for me if you are tired. Good-bye. I'm enjoying my pretty clothes a lot."

Marjorie looked after her in dismay, her heart sinking. Was she really going out with that young man Aiken?

Going to the night clubs after all? But—who had come for her? The doorbell hadn't rung.

Marjorie slipped into the dark parlor and looked out the window. A shabby little runabout was just pulling away from the door. Betty must have been watching for him out the window and gone down at once. They must have had an agreement that he would not ring the bell. She turned from the window and went sadly back to the children whom she was about to take up to bed when Betty came down. She must pray a lot this evening. She wished Ted was at home to help. Or, should she tell Ted? What could he do anyway if he was here? Betty was gone! Poor foolish Betty!

Meantime Betty was discovering that Ellery Aiken was cross at her for not bringing her sister. He wanted to see her. Ellery was great for new girls. Also he sometimes got commissions from men he knew for bringing new attractive girls for the evening, and his exchequer was low just now.

Betty was disappointed too in the car he had brought. He had told her he had the use of a new car, but this one sounded like an old tin pan as it rattled along. Somehow she began to suspect that the evening was going to be as cheap as the car. But she roused herself to throw off her conscience and forget her discomfort at the way she had stolen out and what Marjorie would think about her, and tried to be gay.

It had never seemed to her before that Ellery was coarse. She had always thought him extremely amusing, but tonight he seemed to select the most questionable stories on his list to tell her, and when she did not respond warmly to his mirth he looked at her sharply.

"What's the matter, Baby? Getting high-hat with your glad rags? You better get warmed up or you won't go down a little bit where I'm taking you. I've got a fella wants ta meet ya, some swell! Got millions! Always ready ta spend it on the right kind of a girl. But you gotta be a little interested when he talks. You can't just sit around like a marvelous icicle all the evening. You've gotta get busy and be conversational if you wantta be popular."

Betty was suddenly a little frightened.

"I thought I was going with you, Ellery. I didn't know there were other men along. Perhaps I wouldn't care to meet them!"

"Wouldn't care to meet 'em! What's gettin' ya? Whatcha goin' for, then? You didn't suppose we were just goin' ta sit around and hold hands all the evening together, did ya? I've got other girls ta dance with. I can't just stay with you, ya know."

Ellery didn't state that he was paid by the club to dance with other girls, but that was really the case.

Betty was still a long time. The little tin car was rattling along at a lively pace, screeching its horn at every crossing. Ellery was late. Betty had been slow in coming down in answer to his signal. She had waited to be sure that her mother's door was shut before she slipped down the stairs. Now she began to be greatly troubled. At last she said a trifle haughtily,

"I think perhaps you'd better take me home again, Ellery. I don't think I care to go, after all."

"Aw, you gettin' cold feet, are you? But you don't get out of it now, Baby. I haven't time to run you back and forth while you change your mind a dozen times. Besides, I promised to bring this guy a pretty girl, prettiest girl he's ever seen, and I've got to deliver the goods."

"But I don't care to go with a stranger, Ellery!" she cried aghast. "I had no idea—"

Ellery saw that he was going to have trouble and he had no time for that, so he set himself to soothe her.

"Now, Baby, don't you worry! It's going to be marvelous! You said you wanted ta see the night clubs and I've arranged to give you an eyeful. You just trust me and I'll see you through the evening. B'lieve me you'll be glad you did! It isn't every gal that will get all the attention I'm aiming to have for you. You're some sweetie! I'm proud to be escorting ya! Of course I appreciate your wanting to be with me exclusive, but it can't be done. You're expected to be social and affable and all that, you know. And we have ta be like the rest. But you'll like it, Baby, b'lieve me! You take my word for it, you'll like it!"

Betty felt a strange cold draught about her heart. She was growing more and more frightened. Ellery strung his long arm around her shoulders and drew her up close to him, but she drew away again and sat up very straight.

" 'S the matter, Babe? Ain't sore, are ya?" he said as he brought the car up in front of a sordid looking place. Betty had expected to see glitter in a night club, but this place looked fairly grubby, the more so as they entered. It was blue with smoke. This was a different world, right enough. She shrank back at the door, but he pushed her forward.

"Right over here, Baby! Got a table reserved for four. Nice party! Other girl's real refined. You'll like her. Sit down. We'll have a little cocktail to start things going and get us warmed up."

Betty sat down fearfully and looked about her. She didn't care for the look of the men in the place. Surely this could not be one of the nicer places. She met bold intimate glances appraising her, and shrank in her soul. The women wore more makeup than she liked. It gave them a hard look. Perhaps the haze of smoke that hung over everything emphasized it.

Ellery ordered cocktails, and when they came Betty tried to keep her hand from trembling as she raised the glass to her lips. She must not let Ellery see that this was her first taste of liquor.

But the fumes of it were anything but pleasant to her unspoiled senses, and she didn't care particularly for the taste She kept thinking of what Marjorie had said about drinking Still, she kept taking little sips, scarcely more than touching her lips to the glass sometimes. She didn't like the strange stinging sensation. It frightened her. It sent a tingling down her arms and quickened her heartbeats.

Ellery tossed his off, and ordered another, chided her for being so abstemious.

"Plenty more where this came from, Babe!" he said jovially, so loud that people at the other tables heard him and laughed. They called out remarks over her head. He knew everybody.

They began to come over to be introduced, and Betty didn't feel at home among them They were of another world. She felt herself growing haughty. Ellery kidded her about it.

"You're too high-hat, Betts!" he shouted genially. "Just because you've got a new fur coat doesn't crown you queen!"

Ellery had finished his drink now and reached over and took her glass.

"Here, I'll finish yours and you can get a fresh glass. Waiter, here, double it for us both!"

But Ellery was not himself. He must have been drinking

before he came for her. His loud excited voice seemed to rasp through her sensitive nerves.

Then the other two of the party arrived. A small dark girl with no back to her dress. She had vivid coloring, and her black hair was plastered wickedly to her head with points on her cheeks. She looked Betty over and raised what eyebrows she had left, pursing her lips amusedly. Betty felt herself weighed and found wanting. It made her angry. What was this girl?

The man with her was overweight with a bulging stomach and heavy bags under his small eyes. But the eyes twinkled when they saw Betty. He kept them on her for a full minute and she felt as if he had seen into her soul. She barely kept herself from shuddering. She loathed him. He wore an enormous diamond on his little finger. Another in his tie. His lips were thick and fulsome.

More drinks were brought, and some food. But Betty had no wish for food now, and she lifted her glass only now and then to keep up a semblance of drinking so they would not call attention to her. The floor show that was presently put on was almost a relief to Betty, though in spite of its glitter she was soon disgusted with the girls. In her guarded life she had never seen such girls close by before. But the show did not take the eyes of the men from herself, and she was fairly sickened by the gloating in their faces as they watched.

After the show Ellery asked the other girl if she would like to dance and she arose and floated off with her head on his breast, her cheek to his, till they disappeared in the maze of tables.

Left alone with the other man Betty was terribly frightened. But she mustn't let him see it, of course. She must try to think of something to talk about until Ellery came back, and then she would demand that he take her home at once. But she couldn't think of a thing to say, and the man was looking at her. She hated that. Of course looks, just *looks,* couldn't really *hurt* you, but she felt so ashamed to be sitting there! How terrible if her father, or Ted could see her!

But she must shake this feeling off. Perhaps it only came from hearing Marjorie talk. She had wanted a try at this and now she was getting it, she must accredit herself well. Somehow she must get out of here, and never, never let her family know what she had gone through.

The man asked her to dance but she shook her head.

"Thank you, no, I don't feel like dancing," she said languidly.

He offered her cigarettes but she shook her head.

He looked at her puzzled.

"What are you, anyway? Don't wantta dance, don't wantta smoke, don't wantta drink. Guess you're a kind of a frost, aren't you?"

"Yes," said Betty trying to keep her lips from trembling, "that's what I am, a frost! That's what I'm trying to be—a frost!"

He gave her another puzzled look.

"You're deep! That's what you are, you're deep!" he decided.

"Yes," said Betty quickly, "I'm deep. I'm deep water frozen over!"

"Well," said the man lifting his weight and moving his chair nearer to her, "I've got to look into this. I've got to get to the bottom of this and melt the ice. Let's have a friendly little drink. Here, try my glass. Make it all the better kick for me to drink after you." To her horror his massive arm came out around her shoulders and he lifted his own glass to her lips.

She was on the point of screaming, but she cast a quick wild look about her and realized that she was on her own. This was the sort of thing that was common in this joint. It certainly wasn't the kind of night club she had dreamed about. But whatever it was she must work her own way out, for it was evident nobody else, not even Ellery, was going to help her out. She must use her wits, and she wouldn't get herself anywhere by screaming either.

She suddenly slid her chair away from the encircling arm and the offered glass, and looked at the man with what she frantically hoped was a bright smile.

"I'll tell you what you can do," she said with a shaky little voice that was trying to be gay, "You go and find Ellery Aiken for me and tell him I've been taken sick. Tell him I want him right away!"

He stared at her a minute and laughed.

"Is thish some joke?" he asked. He wasn't exceedingly keen or he would have seen that she was frightened. But then he had been drinking freely and he was somewhat foggy in his perceptions.

"No!" she said sharply. "It's true! I'm sick! Get Ellery for me quick!"

He studied her stupidly another minute and then he said:

"All rightie, darling, if you shay its sho it musht be sho! I'll do my besht!" He got up and tottered off, but then to her horror he turned back again and leaning over her chair said:

"You wouldn't razyer I'd take you home, m'shelf?"

"No, thank you!" she said drawing a deep breath and feeling suddenly faint. The world seemed whirling under her.

But he went off and was lost among the dancers.

He was gone a long time, but she wasn't alone. The informality of the place amazed her. Other men came and sat at her table, tried to get her to dance, to smoke, to drink, and it seemed hours before she finally saw Ellery steering toward her.

She had done her best with the ring of admirers that had come, laughed and talked with them in a dizzy whirl of nothings, told them all she was too tired to dance, and didn't want to drink or smoke. The truth was she was afraid. Terribly afraid. This wasn't the kind of thing she had envisioned when she had longed to go about to the night clubs. This must be a very low-down resort indeed. Her estimate of Ellery had gone down a good deal, yet she was glad to see his familiar form wending its way toward her, even though unsteadily.

"Wha's the matter, Baby? Didn'ya like the millionaire I got for ya, darling? Poor fish been taking too many drinks. I'll get ya 'nuther fella!"

"No, no! Ellery. I want to go home! I'm sick!" she shuddered and certainly did look sick.

"Aw, Baby! It isn't time ta go home. Not quite half past one yet! Never go home that soon! Take 'nuther drink, Baby, an' see if ya won't feel better. Get ya a nice drink!"

"No!" said Betty sharply. "Ellery, if you don't take me home at once I'll go by myself, and I'll tell the people at the office what kind of a place you brought me to!"

"Aw, Baby! Don't get harsh with me! I'm your own

dear Ellery! You wouldn't do that to me! Come on, Baby! Have it your own way then. We'll go home!"

She was glad she had insisted on keeping her coat with her when they came in. Ellery had a terrible time trying to find his overcoat and hat at the checking room, and finally went off with one that didn't belong to him, but she didn't realize until she was down in the car and they were starting off, that Ellery was really drunk. She wasn't used to drunken men. She didn't know what strange things they could do. But when she saw the car start off with a leap and a shock she was more frightened than she had ever been in her life. She wished that she had stolen away without Ellery, after the fat man had left her. She might have had a terrible time in finding her way out of this strange part of the city, but somewhere she could have found a policeman to direct her. She would have had to walk home, for she had not thought to bring any money with her when she came, but anything would have been better than this!

Oh, if she could only get out and run away from this maniac. He was driving like mad, whirling around corners, into alleys and backing out again. The car lurched, and rode over a curbstone, jolting down again, and on around another corner. She dared not ask him if he knew where he was going. She had no knowledge herself of the part of town where they were now.

At last he came up with a jerk under a street sign.

"You read that shine fer me, Baby!" he cajoled. "Hurts my eyes ta read in this light. Is that Ahster Street? We wanta go ta Ahster Street, don't we?"

At last in her terror she begged him to let her out.

"I can easily walk from here," she said, trying to speak pleasantly, though her heart was beating wildly.

"Na, na, can't let ya out. Never let a lady down that way!" said the drunken knight "We'll jusht drive a little farther. P'raps we'll find Ahster Street! Never let a lady out on streetsh at this time a-night. I'm a gentleman if I am drunk!"

He put his foot on the starter and they whirled away like a streak again, Betty trying to still the wild beating of her heart and wishing she knew how to pray!

They were going at such a wild pace now that Betty felt that every moment might be her last. Past red lights they dashed on, and the tears rolled down Betty's cheeks as she gripped the seat and tried to keep her balance.

There were not many cars on the road so late, else they must have come to disaster almost at once. But perhaps some guardian angel was at work protecting Betty.

They had gone a long way. Betty could not tell in the darkness now just where they were, but she steadied her voice and cried out.

"Here! Here! Isn't this Aster Street? Yes, let's stop here! This will do nicely."

"This it? Okay by me! Let's just park awhile an' get a little sleep. Baby!" said the gallant knight, bringing his car up to the curb with such a flourish that he mounted the curb and headed right into the pole that held the street sign.

"Whoa, there, Lizzie!" he called out as he swayed in his seat and put on the brakes. "Pardon me, shir! Shorry ta run ya down, but couldn't be helped. Gotta get a l'il shleep!"

Betty thought the end was coming, and she had a wild thought of her mother, wondering who would tell her. The next second came the shock and she was thrown to her knees with her head against the dashboard of the car, stunned for the minute. Then her senses returned and she could hear Ellery talking, apologizing over and over to the sign post.

"Didn't mean ta disturb ya, shir, just hadta get a little rest. Sure, I'm okay. Not hurt. Fresh as a rose an' twicesh as happy!" and Ellery slumped down in his corner and settled himself for a nap.

But Betty, frightened and bruised and trembling, managed to get the car door open and stumble out to the street.

She looked wildly back at Ellery, but he was unconscious of her presence. Already he was drawing long loud breaths in a drunken sleep. Then she fled up the dark street. She did not know where she was, and her legs under her were very shaky, but she must get away before Ellery came to himself and realized that she had gone. She was more afraid of him now than of any death that could come to her.

Keith Sheridan coming home that evening from a hard drive which had taken him into the country on a road that

had a long rough detour, turned into the city at last with a
sigh of relief. He was tired out and needed a good night's
rest. He had done two operations that day, and had a patient who was going to die, and his nerves were on edge.

As he turned a corner he noticed a car ahead of him
being crazily driven, turning a corner on two wheels and
tearing madly away. A block farther on the same car
came around another corner straight at him, and he barely
avoided a collision. He swerved away from the catastrophe
and looked ahead to where the car was dashing up on the
sidewalk. He heard the crash of the pole and the splin-
tered glass of a windshield, heard a girl's voice cry out in
fear, and then silence!

Quickly he drove to the spot to see if anyone was hurt.
He stopped his car and listened. He heard a man talking,
but there seemed to be no girl, and he was about to drive
on, when suddenly he saw a stealthy form like a shadow
slip out the other door of the car and topple up the street
in the shadow of the houses.

He started his car slowly again and followed, watching.
It was a woman! Was there something familiar about the
way she walked? No, she was almost staggering. She must
be drunk! And yet—maybe it was someone in distress. He
drove his car slowly and followed for another block.

And now Betty was aware of a car, and tried to hurry
faster. Blindly she ran, then caught her toe in a brick of
the pavement and fell prostrate.

For a minute the breath was knocked from her body so
that she thought she was dying, and then she felt someone
lift her, and she froze with horror again. Had Ellery run
after her and caught her? Oh, she wished that she had
died! Rather anything than to be in his power again.

The doctor lifted her very tenderly and looked into her
face, gently lifted one of her eyelids, and in the flare of a
street light Betty suddenly recognized him.

"Oh, Doctor, Doctor, you won't tell Mother, will you?"
she gasped. "It would kill Mother to know I had done
this!" And suddenly Betty burst into a flood of tears and
buried her face in the breast of the doctor's big fur-lined
overcoat.

"Betty! Is it you, dear child!" The doctor's voice was
very tender, and he held her close in his arms an instant
looking quickly up and down the street. Not a soul in

sight that minute, but a car was coming around the second corner above.

He quickly strode with her in his arms to his car, and put her in, shutting the door quickly and hurrying around to get in himself and start the car. He rounded the next corner and drove straight ahead for several blocks. Then he stopped in a quiet street and reaching out drew the still sobbing Betty closer to him putting her head down on his shoulder comfortably.

"You won't tell Mother!" pleaded Betty between the sobs.

"No, of course not, dear child! Now tell me all about it!"

"Oh—I went out—with a young man from the office. —I thought he was all right— He was going to take me to a night club!" Betty was talking very fast, trying to get her breath and tell a coherent story, but her sobs interrupted her.

"He took me—to a dreadful place! It was awful! Everybody was drunk!—I was frightened. I made him bring me home. But I found he was drunk too! He wouldn't stop— and let me out—!"

She gave way in another burst of tears, and he put both arms about her and held her close again, as if he were comforting a little child.

"Oh, I'm so—so—glad you came! I thought he was— chasing--me!"

Keith Sheridan's face suddenly went white and his lips touched for an instant the hot wet lashes that lay on the wet cheeks.

"*And so am I glad!*" he whispered.

Then suddenly he drew his handkerchief from his inside pocket and softly patted her face dry from the tears.

"There," he said in a matter-of-fact voice, "now let's get going! The sooner we get home the less for anybody to worry about. No, of course we won't tell Mother. Now, put your head down on my shoulder and rest and forget it. It's going to be all right. I'd like to get out and whale that friend of yours, but I guess I'd better confine my efforts to getting you home. If he's only drunk he can look after himself. I heard him talking to the sign post as I came by. Now, cheer up, little girl, and don't try to talk about it. I'll fix things up at home for you. Straighten up your face and put on a grin and we'll face 'em out. Ready? Here we are at Aster Street!"

He helped her out most tenderly and went up the steps with her.

The door opened at once and a much scared Ted stood behind it, white with anxiety. Marjorie in a dark robe stood just behind him and their relief when they saw the doctor was almost amusing.

"I brought her home. I hope you didn't worry," the doctor said comically. "She preferred my company to the fellow she started out with, and the pleasure was all mine. I hope I haven't worried you by keeping her out so long. I'll promise never to do so again. But she's been a little worried and I guess you'd better put her right to bed and not ask her questions tonight. She's pretty tired."

"Okay!" said Ted gravely, his face relaxing from its anxious strain. And Marjorie put her arm around her sister and led her upstairs softly. The father and mother were sound asleep with the door shut and hadn't heard a thing.

Betty closed the door softly, faced around toward her sister, and spoke in a low shamed tone:

"Marjorie, I've got to tell you that you were right, and I'm ashamed! I don't know whether it was a regular night club I went to or not, but even if it wasn't, even if night clubs are a great deal different from that one, I *never* want to see one as long as I live! And I never want to see Ellery Aiken again either! I'm cured! And I want you to forgive me for the way I went away and left you, and for the hateful things I said to you."

Marjorie put her arms around her sister and kissed her lovingly.

"You precious sister! There wasn't anything to forgive. I'm only so thankful you are safe home again. Now, don't think another thing about it tonight. Get to sleep as soon as you can."

XX

THEY were just sitting down to breakfast the next morning when a messenger came to the front door with a special delivery letter for Mr. Gay.

His hand trembled as he took the letter which Betty handed him, and the family were utterly still while he opened it. He couldn't understand who would be writing him an emergency letter unless those sharks who took his house away from him before were trying to work some trick again. Marjorie noticed that he was deadly white as he pulled the letter out of its envelope.

Then, as he read, a new look dawned on his face. A look of self-respect in place of the dejection that had been making the corners of his mouth droop habitually.

At last he laid it down on the table and looked at them all and they saw a light in his eyes, and then the light grew till it spread over his whole face.

"Read it, Mother," he said, his voice husky with feeling as he handed the letter over to his wife. "Read it aloud!" and there was a ring of triumph and relief in his voice.

The letter head was of a well known and respected firm in the city.

"Mr. George Gay,
1465 Aster Street,
        City.
My dear Mr. Gay:
    Having known of your connections with the former firm of Hamilton, McIvor and Company, and being in need of the

right man to head our accounting department, we are writing to know whether you are at present open for a position, and whether you would like to come to our office any time this week between the hours of two-thirty and four to talk over our suggestions?

Hoping to hear from you at your earliest convenience,

Very truly yours,

Martin Heath & Company."

Mr. Gay's face was a study in deepening joy as he listened to his wife pronounce the words he had just read, scarcely crediting the evidence of his own eyes and ears.

"Oh! George!" His wife beamed at him, a look such as she must have given him on her wedding day, a look so full of trust and triumph that at last his ability had received recognition.

"Oh, Father!" said Betty her face all shining with relief and happiness.

Marjorie realized that she hadn't understood till then how terrible it had been for her father, and also for the others, to have the beloved father out of a job. Her own heart was throbbing with gladness too. But she mustn't let them see how relieved she was, how thankful to the two lawyers who had helped to bring this about!

In due time the letter was passed to her to read and she rejoiced with the others, noting secretly how tactfully the letter was written, so as not to humiliate him as a man who was out of work, but bidding him to a place of honor, as one who had been accustomed to that place with others. It couldn't have been better. Sometime she would hunt up that lawyer Mr. Bryant, and thank him for his tact and skill in performing so perfectly a delicate task.

"And now," said the mother, when they had all got their breath again after their excitement, "you certainly will have to go downtown this morning the first thing and get yourself some new clothes. You simply can't present yourself the way you are. And now that you have the prospect of a position it needn't hurt your pride any longer."

Mr. Gay turned happy eyes on his eager wife:

"But you must remember, my dear, that I haven't got the position yet. Just getting a bid to come and talk about it may not mean a thing in the world. They may have seventeen others doing the same thing."

"That's all right, Father," spoke up Marjorie eagerly, "but you won't stand as much chance shabby, as you would if you were neatly dressed. Now, please, dear Father, use that check I gave you the other day. Use it now this morning. If it makes you feel any better you can pay me back the day you get to be a millionaire!"

"Fat chance!" said Ted, coming in the back door hungry as a bear, from his paper route.

They all laughed and then they had to tell Ted, and talk it all over again. till Betty roused to the toast and coffee and scrambled eggs that were getting cold, and they all began to eat. Mr. Gay ate hastily. seeming to enjoy every mouthful. and rose before the rest were through:

"Now, if you will excuse me," he said. "I'll run down to the city and get those new clothes that you all insist upon, and then I'm going right over to Martin Heath's. I'm not letting any grass grow under my feet—I mean snow."

"Get something ready-made, George," advised his wife, "and put it on at the store You can send your old things up. Don't think of going without decent clothes."

"That's what I'm going to do." said Mr. Gay briskly, grinning at them all as he left the room and went upstairs.

When Mr. Gay had left for the city and Ted had gone on his busy way the house was tense with excitement.

"How are we ever to get through the day till he gets back?" said Betty, dropping down in a chair and gripping her hands together tightly till the knuckles showed white.

"Oh," said Marjorie quickly. "we have a lot to do! Mother is going to spend the morning writing out a list of things that need to be bought for the children right away, with full directions. And then she's to write another list of things that must be done before we move. Anything that has to be bought especially. I don't believe she ought to do much shopping herself. do you? In these days when things can be returned if they are not satisfactory you and I surely can buy what she wants.

"And while you are doing that, Mother, Betty and I are going to take a run out to Brentwood and look things over," went on Marjorie. "I want to see that plumber I had Ted send there to give an estimate for making everything shipshape and ready for immediate use. The man from the gas company will be there this morning too. I telephoned yesterday. And a man to put in the telephone.

Do you think you would mind being here with the children for a couple of hours? We thought we would take Bud with us. Then you won't have so much confusion."

Betty's face was bright with joy, and Bud shouted, "Oh Boy! I'm going back ta Brentwood!"

Mrs. Gay smiled her willingness.

"Only, dear, I don't think you ought to plan those things for us now when you're going to Chicago so soon. I'm getting much better and will be able to look after things myself pretty soon."

"So you shall, Mother, but I'm having the time of my life spending money just now, and if I left it all to you, you wouldn't spend any, you dear!" So she kissed her mother and she and Betty and Bud went joyously on their way.

Such a happy morning as they had! Betty stood in what had once been her own room at Brentwood and looked about like one who had been shut out of heaven for a long time and had just got back again!

"To think that your coming meant this, too, as well as yourself!" she exclaimed. "But say, Mother wanted me to find out which room you liked the best. She thought maybe you and I would like these connecting ones! That is —but I forgot—I mean, in case you don't decide to stay in Chicago!"

"Keep on forgetting, Betty!" said Marjorie. "That is all what the boys call bologny! I promised to go back and think it over, but I know now just as well as I will at the end of my week of probation what the answer will be. You don't think I could have a taste of a lovely big family like ours, and then want to go back to living alone, do you?"

Betty's face was still sober.

"But—Mother says you might get married, you know!"

"Well, not at present, sister mine, anyway!" laughed Marjorie.

"Oh, but you can't tell what might happen to change your mind!"

"Yes," put in Bud who had strayed into the room where they stood, "if that big mutt that sent you those pair-of-sites should put in his stuck-up tongue you can't tell what she'll do!"

"Buddie! What would Mother say if she heard you talk like that?"

"Well I don't care, he *is* a mutt! I heard Ted say so!" defended Bud. "Say. Betty, would there be any reason why I couldn't set up my 'lectric train in the attic here? That would make a swell place, and I could add to it bime-by and everything."

"Grand!" said Marjorie. "Let's go look!"

So the subject was dropped.

"After you're gone to Chicago, Marjorie," said Betty as they stood taking a last look around before they started home. "I'm going to get Ted to make a fire in the heater, and I'm coming up here with Bud every day and scrub floors and wash windows."

"That's too hard work for you, Betty, with all you have to do at home" said Marjorie, "I told Ted to look up a professional house cleaning firm and we'll have them clean the whole place But I was thinking perhaps you ought to come up every day to see that they are doing it right. You and Ted could come, and be sure every spot was being cared for just right."

"That would be great. But why waste money on house cleaning? If I can do anything I can do that."

"You would just get sick dear. It is a very large house. And besides for the present you have all the housework in Aster Street till Mother is perfectly well and can help. I aim to put the house in your hands ready for use. Then you'll find plenty of cleaning after that!"

"You're simply swell!" said Betty with a sigh of relief. "Will I ever get rich so I can do things for you?"

"Perhaps," smiled Marjorie, "but what difference does it make We'll have a good time anyway!"

When they got back they found their mother had the lists all ready.

"Tomorrow we'll go shopping!" said Marjorie.

There had been no word as yet from Mr. Gay, and of course the strain was still on. The wife went quietly on saying nothing about it, but they were all thinking of him.

"We gotta telephone already, up ta Brentwood," remarked Bud. "If we was up there now he could telephone and let us know what happened sooner."

"Well, we aren't," smiled his mother, "but it is going to

be nice to have a telephone again, although, dear, we could easily have gotten along without that."

Marjorie smiled.

"I shouldn't be happy about you a minute, Mother dear, unless there was a telephone. I only wish we had one here while I'm gone. Then it wouldn't be so bad to leave you alone. That was one reason why I wanted you to move at once. But I guess it is better to wait till I get back."

"Yes, dear,—if you come back!"

"I'm coming back!" said Marjorie with firmly set lips and a little twinkle of a smile. "And now, Mother, there's something I need your advice about. Will you promise to tell me honestly what you think I ought to do about something in Chicago?"

The mother gave her a quick startled look. Was this to be about the aristocratic insolent young man who came on Christmas Day?

"It's about my furniture, Mother," went on Marjorie, "the Wetherill furniture! The lawyer said he had a good offer for the house, and if I sell it, as I probably shall—for anyhow, whatever I did, I couldn't live in a great barracks alone with a retinue of servants—so if I sell it, what about the furniture? It's beautiful furniture, Mother, fine old walnut and mahogany, some of it very rare, some of it antique. I've always admired it. Some of it I wouldn't like to part with. All of it is very lovely. My piano, too. What shall I do, put it in storage out there, or over here. Or sell it somewhere, or give it away? I don't imagine it would bring much at a sale,—except the antiques,—and those are the ones I like the best. Mother, if I should live with you, would you hate to have me bring any of it into your house?"

"Hate!" said Betty who was listening wide-eyed, "I should say not! Why, Marjorie, Mother has done nothing else since she went to Chicago but tell us how wonderfully that house was furnished. When she talked about getting new things for Brentwood she would always say, 'I'd like to get a couch and chairs like those Mrs. Wetherill had! They were wonderful!'"

"Betty, dear!" reproached her mother.

"Well, you did, Mother. You gave us the idea that there wasn't anything more beautiful in the world than the furnishings of that house."

"Well, I felt that way," said the mother, "but I was never envious. It just seemed to me that it was the most ideal way for a house to be furnished one could ever have."

"Yes, but, Mother, that's not saying you would want another woman's furniture in your own home. We could sell these things and buy some more, letting you pick out just what you want," said Marjorie.

"Why, my dear, I don't think I have any feeling against those things. In fact it would be lovely to live amongst them. They aren't hers, any more, they are yours, as you said about your money. It would be foolish to have a dislike for them. I would be delighted to have them in the house and enjoy them. I mean that, dear! And if there is anything that you want to put away to keep, if you don't think you want to use it now, there is plenty of room to store great quantities of furniture over the garage at Brentwood. It would be foolish for you to pay storage! *If* you come, of course!"

"Yes, *if* I come," smiled Marjorie. "Mother dear, I'm thinking that it will all rest in your hands whether I come or stay there. Because, remember, you promised to write the truth to me too after you have thought it over. As for me I can't see that my mind will change a particle."

Then suddenly they heard Mr. Gay's step at the door and all else was forgotten.

He came in with a shining face.

"Well," he said, "I'm hired! Isn't it great? It isn't a job, it's a position. I'm head of the accounting department. I can't understand how it came about. It must be a miracle. But I feel as if I wanted to walk more softly before God all the rest of the days of my life because of this! I—haven't—served the Lord the way I started out to do when I was young. That's going to be different now!"

Ted had come in a few minutes before and now he stood in the doorway his face shining.

"Oh, Dad!" he said joyously.

Marjorie stole up beside Ted and reaching out gave his hand a little squeeze. Ted looked down at her and smiled.

"Isn't God good?" he murmured softly.

But Betty stood there staring thoughtfully at her father, and marveling at the response in her mother's face. Somehow there seemed to be depths in her mother's and father's characters that she had never sounded. It surprised her. Perhaps they knew more about life after all than she had dreamed.

XXI

SUDDENLY the time began to go by at a terrific speed. It was the day before New Year's and Marjorie was to leave the day after. The Gay household went about with sad excited countenances, and Mother shed furtive tears when no one was about. Bonnie and Sunny had a howling match when it all came over them. Bud said: "Aw, can you beat it? It's the limit! Why does she haveta go atall? Why c'n't Ted go get her things? Wha's she want uv things anyhow? We got enough." Betty worked tirelessly getting the nicest meals she knew how so that Marjorie would have pleasant memories.

Ted and Marjorie went out to Brentwood that afternoon to attend to a few things before Marjorie went, and they had a good talk together. It was the first chance they had had since they went to church the first Sunday, for Ted had been busy and there was always somebody else about. The second Sunday Mr. Gay had gone with them, and Bud. So now they had a good deal to say to each other. Marjorie told him about the transaction of the house and how she had done it. She gave him suggestions for things that might be done. There ought to be a fire while the cleaners were at work. There was some painting that should be done at once. Two or three rooms needed fresh paper. She told him to bring a book of samples from the paperhanger and let her mother and Betty choose what they wanted and then see that it was done as soon as possible.

They talked about their father and his going to church with them on Sunday. and what he had said when he came home from getting his job. They spoke of how wonderful God had been to give him that position just when he needed so to feel that he could still do something to maintain his family. He was to start on the third of January. Ted said it was the greatest thing ever, for he had sometimes feared his father would have a nervous breakdown just worrying because he was down and out.

Then they spoke of Betty, the possibilities of her future, that Aiken fellow.

"The poor simp!" said Ted angrily. "I'd like to get him off somewhere and lick him! I could do it, too He's soft. He drinks all the time now. I've been hearing things about him. If he dares come after my sister again I'll make it too hot for him to stay in this town. I know a lot about him."

"Well, don't let Betty know." warned Marjorie. "It might just make her angry so that she would go with him all the quicker."

"I know." said Ted, a softened light coming into his face that changed its belligerence marvelously. "We've got to pray. That's the only thing! You pray too!"

"I am " said Marjorie softly.

"Now. Ted," she said after a little pause, "there's something I want to ask of you. I think I can trust you perfectly to do what I ask I think you understand and believe that I want to come back here and live with you all and be one of you, but you know I wouldn't want to come for a minute if I thought even one of you felt it ought not to be."

Ted opened his lips to protest, but she silenced him.

"Wait a minute till I tell you all. Ted I know you are going to say you are sure. But you know what the agreement is between us all. that we shall take at least a week to think it over So I'm trusting you to let me know if you hear the slightest question or dissension on the subject. You'll let me know at once?"

"Okay!" said Ted with a sigh of relief. "I was afraid you were going to ask something I couldn't do."

"And you'll pray about it, Ted? I want to do what's right about it, you know, even if it isn't what I want."

"I sure will!" said Ted fervently. "I need you. You're the only *saved* sister I've got. We *all* need you!"

Marjorie walked the rest of the way home with the consciousness that there was a very precious bond between herself and this brother.

When they reached the house they found the doctor had dropped in. He stopped a minute or two in the parlor to ask how his former patients were, and then he suddenly got up and sauntered out in the kitchen whither Betty had been hastily called by a smell of burning cookies.

"Say Betty," he said, pausing beside the kitchen table, picking up a cookie that lay on the top of a plateful and taking a bite out of it, "I hear they're having a watchnight meeting over at the Brentwood chapel. Like to go? I might get off about nine o'clock if everything on my schedule comes off on time. I thought perhaps Reaver would like to see us all come in and surprise him."

Betty looked up with delight.

"Sure!" she said eagerly. "I'll go."

So the doctor sauntered back and told Marjorie and Ted, who had intended going anyway.

"We'll walk," said Marjorie. "It's a lovely night, and you and Betty can go in your car."

"No need for that," said Keith Sheridan, "I've got a rumble seat. Room for Bud, too, if he wants to go."

So they went to the watchnight meeting.

It was a very solemn service. Marjorie was glad to have it for a precious memory to take with her as she went. She thought as she watched the beautiful earnest face of the young preacher while he spoke that she had never seen such a look on human face before. It was a holy look. Again she was struck by the utter humility of his bearing, the seeming eagerness to simply pass on the Word of Life as it was given to him, and she fancied she almost understood the hours of prayer that lay behind that address. It was as if it had been given to him from a face-to-face talk with his Lord. Hungrily she listened, breathlessly she put that memory into her heart to keep, sensing there would come times of need ahead of her very soon.

At the close Gideon gave the invitation, if any wished to start the New Year with their Lord, would they come forward while all heads were bowed, just to take a stand in the new life?

Marjorie had not noticed till then that Ted had disappeared from the seat beside her, till suddenly she heard his voice blending with Gideon's, singing:

> "While Jesus whispers to you,
> Come, sinner, come!
> While we are praying for you,
> Come, sinner, come!
> Now is the time to own Him,
> Come, sinner, come!
> Now is the time to know Him,
> Come, sinner, come!"

The singing was very soft and tender. Marjorie's heart thrilled over those two voices, her brother, and this wonderful man of God, working together in this way! She hugged to her heart the precious assurance that she had already come to her Savior, and was now a child of God.

And then she heard a little stir beside her, a low spoken word, intense, earnest, and realized that it was Keith Sheridan speaking to Betty.

"Let's go!"

Her heart sank! Oh, were they angry? Were they going home? Were they going to reject openly the Savior's call? Was he the kind of young man who was going to lead Betty astray?

She began to pray with agonized petition: "Oh God! Oh God!" but her mind could form no other words.

Betty had risen now, slowly, hesitantly, with a deprecating glance behind her, and stepped out into the aisle beside Keith.

Then quietly, side by side, Betty with downcast eyes, Keith with lifted head as if he had just won a battle, they went swiftly up the aisle and stood before the singers.

Marjorie had lifted her head in amazement as she saw what they were doing, and now she looked at the glorified faces of the singers as they perceived who had answered their invitation.

There were others then, several of them, suddenly crowding up as if they feared it might be too late if they delayed. And Bud, stumbling out across a seatful at the last minute, red and determined. Marjorie sat quietly where they had left her and sang hosanna in her heart. What a celebration for the last night before she went home!

Afterwards when they were all together, Betty, shy and half frightened, yet wore a shining look.

"I don't know why I ever did it," she whispered to Marjorie. "but I meant it, and I'm glad I did! I wouldn't have had the courage if Keith hadn't started first!"

Gideon took Marjorie, Ted and Bud home in his car, and they had a praise meeting all the way, Bud nestling sleepily against Ted's shoulder, feeling contented and safe with his brother's words ringing in his mind: "Good work, kid, you'll never be sorry!"

XXII

THOUGH it was late Gideon lingered for just a minute with Marjorie. He knew he must not keep her from her rest, but there were so many last words of rejoicing to say. Then as he turned to go he remarked:

"Oh, by the way, I'm hoping you'll give me the honor of taking you to the train tomorrow evening."

"Oh, that will be delightful!" said Marjorie. "It won't seem so much as if I was going away to have someone I know at the station." .

"Fine, that's settled then! And there's just the least possibility that I might go as far as Harrisburg on your train, if I can get someone from the Bible School to take my prayermeeting tomorrow night. I've just had word that a cousin of mine is being married tomorrow at noon, and she's taken it into her head that I must perform the ceremony. I told her I was too busy, but she's telegraphed again, and if I can arrange it, I'll go. Would I be in the way if I traveled with you awhile? I'd drop off at Harrisburg before midnight, you know."

"Wonderful!" said Marjorie. "Then I shall have opportunity to ask you a lot of questions that have been crowding my mind ever since I first heard you preach."

A light flashed into his eyes.

"I'll be only too glad to answer anything I can," he said. "That's settled then. I'll be here in plenty of time. Your train leaves at six fifty-five. Time enough if we start at ten of six. Well, good night, and don't stay awake too long rejoicing. My! How we are going to miss you! I hope Chicago doesn't claim you long."

Marjorie, watching his car spin away into the winter night, had somehow a happier feeling about going, now that she was to have such good company part of the way.

Betty and the doctor came in a few minutes later, Betty wearing a shining look, so different from the one she wore when she came in the night before.

They talked a long time after they got to bed, in soft whispers, close to one another.

"I'm happy!" said Betty. "It's so strange! I think I'm happier than I ever was since I was a little kid. It seems as if everything is all changed. I think if you weren't going away I'd feel as if I was in heaven."

"Oh, you dear!" said Marjorie. "And I was afraid to come here! And didn't know what I was missing. I'm going to miss you terribly. If it wasn't that Mother isn't fit to be alone yet I'd be tempted to take you along. But then we couldn't carry out the contract, could we? For I should only be getting deeper and deeper in love with my family. However, it won't be long till I'm back to stay!"

"Are you sure, Marjorie?"

"Yes, sure as one can be in this world," said Marjorie happily. "I'm just crazy to get into the Brentwood house, aren't you?"

"*Am* I?" said Betty. "Watch me and see!"

So at last they fell asleep.

But the next day wasn't half long enough, and sped away so fast they were aghast. Marjorie was here and there and everywhere, with her mother and the children, and everybody restless because the time was getting shorter and shorter. How they were going to miss her, the daughter who had only known them a few short days!

Ted came home in the middle of the afternoon with a box of candy he had bought for her journey. Father said he couldn't get home early enough to see her before she left, but he would step over to the station and meet her at the train to say good-bye. Sunny and Bonnie each scribbled a queer little letter for her to read on the train, and Bud took some of his cherished Christmas dollar he had found in the toe of his cherished Christmas stocking and bought her a magazine to read on her way. Then her mother folded her in her arms and kissed her, fastening a thin little chain around her neck with a tiny gold locket on it.

"It was mine when I was a child," she explained. "Wear it till you come back to me, dear! Maybe it will remind you of me. It is long enough to drop down under your dress and not show. You won't be ashamed of it, will you?"

"Ashamed! Mother dear!" said Marjorie, on the verge of tears. "Oh, Mother, I think it was all wrong of me to go back at all. I should just take you all along, and then we could pack up together and do as we like about everything."

"No, no, dear! It's right for you to think it over. I'm not crying! There! Go quick! They are calling you. The minister has come. So nice of him that he is going part way with you. I shall feel better about you. I know Ted was terribly disappointed he had to go to work and couldn't see you off!"

And so at the last minute she hurried away, smiling and waving and throwing kisses to the children.

But Ted was at the train after all. He met Gideon's car at the curb, and stood there grinning to open the door for his sister.

"They had to send somebody down to the station to get a reservation for the boss to go to New York tonight," he said, "and didn't I volunteer! I'll say I did!"

A few minutes later Marjorie and Gideon were seated in the train as it moved off, waving to the father and Ted. Then the train swept out of the station and they were alone.

"Isn't this wonderful of you!" Marjorie said. "You can't imagine how forlorn I felt going off alone like this after I've had such a nice big family! It seems like a miracle arranged entirely for my benefit that your cousin should select tomorrow for her wedding when there were all the other days of the year she might have chosen from, and it wouldn't have affected me in the least."

"Well, of course," said Gideon, "I felt that the benefit was all mine, however I won't grudge you a share. And now, what were those questions you wanted to ask? I'm eager to hear them."

"Oh," said Marjorie, "I want to know how to walk with God, and I want to know how to study the Bible, and then all about grace."

Gideon laughed.

"Rather a large proposition for one short evening," he said, "but those are the best things I talk about. Where shall we begin?"

They settled back on the comfortable cushions and began a talk that neither of them will ever forget, and the record of which is surely in heaven.

The minister got out his pocket Bible, and again and again the two heads were bent over the text. Marjorie took out her pencil and note book and kept a great many references for her help when she got back to Chicago alone. So the time flew fast. It seemed only a brief space before Gideon had to put on his overcoat, seize his hat and suitcase, grasp her hand for a quick instant, and hurry to get off at Harrisburg.

He waved to her from the platform an instant, and then the train moved on and she was alone. A great desolation came over her. Would she ever see him again?

But he had her address in Chicago, and he had promised to send her some booklets to help her in her Bible study. That was something to which to look forward.

Then the porter came to know if she would like her berth made up, and she was glad to put her head on the pillow and rest, thinking over the evening and all the wonderful days since she had come out on this pilgrimage to find her family! Her dear family!

Ah, she did not need to take even a week to consider whether she wanted to be with them. She knew now. Just this brief separation had made her sure, if she needed even that! She thought back to the tiny house on Aster Street and wondered if they were all sleeping now! Had they missed her during the evening? Had the children in their evening prayers remembered her as they had so earnestly assured her they would do? Were her mother and father talking about her now considering whether she ought to come back?

Then her mind went to Gideon again. How handsome he had looked as he stood there waving to her on the platform. How suddenly hard it had become to see him go!

It was strange the next morning to waken and find herself almost back in Chicago, to dress hurriedly just in time to get out and to find her own chauffeur waiting at the station with her car according to orders, to drive through the familiar streets and see everything just as it had been when she left it. It was as if she had been moving in a happy dream for a season, and now was awake again. Would the joy vanish as quickly as the dream was doing? Were her father and mother perhaps right. did she really need to come back in order to get a practical vision of things? In order to find out what she really wanted? She put the thought from her frantically, a kind of fear growing in her. No, it could not be that she would ever be content to go back to the old life, even with all its luxuries and amenities, and forget her beloved family, to settle down to a life here where she had always been. A life that would include Evan Brower instead of them all! Evan Brower instead of the wonderful man of God, who understood the precious vital things of life! No! A thousand times, *NO!*

And suddenly she knew what she was going to say to Evan Brower.

The house was immaculate, the servants all there in their places, welcoming her, thanking her for their holiday, apparently ready to go on with life as she had left it. She could settle down now and every day would go smoothly, engineered by these trained workers. She wouldn't have a care except just to please herself. But oh, the emptiness of it all!

She ate her dainty breakfast, and heard them tell her what a happy time they had had, and how they enjoyed the Christmas remembrances she had given them. Then she began to wonder what she was going to do about them, supposing she sold the house and went away? It was not thinkable that her father and mother would want a hoard of servants trained by others. She did not want them herself, although she was in a way attached to them all. Yet she felt it would be so much better that there should be new servants in the new life if she went away, servants that her mother should choose. Was this another of the elements that her wise father and mother had known she would have to meet and reckon with in her decison?

After breakfast she went from room to room and tried to take up the thread of life. For this one week at least she was committed to do nothing definite about leaving her home. But that did not include Evan Brower. In the afternoon she wrote a note to him.

"Dear Evan:
This is just to tell you that I got home today and shall be glad to see you whenever you feel like calling,

Sincerely,
Marjorie."

She mailed it late in the afternoon. He would not get it until the next morning. She could have telephoned him of course but she wanted one free evening to consider what she should say to him. He could not likely come until the next evening.

Next morning she went up in the attic and went over the things there, considering what should be looked over and given away whether she went or stayed. There was no point in wasting all this week. Some of the old papers and letters and garments might as well be put out of the way. Also she could write out lists of things she wanted to get rid of if she went away.

The morning passed very quickly and in the afternoon she went to see her lawyer and check up on business matters. Then just after dinner Evan Brower came.

She had been reading the little book that Gideon gave her, sitting in the library before the open fire, when he was announced. His coming brought her suddenly back into the present, exchanging the memory of Gideon Reaver for the reality of Evan Brower.

Evan had brought her flowers, dignified long-stemmed aristocratic roses, dozens of them. Thelma the waitress knew just what to put them in, one of the deep crystal rose jars. She brought them presently and put them on the low table between Evan and Marjorie. Marjorie had a quick thought of how it would always be like this if she married Evan. Always sitting there or somewhere else with Evan, always the most expensive flowers on all occasions, the best music. He had suggested a concert the next evening he thought she would like to attend. He took it for granted she would. Their life together would be well-ordered and peaceful, meticulously perfect in every human way. But he would have no thought of the things that had come to mean so much to her. She grasped the little book warmly. It seemed to her a bond between herself and the things she had left behind her in the east. Was it going to be humanly possible for her to cut herself off from those things for even a week, and with unbiased mind consider what she had promised her parents to consider?

Evan told her of the news since she had been gone, spoke pleasantly like the old friend he had always been, with no mention of their differences when he had seen her last. He told her of affairs that were going on in their social world, said his mother wanted her for a quiet visit, suggested things they might do together, and at last he got out the little velvet box again.

"Marjorie," he said in a calm voice, "I want you to put my ring on now and wear it. It will be a sort of protection for you while you are alone, and I shall feel a great deal better about you if you are wearing it. I do hope you are willing to see things in a reasonable way by this time, and that we can soon get our affairs settled. I hate so to have you unprotected. Of course, if you feel that you must wait a little longer to get married I will be willing, though I am quite sure everyone will see that it is the sensible thing, alone as you are. No one will criticize you, I am positive, for having a quiet wedding so soon after Mrs. Wetherill's funeral. She would have wanted you to do this, I am certain."

Then Marjorie grasped her little book softly, like a talisman, looked calmly at Evan Brower and answered in a clear voice:

"Evan, I do appreciate your kindness and your thought for me, and I feel sorry that I had to be so uncertain in the past when you talked to me about these things. But now that I am home again I have thought it all over and made my decision. Evan, I am not going to marry you, either now or at any other time. I am quite sure that I do not love you as a woman ought to love a man she marries. Perhaps I ought to have known this before, but I didn't. But now I know, and it would not be right for me to keep you waiting any longer."

Evan Brower looked at her steadily, calmly, and slowly put the ring back in its box and the box away in his pocket.

"Very well," he said quietly, determinedly, "if you haven't come to your senses yet I can wait, of course, till you do. Undoubtedly you will get over this phase pretty soon and be sorry. In the meantime I am at your service. Are you willing to be friends? Are you willing to go to the concert with me tomorrow night? It is a very quiet affair and we can sit in Mother's box at the Opera House. You will not necessarily be in the public eye."

Marjorie looked at him and smiled.

"Yes, Evan, I'll be glad to be friends. Friends just as we used to be. That will be nice. And yes, I'll go to the concert tomorrow night if you want it. You are really very kind."

He did not stay long. He was a lawyer and canny. He thought he saw that he must take a new line entirely and drop back into his old role of friendship without urging her into anything new at this time. She would change presently, of course, when she got used to the idea of his being her constant attendant everywhere. He would be patient.

So presently he took his leave and Marjorie went happily back to her new study with her little book in her hand and her Bible open on the low table before her, and forgot entirely that she had just refused one of the most sought after young men in Chicago.

XXIII

THE week of probation dragged its slow length along, and Marjorie began to realize how impossible it was to really fix her mind on the question in hand. Somewhere in the back of her mind the matter seemed to be settled and sealed and there was no more possibility of considering it.

As the days went by developments made her feel more and more that everything was working out to show her that her conclusion had been right. To begin with, the third day after her arrival, Thelma, the waitress came to her blushing and told her that she was going to be married, and she had to give notice.

Marjorie congratulated her, and did not feel the sense of loss as she would have done if she were convinced she was going to remain in the Wetherill house. That was perhaps the first happening that made her see clearly that she wasn't even considering staying.

She went out two or three times with Evan Brower, and was sweet and pleasant with a kind of vague-eyed detachment that much annoyed that entirely assured young man, but he shut his lips thinly and went forward in his campaign as he had planned. Marjorie would be his in the end. She didn't seem to care for anyone else, why shouldn't she turn to him eventually?

The fourth day after her homecoming the old Scotch housekeeper, her former nurse, came to her in great distress with an open letter in her hand. Her youngest sister back in the old country was very sick with a lingering illness and wanted her to come home and nurse her. Tessy felt she ought to go.

So Marjorie gave her her blessing and sent her on her way to catch the next boat. Another tie to her old life was broken without her lifting a finger! God was working her way out for her.

But, suppose at the end of the week there should come a letter from her Mother saying—oh, very sweetly of course--that they felt it was best for everybody concerned that she should not come to them? Well, yes, she would then be rather cut off from everybody who could serve to make her life pleasant, Evan, and the servants. But she hadn't done it herself, and there would surely be some way, even if it were a way of heartache.

Then there came a letter from Gideon and her heart leaped up to welcome it singing a little song even before she opened it. It wasn't a long letter. It was mostly about his work and the questions she had asked, and some books he was sending. But it did say how much they missed her, and it started a lilt in her voice and a joy in her eye that even Evan Brower noticed when he dropped in with gardenias.

The next day Gideon sent flowers. Marjorie thought they were some more from Evan, and forgot to open them for almost an hour till Thelma, not yet departed, asked if she should put them in water, and brought the card to her. She opened it idly, expecting to find Evan's name as usual inside, and found instead Gideon Reaver's card. The soft color came into her face then and her eyes shone with joy. She got up and came over to them. They were crimson roses, deep and dark. She buried her face in their sweetness and closed her eyes as she carried them upstairs to her own private sanctum. She did not want them out of her sight. But Evan Brower's stately flowers remained downstairs in the reception room.

That same day the lawyer called her up. The man who wanted to buy her house was insistent. His plans had changed and he wanted to move at once. Could she give an answer within the next two days?

Marjorie could and would. The week was up day after tomorrow. She would give an answer then, she told Mr. Melbourne.

Later in the day the chauffeur who had served the

Wetherills so many years presented himself apologetically, and with many a hem and a haw made bold to ask if it was true that she was going to sell the house and move away, as rumor had it? If she was he would like opportunity to see a man about another place he had heard of that paid very good wages, and was well-fixed with a tidy house for the chauffeur and his wife.

Marjorie smiled and told him to go and see it, that she would let him know in a couple of days. And so the ties were one by one broken and again without her making a single move. It was all very wonderful. She wondered if it was because so many people were praying about it. There was only the old cook left now, and she was hinting she might give up work and go and live with her sister. She was getting old and rheumatic and wanted a rest.

And then the week was up.

Marjorie arose with a feeling that great things might happen today. Would her mother write at once, or wasn't the week long enough for them to decide? *She* had decided. She was only waiting for their word. Would the morning mail bring her answer?

But it came sooner than that. Thelma brought it up to her before she was dressed. A telegram:

"We have kept our contract. The time is up. We want you with all our hearts. We feel that this is your place if you still want to come to us. But not unless you would rather come. Letter follows."

It was signed with all their names.

Marjorie wasn't long in answering that. She caught up her telephone and dictated a telegram:

"Was coming anyway, whether you wanted me or not. Could not stand it without you. Brentwood for me! Love to you all. Glory hallelujah!

Marjorie!"

Then she telephoned her lawyer and told him to go ahead and sell the house. She was moving today. She also called up a mover and asked him to come at once and arrange about the moving. Then she got out her lists and began to pack her personal belongings.

Next morning Ted appeared on the scene. A very properly-clad Ted, looking handsome and capable.

"Mother said I was to come and help pack," he said simply. "She said you oughtn't to be alone. Dad would have come but he couldn't leave his new job, of course."

And then when his sister fell upon his neck and embraced him, crying for very joy, he remarked quite casually though in a jubilant tone:

"Gideon Reaver said he was coming over on Monday to drive us back home. He said you said you were bringing your car, and I haven't any driver's license yet. He said I was to wire him when we would be ready. He said he might bring Bud along for the ride if you wanted him. He's crazy to come!"

"Oh, wonderful!" said Marjorie looking up with shining eyes! "Won't that be great! I was planning to have the chauffeur drive the car over, but now I find he's got another place and they want him right away this week. That will solve the problem. And what fun we'll have!"

"It might be bad weather," remarked Ted, revealing that the matter had been discussed at home.

"Of course, but there is a heater in the car, and we don't mind weather! Won't it be great?"

They were hard at work packing, and there was a large van drawn up before the door taking away furniture, some that was to be sent to the auction rooms for sale, and some that was to be given to the mission, when Evan Brower arrived. He had come to take Marjorie over to the park to see some professional skaters who were said to be very fine. He stood in the denuded parlor where furniture was shrouded in summer slips, and rugs were rolled up in bundles, and looked blankly about him.

"What in the world does this mean?" he asked sternly as Marjorie came to greet him.

"Oh, I'm so sorry, Evan," she said. "I completely forgot you were coming to take me somewhere. I should have let you know, but I've been so busy everything else went out of my head. You see, I've sold the house, and I'm moving. It all happened quite suddenly or I should have called off our engagement. But you can see I can't possibly go today. I'm sorry. And I guess there won't be any other time, either, Evan. You know how it is when people move."

"Moving?" said Evan angrily. "You don't mean you've

sold this house without letting me know? Without saying
anything to me about it?"

He glared at Marjorie and then he saw Ted standing
straight and unsmiling beside his sister. He hadn't seen
him come in, but there he was!

"Good morning, Mr. Brower," said Ted, "I think I met
you at Christmas time while my sister was east."

Evan Brower glared at Ted with scarcely an inclination
of his head, and then he said savagely to Marjorie:

"Can I see you alone somewhere?"

Marjorie gave him an absent-minded smile.

"Why, yes," she said, "for just a minute, I guess. The
mover will be here in five minutes or so, but we can go
into the library. That isn't so much torn up yet."

Ted didn't follow, except with his eyes but he worked
outside in the hall making enough noise to let it be known
that he was there. If his sister needed assistance he would
be at hand. He certainly would like to wallop that insolent
chump before he left Chicago, but of course he couldn't.

What was said behind that closed door Marjorie never
told him, but it must have been decisive for the caller presently came out walking as if he were following to the
grave after a dead hope.

Marjorie's face was calm however as she came after
him briskly and went with him to the door.

"I'm going to make time somehow to see a few people
before I leave of course, Evan, and I'm coming to your
mother first of all," she said pleasantly.

"Most kind of you," murmured Evan Brower haughtily,
"but I beg that you won't put yourself out in the least for
us. Since you have been so self-sufficient in all your arrangements I suppose of course there is nothing we can do
for you. You have chosen to make your plans without taking advice from us who supposed we were your best
friends. I hope you will not inconvenience yourself to
call."

"Oh, but I want to see you all before I leave," said Marjorie brightly. "You will run in again won't you, Evan, of
course? We shall not be leaving before Monday or Tues-
day."

He whirled then and looked at her full in the face, and
Ted in the back of the hall heard his voice savagely say:

"Do you really mean to tell me that you are giving up

this lovely home and going to live in that little untidy
dump where I found you at Christmas?"

Marjorie laughed.

"Oh, no," she said. "That was just temporary. I am
going to live in my father's house that he has owned for
several years. He is moving back to it next week. We'll be
glad to see you out there some day when you are in the
east. It is a lovely home. My father is with Martin Heath
Company. Perhaps you know the firm. I'm sure the family
will be glad to entertain you whenever you are in our vi-
cinity. I have told them what a good friend of the family
you have always been."

"Some sister!" murmured Ted from the depths of the
back hall where he had been rolling up more rugs. Then
under his breath, he added, "and *some mutt!*"

They were ready to leave Wednesday morning. Marjorie
had made her calls, although she had not found Mrs.
Brower at home and had to write a note for good-bye. She
had called up some of her friends on the telephone, and
written to others announcing her sudden departure, and
she hadn't a regret. Chicago had been dear, but Brentwood
was dearer. Even Bud was satisfied with the single day of
sightseeing which Ted and Gideon had given him. He said
Chicago wasn't so much, though he was glad he'd seen it;
he liked Brentwood a lot better.

The last truck was filled, and started on its way; the
cook had wept a farewell and had been taken to her train
en route for her sister's in the far west; the house was
locked and the key handed over to the lawyer's representative for the new owner; and they were all comfortably
seated in the big luxurious car ready to start.

"It's a beautiful house," remarked Gideon. "I'm so glad
to have seen where you were brought up," and he smiled
at Marjorie. "Yes, it's a lovely home. But you're going to
one just as pleasant, I think!"

"Sure thing!" said Ted fervently. "Though this one's all
right," he added as if he feared Marjorie's feelings might
be hurt.

"Some dump, I say!" remarked Bud contemptuously
looking toward the fine old house in its setting of ever-
greens, with the distant blue of winter water edged with
snow behind it. "No place ta play baseball anywhere about
it, and that old lake out there always behind yer back.

'Spose it might rise some day like the river and drown ya out? Course it would be nice ta wade in summers, but I'd rather have Brentwood. Give me Brentwood every time!"

They all laughed merrily at Bud, and it helped to drive back the sudden smarting tears and the choking sob that threatened Marjorie as she gave one last wistful glance back and realized that the old life was done with forever. Yet she was not sad, for Brentwood was ahead, and Brentwood represented a new life of love and service, companionship with God, and with dear people who loved her. She was glad as they drove away into the new life that she had chosen Brentwood instead of Chicago.

Then they wound down along the lake shore, into the city and out on the highway for Home.

And such a drive as they had!

They had arranged that the trucks should not get to Brentwood ahead of them, for Marjorie wanted to be there to give directions. But they did not have to hurry. The day was bright and clear, and the four were happy and together. It seemed like a great picnic, and every moment was a treasure to be remembered always.

Especially was it a happy time for Gideon and Marjorie for during that two days of drive they bridged the years that had gone before, and got really acquainted with one another, so that by the time they reached their destination they were like old friends.

Evan Brower had not been present to see Marjorie off. When he had stopped in the night before for a moment, hoping even yet to persuade her of her folly and turn her from her purpose, Gideon had opened the door for him and told him that Marjorie had gone with Ted to take some jellies and fruit to an old washwoman who lived a mile away. Though Gideon had cordially invited Evan to wait in the almost empty house until they returned, Evan had declined, and gone away in a huff, leaving only his card behind him for farewell. Marjorie would have to learn her mistake by sad experience, he decided. But when she discovered it, it would probably be too late.

So the four journeyed back to the east over a hard white road under a blazing sun, and had a happy time, and never once thought of Evan Brower all day long.

But oh, that home coming. How precious it was! To be folded in her mother's arms and to know that she was at home! To watch the lovelight on her father's face as he said: "Welcome home, my daughter!" To feel the children's eager sticky kisses and hear their screams of welcome. To see real joy in Betty's face, real welcome! Ah! That was better than all the other world had to offer her.

And then to drive hastily over to Brentwood and meet the trucks which had just arrived, and with Betty direct where things should go. It was great!

They had reached home early in the afternoon and by evening all the trucks were empty and the house in fair order.

Ted had had the floors done over, and they laid the rugs down first, so that everything could be set in place at once.

There were many hands to work. There was Betty in the parlor with Keith Sheridan to help, taking off the covers from the upholstered furniture. There was Bud bringing in endless armfuls of wood to the woodbox, and under Ted's strict directions carefully laying a fire in the fireplace for later in the evening. And there was Gideon going quietly about doing things without having to ask what to do next, just as if he were a son of the house and had always lived with this furniture and these rooms.

"You want this here, don't you, Marjorie?" he would say, and proceed to put it there.

And once in the back hall, toward dusk, those two came hastily upon each other. Marjorie from the way of the kitchen, and Gideon from the big pleasant library where he had just deposited an armful of books that had been misplaced by the now departed movers, and they ran right into each other. Gideon put out his arms and enfolded her, perhaps to save her from falling, but it became more than that of itself as suddenly they were close to one another, and Gideon stooped and placed a tender kiss on her lips.

Then, just as suddenly, while they were still under the spell of the wonder of each other's lips, and did not know anyone else was in the world for the moment, there stood Betty and Keith hand in hand.

"Might a mere brother-in-law offer congratulations?" saluted Keith joyously, "because we're in a position ourselves to understand."

He grinned and bowed low with his hand upon his heart. That is, one hand. The other Betty had.

Then he looked up at the embarrassed two who had been taken unawares and grinned.

"It's a little soon, I suppose, to spring all this on the assembling multitudes," he offered. "Wouldn't it be as well if we were to unpack the supper that I understand is awaiting us in baskets in the dining room? I thought I'd just let you know that Ted is at the door with the rest of the family, in case you didn't want them all to become aware yet of what has happened. I humbly ask your pardon if I have intruded."

Marjorie with glowing cheeks and dancing eyes was laughing now.

"We didn't know anything about this ourselves till a minute ago!" she announced shyly.

"I believe you!" said Betty solemnly. "That's the way it came to me, all suddenly."

"Well, I'm not ashamed of it, though I didn't think I dared announce my intentions so soon. But I'm glad!" said Gideon solemnly.

"Yes!" said Marjorie. "Aren't we?"

"Where are you all," rang out Bud's clarion voice. "The whole family's here! Where's everybody? Say, I'm *hungry!* When do we eat? Say, whyn't ya start the fire?"

But the rest were scurrying to the front door to welcome the family.

The mother walked into her house and stood and looked around with eyes full of wonder. There was Marjorie's piano open, just as if she were going to play; there were the beautiful couches and chairs and tables just as she had dreamed she would like them, and beautiful paintings on the wall. Ted had scratched a match and sent the flames licking up in the fireplace. It was like having a dream come true.

"Oh, it's too good to have all these things at once!" she said. "My girl come home to Brentwood, and all my children here!"

"Yes, Mother dear," chirped Betty from the doorway, her hand again in Keith's who winked across at Marjorie and Gideon, "even more children than you had bargained for!"